ENEMY EXPOSURE

Also by Meghan Rogers

Crossing the Line

Enemy Exposure

Meghan Rogers

PHILOMEL BOOKS

PHILOMEL BOOKS
an imprint of Penguin Random House LLC
375 Hudson Street, New York, NY 10014

Library of Congress Cataloging-in-Publication Data
Names: Rogers, Meghan, author. | Title: Enemy exposure / Meghan Rogers. | Description:
New York, NY : Philomel Books, [2017] | Series: The Raven files ; 2 | Summary: "Jocelyn's cover is
blown, and now she's focused on taking down KATO. But in order to do that, she needs to turn
some of their own against them"—Provided by publisher. | Identifiers: LCCN 2016014588 |
ISBN 9780399176180 (hardback) | Subjects: | CYAC: Spies—Fiction. | Adventure and adventurers—
Fiction. | Classification: LCC PZ7.1.R66 En 2017 | DDC [Fic]—dc23 | LC record available at
https://lccn.loc.gov/2016014588

Printed in the United States of America.
ISBN 9780399176180
10 9 8 7 6 5 4 3 2 1

Edited by Jill Santopolo.   Design by Semadar Megged.   Text set in 11.5/17.5-point Adobe Devanagari.

To Andrea, for your friendship, inspiration, and belief.

And for always sitting on my couch and helping me
fix my writing problems.

This book needed you badly.

Chapter One

PARENTAL DEVELOPMENTS

I pounded the punching bag hard—harder than I should have for my first real post-gunshot workout. It was lunchtime at the Wilmington, Delaware, headquarters of the International Defense Agency, so I had the training facility to myself. I promised Dr. March I would ease myself into a regular workout, and I had meant it at the time. But now that I was punching, I couldn't slow myself down. My anxiety had been building the past few weeks and it seemed to be erupting now that I finally had an outlet. Each punch held a memory.

Me, back inside KATO, seconds away from a Gerex injection.

My former handler, Chin Ho, standing over me with a gun, realizing I'd betrayed the agency.

Me and Travis barely hidden in a train car with North Korean military feet from us, on the verge of being recaptured.

I hit the bag with even more force. There was some aching and tightness in my shoulder, but overall I felt strong. Which was good. I *needed* to feel strong. KATO knew I wasn't their agent any longer. I had been able to keep them in the back of my mind while I was recovering, but I knew they'd be after me. For the time being, though, I was inside the IDA. I was *safe*. That was enough to get me through the worst of my injury pain and Gerex cravings that came with it.

The illusion of safety dissipated the day I left the medical wing.

I should have known better than to check KATO's message boards—in fact, I *did* know better. Yet, I couldn't make it twenty-four hours before my curiosity got the better of me. KATO had used these boards to contact me when they'd sent me into the IDA as a double agent. If they had anything more to say to me, I would find it there. My chest constricted when I saw that there was a message waiting. I let the cursor hover over the post, bracing myself, before I finally found it in me to click.

I clenched my fist until my nails dug into my palms.

You have shamed and humiliated this agency. We will find you, and you will be punished for your actions.

The message was written in plain English. Not only were they coming for me, but they didn't care who knew. There were no descriptions or details about what kind of punishment would be waiting for me. They'd left it all up to my imagination, which was so much worse than anything they could have described.

I hadn't told anyone at the IDA about this message. It wasn't unexpected, and it didn't reveal anything new about KATO's plan going forward. But it had reminded me just how vulnerable I had become. My dreams had also come back with a vengeance. I could barely sleep without waking up sweating, and trying to shake the feeling that I was tied down in some kind of KATO torture chamber.

I focused on beating the punching bag.

The training room door opened behind me, but I never slowed my punches. It felt too good to move like this. Dr. March had kept me in the medical wing for a week after I got back from KATO before clearing me for a cardio workout routine. Then finally this morning, nearly four weeks after I'd been shot, she said I could throw a punch if I promised to take it easy. I had gone right from her office to the training facility.

"Hey." Travis's broad form moved just inside my range of vision. "Do you want to cool it for a second?"

I stepped back from the bag, shaking my arms and forcing myself to rein it in. Travis shifted in front of me. He had his arms crossed and eyebrows arched, and I knew he was ready to tell me I was going too hard. I didn't give him the chance. "Please don't," I said. "I've needed this for a while."

He tilted his head to the side in mild exasperation. "You're going to re-injure yourself."

"I've had more time to heal here than I ever had at KATO. I know my limits." I rolled my shoulder. I wanted to hit until I felt ready to face them. "They're coming for me, and I'm going to be prepared."

"I realize that," he said. "But this isn't the way to go about it."

I wasn't in the mood for a lecture. I bit my tongue to keep myself from snapping at him. "Travis, I get that your heart is in the right place here, but I need to do this my way. So you can either help or step aside."

Travis eyed me intently, and I was sure he was going to keep arguing, which was why I was thrown off when he nodded. "Okay." He took his sweatshirt off and tossed it aside. "But we're sparring. At least that way, you can swap out a few punches for kicks."

I shot him a grateful smile. The punching bag was a good workout, but I was aching for something more. It had been a while since Travis and I had fought, but we fell back into step easily on the mats. Keeping pace with him took all of my energy and focus. It was the best release I could have asked for.

Travis started with a hit to my side, which I blocked easily. I fired back with a shot to his shoulder, forcing him to duck. Each of my hits were still harder than they should have been, but it felt too good to stop.

"You're more wound up than I realized," Travis said once we really got into it.

I gritted my teeth together, feeling exposed. "There's a lot going on."

"You know they can't touch you, right?" He attempted to sweep my feet out from under me, but I jumped over him, jabbing a quick hit to his stomach.

"If KATO wants me, they will find a way to get to me." He had to know that. I spent my entire time at the IDA trying to keep my traitor status a secret from KATO and now they knew the truth. It was everything I had been afraid of.

I launched a kick at Travis. He dodged it and threw another punch. I caught his fist with my right hand. He reacted quickly, grabbing my wrist and twisting me down onto to the mat. He took care to make sure I landed on my uninjured right side. I put my foot on his stomach, bracing my hands on his biceps to keep him at bay. He leaned into it, hovering over me and refusing to back away until I looked him in the eye. "I won't let them take you. No one here will."

I bit my lip to keep my frustration from showing. The fact that he thought this was something he or anyone could protect me from showed that—despite his best intentions—he didn't completely understand what I was up against. "It's not that simple."

He opened his mouth to disagree, but I'd didn't want to debate this anymore. I rocked up slightly, gaining momentum, then rolled backward, flipping him over me. He landed behind my head.

I popped up quickly and pressed my foot to his chest, pinning him in place. "Do me a favor and stay focused next time," I said, giving him a pointed look. "It's not much of a workout if your head's not in the game."

His expression hardened the way it did when he knew I was being evasive, but a throat was cleared by the door before he could challenge me. It was only then that I realized we weren't alone. Simmonds was watching us, and so was someone else. He was tall, and he had his hands crammed into his jean pockets. I recognized that jaw. The shape of his mouth. My heart sped up.

It was my father.

His hair was longer and the creases in his forehead were deeper, but it wasn't until I got a good look at his eyes that I saw the true difference. They used to be bright—full of life and energy. Now there was a darkness to them. He stared at me with disbelief.

"Jocelyn." There was a smile in Simmonds's voice as he approached us. "There's someone here to see you."

My father followed behind him, his movements rigid.

My stomach twisted with a mess of conflicting emotions. We'd missed ten important years together. Ten years where I had worked for the people he had spent his life fighting against. I was glad to see him—at least, a part of me was—but I didn't exactly know what to do with him either.

I felt unprepared. It had been nearly a month since Agent Lee burst into my room in the medical wing telling me he had been found. At the time, all she had was a confirmed location. He was on some remote island in the South China Sea, which meant the whole time I was in KATO, he was closer to me than I ever could have imagined.

"It'll be a little bit until we get to him," she had said. "But we're positive he's there." She beamed at me the whole time she spoke and I forced a small smile, if only to hide the fact that I was relieved to have more time before I had to face him. I had done *terrible* things for KATO, and while I believed I did what was necessary to survive, I didn't want him to know the details.

My childhood came back in a flash. We used to play games—a lot of them. My favorite was a seek-and-find game. About a year before I was taken I had found a rock shaped like an elephant in our yard. My dad used to hide it and leave a trail of clues for me to follow. At first, it had been enough of a challenge just to find the rock, but as I got better, the hiding spots got more complex. He'd stick it in tree trunks that were just a little too tall for me to reach and divots a little too small for my hands to fit into—places that required some skill to be successful. I didn't realize it at the time, but it was almost like a retrieval game. The part that stuck with me the most was how proud he was of me every time I was victorious.

Studying him now, I wondered if I'd ever see that look from him again.

I was vaguely aware of Travis next to me, throwing eager looks my way. But I couldn't face him. I couldn't tear my eyes away from my father, who seemed to be just as uncomfortable as I was. He gave me a once-over and I found I couldn't read him. I fluffed the curls in my side ponytail, making sure the burn scar below my left ear was covered.

"Chris," Simmonds said after a moment. They were standing at the edge of the mat now, feet from Travis and me. "This is Jocelyn." I swallowed hard. It felt so strange to be introduced to my own dad, but it also felt necessary. It had been ten years and I had changed a lot more than he had. I wondered if he would have recognized me if he wasn't expecting to see me.

I stood up straighter, searching my brain for what to say or do, but my thoughts moved too quickly to latch on to one.

My dad glanced back at Simmonds, his expression growing momentarily piercing. "I've got it from here."

Simmonds tensed in a way I wasn't used to seeing, but nodded curtly. "Of course." His voice was stiff. "I'll leave you two to get reacquainted."

I caught a bead of tension between them, but I was quickly distracted by Travis next to me. He took a step away and I knew he was about to follow Simmonds out. "Don't forget to ice your shoulder," he said to me. I fought the urge to grab his arm and keep him in place. I wasn't ready to be alone with my father—not yet. But I didn't know how to say that. So instead I watched as Travis grabbed his sweatshirt and headed for the door.

And then it was just the two of us.

My heart started to beat faster. I knew I had to say something, or *do* something. But what? I drew a tight breath and settled for a simple *hi*. It came out hoarse, which irritated me. This was far beyond the scope of any mission I had ever been prepared for. My arm started to shake slightly and I clenched my fist to stabilize it. I'd felt more anxious and on edge since I'd gotten back from KATO. Dr. March said it was probably a combination of being further removed from the drug and recovering from a gunshot wound without any medication. The pain had, for the most part, faded. The edgy anxiety stuck around.

My father's eyes slid to my shoulder. I wasn't sure if it was because of what Travis had said or if he'd been briefed.

I tugged at my hair. Part of me wanted to move to the side and sit down on one of the benches, but that felt too relaxed.

We held our positions, staring at each other, until my dad finally broke the silence. "That was impressive," he said. I knew he was referring to the fight, but I didn't know how much of it he had seen. "Roy says you're a pretty good agent."

I wasn't used to hearing Simmonds's first name, so it took me a minute to realize who he meant. I pressed my lips together, trying to push my nerves aside enough to think. The last thing I wanted to talk about was what kind of agent I was. That would lead to talking about what I've done for the IDA, which was almost entirely KATO-related. And then we'd be talking about KATO, which wasn't something I wanted to discuss today. "I can hold my own."

He nodded, watching me carefully, considering. The silence around us felt hollow.

"What happened to your shoulder?" he asked after another stretch of silence.

I studied him. Did he really not know, or did he just want to hear it from me? I kept my answer short and safe. "I got shot."

My father's jaw tensed in response.

I looked around the room, just so I didn't have to focus on him. This was one of the biggest spaces on the IDA's campus, but right then it felt entirely too small. He stood on the edge of the mat, at least ten feet from me, and I wished there were more space between us. I took a beat to think. If I wanted to control the situation, I'd have to be the one to speak next. The only thing we had in common was the IDA.

"So," I said, hoping my voice didn't sound as shaky as it felt. His face lifted a fraction, as if he was surprised I said anything at all.

I pushed on. "What did you do when you were an agent here?" It seemed like the safest topic. We were talking about spying, but we weren't talking about me.

His eyes hardened briefly. "I did a lot." He shifted slightly. "Mostly fieldwork." He didn't elaborate beyond that and I didn't ask him to.

After a few minutes of silence he came a little closer, so he was standing on the mat, his head bowed slightly. His step forward made me want to back away, but I held my ground. "Roy also said you've been here for a few months now." He glanced up, looking at me through his eyelashes. There was a touch of irritation in his voice, but it disappeared when he continued. "I'm sorry it took me so long to get here."

I shook my head hard. He shouldn't be apologizing to me. Not when I spent a decent portion of the past few months praying he wouldn't be found. "It's fine," I said. "I wasn't really expecting you."

I caught his eyes in time to see the flash of pain they held before he buried it. Guilt settled in my chest, but only for a moment. He opened his mouth to say something I was sure I didn't want to hear, and then the door to the training room opened behind him.

"Hey," Nikki said, crossing the threshold. "When you weren't at lunch I figured you were cleared to—" Then she caught sight of my father. She looked from him to me as she put the pieces together. "You're Chris." Her eyes were wide with excitement, which I knew was on my behalf. "I mean, Agent Steely. You're her dad." She looked to me and beamed. Next to her, my dad had a fraction of a smile peeking through his rigid expression. "I'm Nikki Edwards. It's *so* nice to meet you." She extended a hand, which my dad seemed relieved to accept.

"You too," he said.

Nikki gave him a nod before turning back to me. "I'll find you later."

"Now's fine." I couldn't get the words out any faster. I wasn't sure what else to say to my father, and the longer we were left alone, the more uncomfortable it would become. "We were finishing up, and I have classes anyway." I had never been so eager to get to Agent Lee's.

My father stood up straighter, his small smile fading. "Right," he said. "Of course." He shifted on his feet, his eyes roaming around the room before settling again on me. "We'll talk more, though?"

My muscles clenched at the thought, but I nodded. "Yeah," I said. "Absolutely." I walked past him, shoving Nikki toward the door.

Still, he called after us. "After class?" I froze feet from the exit, biting my lip hard. I turned around to find him watching me expectantly. "I'll meet you?" he asked.

My heart was pounding harder than it should for something like this, and I forced myself to nod. "Sure."

His face lifted. "Great!"

I pushed Nikki before he could stop us again. She pulled away from me once we were outside. "What was that about?"

I eyed her wearily. "I don't want to talk about it."

Her eyebrows knitted together. "Did it go badly?"

I shook my head. "It was mostly just—strange."

She shrugged. "You guys have missed a lot of time. I'm sure things will get better."

"Yeah, you're probably right," I said, rolling my injured shoulder as if I could shake away the extra tension.

"I *am* right," she said. We came to a stop in front of the academy building. "I grabbed this from the cafeteria." Nikki pressed a wrapped sandwich into my hand. "I figured if you were cleared to train, you'd get caught up in it."

My stomach growled as she shot me a knowing look. I smiled lightly. "Thanks, Nikki."

"Let's not make this a habit," she called over her shoulder. I ate my sandwich before heading inside.

Chapter Two

OVERLOOKED

My quick escape from my father had made me a little early for class. Our brief conversation was enough to drag up old memories and I found myself caught up in the past.

I was six years old, lying on the floor on my stomach, across from my dad. Cards were spread out facedown between us. We were playing a memory game. With eight cards left, I was winning. I had never beaten him before, and it was my turn. I flipped a card over. It was a penguin.

"Come on," my dad said. "You know this."

He was right, I did. I collected the match and turned over another card. I found that pair too. Before long, I had gathered the remaining sets, not giving my dad a chance to stage a comeback. I stared at him for a moment, with a smile as big as my face, almost afraid to believe I could really have beaten him. "I won." I kicked my toes against the carpet.

Across from me, my dad smiled back, his eyes twinkling in triumph. "Yeah, kid. You did."

It was what I needed to hear. I jumped up, bouncing around the living room in sheer excitement. "I won, I won, I won, I won, I WON!"

My dad laughed and I stopped running around long enough to look at him. He was all smiles. "That's my girl."

I snapped back to reality, squeezing my head at the temples.

I was his girl.

I was sure he knew enough of KATO to have an understanding about what things may have been like for me, and I hated the thought of him ever learning the specifics of my time there. Because I wasn't that girl who ran around the living room anymore.

"Whoa," Gwen said as she and Olivia arrived. "You're having some deep thoughts."

"It's nothing," I said, sitting up straight.

Gwen's forehead crinkled as she scanned my face. "It's not nothing," she said. "But it's nothing you're ready to share."

I raised an eyebrow at her. "You're good." Her observations were small, but specific and incredibly accurate. She always said she was skilled at reading people, but I hadn't realized she was this talented.

Olivia nudged Gwen. "Don't let it go to your head."

"You could be good too," Gwen said. "If you gave in to your natural instincts."

Olivia turned away. "Don't start with that again."

Gwen shrugged. "The sooner you decide to accept your path as a strategic planner, the happier you'll be."

Olivia scowled at her. "Seriously. Stop," she said, before spinning around to face the front of the room.

Gwen held her hands up in surrender and looked at me. "It's a touchy subject."

She turned back as Agent Lee started class. This issue had been debated for as long as I'd known the two of them. Gwen was planning on being a future grifter for the IDA. Olivia was looking to go into observational intelligence, which would mean she'd blend into the shadows of a given situation and pick up whatever intel she could. Gwen believed Olivia to have more of a big-picture mind, and that she would be better suited for planning operations. Based on what I'd seen, I thought Gwen had a point.

A few minutes after Agent Lee had begun teaching, Sam Lewis sauntered in, taking the seat next to me.

Sam was the most advanced tech student in the IDA. So much so that he had helped me out on several occasions, including my mission into KATO a month ago.

"It looks like we're getting close to cracking the files," he said.

My head snapped in his direction, and I tried not to be too eager. Travis, Sam, and I were working on retrieving Eliza Foster, a girl KATO had kidnapped to force her father, a known weapons expert, into working for them. It was just like KATO had done with me and my mom. Travis had been responsible for keeping Eliza safe before she was taken, but things went sideways and he wasn't able to. I managed to get an approximate location on her when I was in their headquarters, but now we were having a hard time pinning down the specifics. Our first goal was to get Eliza back—she was taken under the IDA's watch, which made her our responsibility—but we also had to consider what retrieving her would mean.

My main goal when I came to the IDA was to shut down KATO's agent training program, which could be done most effectively by targeting their satellite safe houses. These houses were primarily used for agent housing and training. Shutting them down would almost certainly cripple the entire agency. Eliza was being kept in one of them. If we went for Eliza, we'd be showing KATO we could get to their houses, which would run the risk of them raising security across the board. The ideal scenario was that we'd be able to hit them all at once and get Eliza back that way. Though it was proving to be challenging enough to find her house, let alone the others. However, we did have one potential lead.

It hadn't gone unnoticed by Sam that I'd taken the time to look up Eliza's location when I was in KATO. What I didn't know at the time was that when Sam saw where I was poking around, he figured it had to be important. He copied as many files connected to Eliza's as he could in ten seconds, but he hadn't said anything until a week after the mission.

"By the time the files ended up on our servers, they were seriously encrypted," he'd told us when Travis and I met with him in Simmonds's office. "I wasn't even sure I came away with anything we could use."

"But you did?" Travis asked, making no attempt to hide how eager he was.

"It looks that way," Sam said. He explained that he hadn't anticipated the protections KATO put on copied files. Despite the fact that we had infiltrated their system, copying the files triggered an automatic encryption so sophisticated and layered that even with the IDA's most advanced technology it would take weeks to crack. Sam and the tech team had been working on it since we'd gotten back, which is why it meant so much to hear there had been progress. It was our hope that the other files would give us insight to other locations just as Eliza's had.

"How close is close?" I asked Sam, trying to tamp down my excitement.

He shrugged. "Hard to tell exactly, but it could be anywhere from a few hours to a few days."

A few days seemed like nothing compared to the weeks it'd taken so far, yet still not soon enough. "You'll find me?"

He looked at me out of the corner of his eye. "Don't ask stupid questions, KATO girl." He remained the only person who could get away with calling me that. He looked back at his phone.

"As soon as Lewis and Steely are ready, we'll be starting our individual and team assessment unit," Agent Lee said, looking directly at the two of us. I gave her an apologetic look as Sam put his phone down.

She nodded in brief acknowledgment before continuing her lesson. "Our goal for this is to have a better understanding of how to recognize the strengths of an individual, and how to either utilize them on a team or work around them in an enemy." In front of me, Gwen was staring at Olivia, who was very pointedly ignoring her. Agent Lee turned to the whiteboard. "Strengths can primarily be sorted into two groups—physical and intellectual—but within each group is a wide variety of skills."

She proceeded to list the different physical and intellectual strengths a person can have, and I forced myself to push my other problems aside and focus.

The rest of my classes passed without much else to note—until I reached Agent Harper's room. He'd spent most of the year going out of his way to get under my skin, mostly by using my history at KATO to embarrass me in class. I had gotten a brief pass after I'd left the medical wing, but that only lasted for a few days. Since then, he'd been growing increasingly hostile—pushing every KATO button he could think of. The edginess I'd felt since I got back from North Korea had only made the situation worse.

"Viper." Harper's voice cut through the pre-class chatter, effectively silencing the room. My stomach tightened as Sam, who had just crossed the threshold, caught my eye. Then he glared at Harper and stepped purposefully in front of him on his way back to his seat.

My eyes locked back on Harper, who was unfazed by Sam, while I pressed my palms into the table. I was in no mood for anything that might come next.

"I've been thinking." Harper's tone was perfectly innocent, but his lips were twisting in a way that was anything but. "In order to better understand the enemy, it would help if we knew how one thought. I'd like you to tell the class what it's like to kill someone."

Everything went quiet and there was a ringing in my ears that I couldn't seem to shake. It was just loud enough to make me think there was a possibility I had heard him wrong. "What did you just ask me?" I couldn't help the growl in my voice.

Harper smirked, his cockiness reaching unmanageable levels. "What is it like to kill someone?" He asked the question slowly, leaving no room for error. "More specifically, what is it like to *want* to kill someone?"

A fire ignited in my chest and quickly spiraled through me.

Harper came closer when I didn't answer. He stood next to me, towering over me in what I was sure was some kind of power play. "Plenty of people in this room will fight killers like you—"

He never got to finish his sentence. I'd had more than enough of Agent Harper and his questions. I barely thought about what I was doing when I found myself standing over him, my hand around his neck, holding him to the table. Harper's eyes were wide with surprise and a flash of fear. I felt like I had in the training room earlier—like I finally had a release from all the tension that had been building over the past few weeks—or even months.

I forced myself to let go of him, but I didn't back away. I stayed hovering over him. Sam shot me a series of questioning and concerned looks, while Gwen, Olivia, and the rest of the class stared at me wide-eyed. I heard someone on the other side of the room mutter that it was about time. As much as I was mad at myself for giving in, the kid wasn't wrong. It *was* about time.

I leaned in just a little bit closer to Harper. "You're not going to tell *anyone* about this," I hissed at him. "Because if you do, I'll tell Simmonds what it was that pushed me." I strangled a teacher. If it got back to Simmonds, I would most definitely be in more trouble than Harper would be for provoking me. But he had been crossing the line with me since I showed up on campus. I knew from Olivia that Harper was too young to be assigned in-house, which meant teaching had to be some kind of punishment. He couldn't afford another black mark on his record, no matter how small.

He gritted his teeth and glowered at me in a way that told me I had him. I stepped back, giving him the chance to get up. Harper hurried to the front of the room, staring straight ahead as I attempted to burn a hole in his skull using only my mind. He threw a worksheet at us and spent the rest of the class hiding behind his computer screen.

As good as it felt to put Harper in his place, I was still agitated that he'd dragged up my history again in the first place. I was so distracted that I completely forgot my father would be waiting for me after class. I stopped short when I saw him standing across the hall.

There were days in KATO where I dreamed that something like this would happen—that I could actually find myself face-to-face with either or both of my parents. But I thought KATO had killed them both, so I never believed this could be a reality. It was something I'd made peace with a long time ago. Now I was seeing my dad for the second time that day and it felt overwhelming. I still had that six-year-old running around my mind. I couldn't stop comparing who I'd become to who I used to be.

I crossed my arms to keep from fidgeting.

Behind me, Gwen and Olivia slipped out of the classroom, congratulating me on my victory as they passed.

"What's that about?" my dad asked.

"Nothing," I said, shaking my head. "You wanted to talk?"

"Right." He shifted his weight awkwardly, glancing around as if he had forgotten why he'd come here. "I saw an empty meeting room down the hall. I thought we could use that."

"Yeah." I bit my lip. "Okay."

He took a hesitant step toward the room and I followed. The space was no bigger than a classroom, but arranged to look more like a conference room. There was a long table in the center with a large monitor behind one end and a whiteboard behind the other. My dad took the seat in front of the monitor and I sat down next to him. He wheeled his chair over so we were sitting across from each other without the table to separate us.

For a long moment neither one of us said a word. He studied me, seeming to be waiting for something, though I didn't know what. Eventually he spoke. "I know this might be strange."

I arched an eyebrow. "Because we've haven't seen each other for ten years?" I asked. "Or because you thought I was dead?" His jaw clenched. "It's okay that you did." I sat up straighter. "I understand why you would. KATO isn't exactly known for turning enemy kids into spies. Aside from me, there are only two other foreign agents I've come across." I killed one of them in a KATO training exercise, but he didn't need to know that. "Plus, I thought you were dead too."

He held his hard expression and watched me steadily. "I—" He struggled to get the words out. "I figured out pretty quickly that KATO wanted your mom for her science background. And if that was true, it had to mean that you were leverage." I swallowed hard and he continued. "I spent three years doing *everything* I could to get to you. I knew you had to be in KATO's headquarters, but I could never get a lock on their location." He paused, and when he spoke again his voice had softened. "When your mom turned up—when her *body* turned up—I was certain you wouldn't be far behind. KATO had my full attention for three years. I thought I understood how they operated. Everything I'd found said that they killed the people they were finished with. So if your mom was dead it meant they didn't need you for leverage anymore. And I couldn't handle seeing you like that." He gave his head a hard shake. "I shouldn't have given up so easily."

"It wouldn't have mattered," I said, looking away from him. I wasn't going into this any deeper. Not now. "Even if you found out I was alive, you wouldn't have gotten close to me." He drew a sharp breath, and I couldn't tell if he was hurt or angry. I paused for a beat then tried again, speaking more gently this time. "This isn't your fault." His eyes sharpened considerably. "It's KATO's. There was nothing you could have done."

Pain flashed across his face, and he took a moment to find his voice. "We can get away from them now."

My stomach jumped into my throat and I wasn't sure if it was fear or excitement. He couldn't mean what I thought he did. "What are you saying?"

A smile fought its way onto his face. "I'm saying I can get you out of this world. We can leave together. I can make us disappear."

I bit down on my tongue, not daring to speak until I was certain I had heard him correctly. "No."

He stiffened. "What?"

"I said no." I crossed my arms and shifted away from him, leaving no room for misunderstanding. "I have too much to do here."

His face wrinkled with confusion. "I don't know much about what happened to you over the past ten years, but I got the highlights of what's gone on since you've been back. I heard you're being *hunted*." He leaned forward, invading my space. "I can get you away from that. I know how to stay hidden."

I pushed myself out of the chair and spun to stand behind it, gripping the back tightly. "I don't *want* to stay hidden! I didn't come here just so I could get away from them. I came here so I could *hurt* them. I'm not finished with that."

Of course, part of me loved the idea of falling completely off the grid; the damage KATO had done over the years has been devastating, and they used *me* as a tool. But I was too far in to let them get away with it.

He blinked a few times, clearly struggling to comprehend. "What's the point in hurting them if it gives them the chance to hurt *you*?"

"They already *have* hurt me!" The words came out before I could stop them, and I saw the anguish on his face. I tucked my head, giving myself a moment to get it together before looking back up at him. "I'm not going anywhere."

The silence buzzed the air.

"This wasn't how your life was supposed to play out." His voice was barely above a whisper, and it still seemed too loud. "You didn't choose any of this."

"That doesn't matter anymore," I said. "This is the life I have. I don't know if I'll be doing this forever, but I do know that no part of my future involves running. So for now, I'm a spy with a mission. Once that mission is complete, I'll figure out what comes next."

"Jocelyn—"

"No." He was gearing up for an argument. I could see it all over his face. "I don't know how to do this," I said. It was enough to keep him quiet. "I don't know how to be a daughter after nearly a decade of thinking I was an orphan. But I do know that this is my life. You don't get to show up and change it."

He leaned back in his chair, taking me in, his expression completely blank. He opened his mouth to talk, but I cut him off. "I need to go," I said. "I have work to do."

He blinked, looking somewhat stunned. "Right." His voice was hoarse. "Of course."

I didn't waste any time finding the door.

. . .

The IDA had a handful of mission prep rooms that were set aside for long-term planning. Simmonds had assigned one to me and Travis so we could keep track of everything related to KATO, their safe houses, and Eliza. Travis and I were focusing on locating the safe houses and trying to detect any movement from the agency.

Since Travis had a special interest in Eliza, Simmonds had tasked him with looking specifically for Eliza's safe house, which we knew to be in the vicinity of St. Petersburg, Russia. Locating her was the unquestioned priority, but the ultimate goal was still to find all of the safe houses. Travis and I worked together on that. In addition, I had also been asked to focus on KATO's broader goals. We had invaded their headquarters, which meant they were going to be looking to relocate and rebuild. Simmonds needed someone who could pick up on their more subtle moves. That was where I came in.

I headed straight to the prep room after my talk with my father and wasn't at all surprised to find Travis already there. The two of us had been spending every minute we could get in that room. Travis was finally closing in on the Russian location, having narrowed it down to four places. And while we didn't have a lock on any other houses, we had twenty potential host countries we were monitoring.

"Hey," Travis said, looking up from his computer. "How did things go with your father?"

"Great." I spit the word out as I flopped down into the chair next to him. "He just cornered me and tried to get me to leave. He has some plan to make us disappear."

His eyebrows shot up. "You're kidding."

"I'm not."

He wheeled even closer—closer than my father had been to me, though with Travis I didn't mind. "So how'd he take it when you told him no?"

The fact that he never questioned what my answer would be made me smile. "Not well."

"Given your history, he probably thought he was doing you a favor." Travis nudged my knee with his. "It'll take some time, but he'll get used to you."

I exhaled heavily. "Can we just focus on KATO?" I asked, powering up the computer in front of me.

Travis rolled away, but he hadn't taken his eyes off me. "There's nothing else you want to tell me?" he asked. "You didn't do anything—*unusual* in one of your classes?"

My head snapped back in his direction. "How did you find out?"

"Sam stopped by," Travis said with a laugh. "He was very excited."

I rolled my eyes. "I know he was."

"So." He turned to face me again. "What did Sidney do?"

I shook my head. "It's not your problem." His eyes narrowed. "Really," I said. "I handled it, and we have enough to worry about." I tapped his monitor. "What have you found?"

Travis looked a little disgruntled that I wasn't sharing, but his mood lifted when he turned to his screen. "We can officially discount the northern location. We got some field photos from another IDA assignment and it looks like the people that live there are European." He zoomed in on the map that was on his screen. There were three red dots at various points across the country. These locations were all purchased around the time we believe KATO would have been looking to buy, and we had difficulty locating the purchase information. It was likely that KATO bought one of them.

"Does that mean there are teams on the ground?" I asked. Simmonds had said that once Travis narrowed the possibilities down to three, he would authorize a reconnaissance team to investigate.

"I met with Simmonds a couple hours ago. He said there's already a team in the area, so he retasked them to Russia," he said. "I'm going to keep working our intel just in case none of these are what we're looking for."

"It has to be one of them," I said. Travis had been too careful to get this wrong. "And Sam told me that the files are almost decrypted."

"He mentioned that when he dropped by," Travis said. "But until we have something definitive to work with, we need to stay focused."

This had been our approach since we'd learned about the files Sam pulled. We were hoping for something useful, but there was no guarantee it would get us closer to Eliza or KATO. For now, we had a recon team on the ground, and the tech team was doing their best to pick up on KATO's movement via satellite. There were also observational intelligence agents around the world with their ears to the ground, reporting daily on global developments, so we had plenty of intel to sift through while we waited for word.

The prep room's walls were mounted with several monitors, but also a corkboard. We had filled it with satellite photos of locations we were investigating, along with all of the other data we had collected.

However, when it came to KATO's activity, I wasn't having too much luck, which was extremely concerning. KATO seemed to quiet down only when they were working on something big, like they had been in the year leading up to the attempted missile launch. But they shouldn't be too quiet now. We had completely blindsided them, invaded their headquarters, and even gone as far as to set off a small explosion. It should have sent them scrambling to rebuild. No matter how hard they worked to stay unnoticed, we should still be able to detect some kind of activity. But we hadn't.

After another hour of poring over the IDA's satellite images and field reports that got me nowhere, I found myself staring at the corkboard. We had laid out everything we knew about KATO, the safe houses, and Eliza in chronological order. Behind me, I noticed Travis had stopped working and was watching me instead. "What's up?" he asked.

"We're missing something." I raised my chin, studying the board from the top. "They have an entire network to rebuild thanks to us and we're not seeing any sign of it. The only reason they would be keeping this low of a profile is if they already have a major operation in motion that they need to protect." I traced the timeline, hoping to find something we might have overlooked.

Eliza was taken over a year and a half ago. I knew she was briefly brought to headquarters before being relocated to the safe house in India. Then a little over two months ago, she was moved to the Russian house. I had gotten the specifics of her location when I was in KATO, but we had actually received a report months before that. On my first mission with the IDA, Travis had been sent to retrieve KATO intel from the Chinese. When he didn't make it back, I'd gone in after him. We returned with several KATO files. One of them was a coded message about Eliza's relocation, though we didn't realize that at the time. A translation of the message was pinned to our board. My fingers froze on it.

The snake is hidden in the frozen forest. The job is nearly complete.

"What is it?" Travis asked, coming to stand next to me.

"I think we're looking at this all wrong," I said. Pieces were starting to fit together in my mind. "We've been using my experience to guide us with Eliza, but what if she's different? What if she isn't just leverage that KATO turned into a spy?"

Travis's forehead furrowed. "You think they're using her for more than that?"

"I'm not sure of anything," I said with a halfhearted shrug. "But I think we've overlooked this." I ran my finger under the message. "We assumed KATO was keeping track of her because of Dr. Foster's involvement. But this is KATO, and we know from my history that they had no intentions of ever releasing her. She became a future KATO agent the second she was taken, just like every other girl in their program. But if that's the case, then why would KATO send a coded message about her relocation?"

The understanding spread across his face. "Once they didn't need her as leverage, she would have become a normal agent-in-training. So they would have just moved her and been done with it. There shouldn't have been a reason to follow it up with a memo—especially a coded one."

"Exactly," I said nodding. "And think about where we got this intel from. Everything else on that flashdrive is tied in to KATO's bigger goals to gain more power and global control. Why would this be any different?"

Travis crossed his arms, and I could almost see his mind spinning. "What could the daughter of an English scientist, who was taken purely as leverage, have to offer them?"

I shook my head. "I don't know," I said. I glanced cautiously at Travis. "It was bad enough when she was collateral damage. If she's *special* to them—"

A knock on the door cut me off, but it wasn't a sentence I needed to finish.

"We need to get those files decrypted," Travis said as I opened the door.

Sam stood on the other side, smiling. "Then you must be really glad to see me."

Chapter Three

PIECES

S am went immediately to Travis's computer and started typing. "I asked Simmonds if I could brief you." He clicked a file up onto the screen. It was Eliza's. "Hers is the only one we have right now. For some reason, her encryption was more complex, so we had twice as many people working on it. The others should be finished within the next couple days." Given what Travis and I had just worked out, I didn't like knowing Eliza's file was more secure.

"It's okay, hers is the most important." I may have gotten a look at the file in KATO, but I didn't have time to do more than locate the information I needed. Her picture was on the upper left-hand corner. Next to it was a grid of some facts, followed by blocks of notes below. It ended with a single line, and then the note about her relocation, which was what I saw when I pulled up her file inside KATO headquarters. The text was still in Korean, but aside from the last line, it didn't make any sense.

"It looks like they've only been decrypted," I said, finally tearing my eyes away. "Not decoded."

"Right," Sam said. "We got through the computer encryption, but the translation and coding team said none of the ciphers you gave them worked. They're still working on cracking it, but they thought you might be able to do it faster."

I'd need to get a good look at the language. Hopefully my experience with KATO would allow me to pick up on something that would help.

Travis hadn't said a word. He stood rigid as he studied the screen, and I knew he had to be thinking of every horrible thing KATO could be doing to her. A part of me wished I'd told him less about my experience so he wouldn't have as much to work with.

I came to stand next to him, if only because it seemed like he needed me to. "We need to know what this means," he said.

"I'll get started on figuring that out," I said. "But no matter what it says, we need a confirmed location before we can act."

"Right." Travis inhaled sharply and pulled his eyes away from the screens, snapping back to reality. "You work on the code, I'll work on the safe house."

I nodded to him.

"I'm going to get back to the other files," Sam said. "We should have more for you soon." He headed out, leaving Travis and me to get to work.

. . .

The decryption team was right; the wording was bizarre even by KATO's standards. Traditionally, their codes look like random characters thrown next to each other, but in this case, parts of the sentences and phrases seemed to make sense. It looked like the document was only partially coded, which was probably because it was an in-house document. It shouldn't be too hard to work out, but I was sure the IDA's coding team hadn't come across this before. I had cracked one of KATO's upper-level ciphers in the past, and this didn't seem as complex.

I wrote the phrase out on a piece of paper so I could work with it more easily. I tried rearranging the words, first of the whole sentence, then only the words that didn't make sense. I started with the more obscure codes—the ones most KATO agents at my level weren't supposed to know—but after I played with that for an hour, I decided to give the more traditional ones a try. I was surprised when the first decoded word made sense in the sentence. A spark of excitement shot through me. I tried the next word.

It didn't fit.

I rubbed my forehead in frustration. I still felt close, but I was missing something.

Then it hit me. I hurried to put my theory to the test and before long I had cracked the other word. "I figured it out," I said to Travis. He wheeled over to my area, which was scattered with paper. "The last time I had to crack one of KATO's higher-level ciphers I had to move the entire message through a series of cipher keys. For this one, each coded *word* has a different key."

"So you have to try a different cipher for each word until the sentence is decoded," Travis said.

"If you're someone who is supposed to read the message, you'll know what ciphers to use—it would take less than a minute," I said. "But for us, I think we'll know we've cracked it once the phrase makes some kind of sense."

I had three more words to work out. Travis watched me scribble. It should have been annoying but it wasn't.

When I finally got the last word cracked, I met Travis's eyes. "This is it," I said. "This is what we needed." I looked at what I had just de-coded and dread spread through me.

"What does it say?"

I glanced at him uneasily. "A rough translation is that she is the future of KATO training and control."

Travis's face contorted in horror. "How could they control their agents any more than they already do?"

"I don't know." I let my mind slip briefly to my time at KATO and my stomach turned at the thought that it could be worse. "But if she's the key, we need to get her away from them. Now."

"We're still waiting on a location," Travis said.

I bit my lip to keep from showing too much frustration. So we waited—there wasn't anything else we could do. It was just over half an hour later that Travis's pager went off.

He read the message and looked to me with a fire in his eyes. "We've got it," he said. "Let's go to Simmonds."

. . .

Travis leaned against the wall in the hallway, waiting to get into Simmonds's office, while I paced. His arms were crossed and his jaw clenched. I knew he'd been waiting for this moment for over a year and a half.

Travis and I both straightened abruptly when the door opened, and Simmonds's eyebrows rose slightly when we entered. "What can I do for you two?"

"We have something we need to move on," I said. I told Simmonds I'd cracked the code on Eliza's file and gave him the key so the coding team could decipher the rest of them for us. Then Travis and I launched into everything we'd uncovered.

"You're saying Eliza Foster is essential to KATO's training future, and we have a lock on her location?" Simmonds said when we had finished.

"Yes, sir," Travis said, rocking forward on the balls of his feet. "We can get her." He was fierce and determined, and clearly ready to walk out of that office and on to a plane.

Simmonds hesitated, and judging by the look on his face, we weren't going to like what we were about to hear. "I'll authorize it." A surge of adrenaline rushed through me.

"Thank you, sir." Travis was already headed toward the door.

"We're not finished yet," Simmonds said. Travis pivoted back and glanced at me. When I shrugged, he looked to Simmonds. "Elton, you will not be going on this assignment."

And there it was.

Travis stared ahead at Simmonds, the wave of emotion washing over his face. "What?"

Travis had been suspended for accidentally spilling details about my relationship with KATO to other IDA agents. I hadn't thought that would apply here. And judging from Travis's reaction, he hadn't either.

"Sir." I took a step forward. "Travis has been working on this. He knows the situation better than anyone."

Simmonds flicked his eyes to me. "This is an operational matter that does not concern you." His icy tone was enough for me to keep my mouth shut. Simmonds turned back to Travis. "I allowed you to go to North Korea because you were essential in that operation," he said. "But you're still on field suspension. While you would be helpful on this assignment, other agents can do the job."

"I've been working on this for over a year," Travis said. His voice was quiet. He was beyond anger—he was devastated.

"Your goal was to get her back. That will still happen."

"Sir, *please*—"

"It's not much of a consequence if you don't mind missing the assignments you're held back from," Simmonds said. Travis's breath rattled, and he seemed to be struggling for control. "You can, however, watch from the command center."

Travis's face started to turn red, his anger surfacing. "Sir, you know—"

"Agent Elton, this decision is final." Simmonds spoke with the power and authority he seemed to reserve for moments of extreme finality.

A vein throbbed in Travis's neck, but he didn't dare say a word. If he did I was certain he would have erupted. Instead, he spun away from Simmonds and left the office, slamming the door so hard I was surprised it hadn't broken.

I swallowed and faced Simmonds. "When do I leave?" I asked, my voice soft. I hated the thought of acting on this without Travis, but it was still a mission—and an important one.

"I'll have something ready within hours," Simmonds said. "I'm assigning Mathers, Hawthorne, and Edwards to the team. Check in with Dr. March while I brief them. You can meet up after in the mission prep rooms to go over your plan." He met my eyes firmly. "Your mission is to get the girl, and only the girl. There will be others in that house. You have to leave them there."

I wanted badly to argue, but instead I nodded. I knew it wouldn't be easy, but he was right. "She's the job. I got it."

Simmonds dismissed me after that. I hurried to the door, planning on tracking down Travis before I did anything else. It turned out I didn't have to look very far. I found him in the hall outside of Simmonds's office.

He was pacing, his fingers laced together behind his head with his elbows jutting out. He came to a stop and dropped his arms when he saw me.

"I'm sorry—"

He cut me off with a wave of his hand, defeated. "Just get her, okay? If I can't—I need you to come back with her."

I looked him dead in the eyes. "You know I always complete my missions."

His jaw set, not seeming all that comforted. "Be careful." He enunciated each syllable, refusing to let me leave until I promised him I would.

Chapter Four

IN RUSSIA

I was in charge of prepping Nikki, Rachel, and Cody for what they might find inside a KATO house, but there was ultimately only so much I could do. I knew what a KATO training facility might look like, and that we should expect to find two handlers in the house, but these safe houses were completely unfamiliar to me. Still, if I had to guess, most of the training would take place in the basement. The facility was in the middle of nowhere, but KATO would want to limit the exposure of their agents. The best way to do that would be to keep them underground.

I rubbed my palms along my thighs. The acupuncture treatment Dr. March forced on me was only so effective this time. As glad as I was to be going after Eliza, it also meant going into a building that was operated by KATO. No amount of preparation could change that.

Nikki sat next to me on the plane with Cody and Rachel on the other side of the aisle. They seemed to be going through the file one last time. Rachel glanced up and caught me watching. Her forehead creased and she seemed to be battling her own thoughts.

"You'll have his back?" she asked finally, gesturing to Cody. He and I were partnered on this assignment. Out of the four of us, we were the strongest fighters, which was why we were directly tasked with getting to Eliza.

"Rach—" Cody shot me an apologetic look.

"No, it's okay." I cut him off and turned back to Rachel, giving her my full attention. "He's covered."

She studied me for a long time. "He better be." Her eyes were as hard as her voice. She held my gaze as she crossed her arms and sunk back into her seat.

I nodded once, in acknowledgement, biting my lip until she finally turned away. I didn't blame her for questioning me, even now. No matter how understanding she had been after the last mission, I had hurt her badly when I was fighting for the other side. A part of me wished I could remember what I did to her. Though, judging from the details I had picked up here and there, maybe it was better that I didn't. I was haunted enough by my KATO assignments as it was.

I ran a hand through my hair and opened my own mission file, putting my focus where it needed to be. This had to go flawlessly for so many reasons. And if I was honest, I really didn't like doing this without Travis. Not just because of what this mission meant to him, but because after years of solo assignments, I had come to rely on him to have my back. Even though I trusted the others, his absence made me feel strangely off-center.

I didn't realize my knee was bouncing until Nikki put her hand on my leg, driving my heel into the ground. "Try to relax." Her face was open, with a tranquility that she seemed to be trying to transfer to me. "We've got this."

"I know." I pressed my fists into the seat. "It's just—"

"KATO," she finished for me. "Believe me, I get it." I relaxed a fraction. "Can I ask you something?" She waited for me to nod before continuing. "Why are KATO agents always girls?"

I noticed Rachel and Cody listening from the other side of the aisle. In all my time at KATO, the answer had never been spelled out for me in any capacity, but I had overheard enough conversations to have a good idea. "From what I can tell, it was more important to them to have the men in the military," I said. "Men got KATO off the ground, but the agents for something like this were meant to be expendable. To them, men aren't, which is why they wanted women. I also think they wanted women because they thought we'd be easier to control."

A long silence followed, and I looked away from all of them.

"Well," Nikki said. "You showed them, didn't you?"

I smiled lightly at her, though it was hard to know if I had really shown them anything.

Nikki shifted away from me, and I took advantage of the quiet. I rested my head on the back of the seat, doing my best to find some sense of peace.

. . .

We landed about ten miles from the safe house. The house itself was essentially in the middle of a forest, but the last thing we wanted was to give the handlers any reason to suspect something out of the ordinary. As anxious as I was on the plane, I found myself snapping into mission mode once we hit the ground. I let the adrenaline push my nerves aside and control my focus. The IDA had sent a two-man advance surveillance team an hour ahead of us to get a couple cars on the ground and eyes on the house. The two agents, Parker and Mills, met us when we landed.

The first thing I noticed was the cold. It threw me off even though I was prepared for it. We were dressed in layers—the last of which was a thermal hooded sweatshirt. Mine was zipped up to my chin.

"We didn't learn anything new," Agent Parker said. He looked like he might be a little older than Cody. "We managed to get close enough to put a tap on their security system, so Command has access to it. They're waiting for your word to shut it down."

"Excellent," Cody said. As the most experienced and highest-ranking agent, he had point on this mission. Though he and everyone else deferred to me fairly regularly.

Agent Mills started her car while Parker jumped into the second one. We partnered off. Cody and I took the backseat of Mills's, while Nikki and Rachel took Parker's. We went in opposite directions. The plan was for each team to approach from either side of the house, which would ideally reduce our visibility.

"You guys are clear on the extraction protocol, right?" Mills asked before she dropped us off.

"We're good to go," I said, answering for both of us. Two cars brought us in, but only one was picking us up. Our plan was to gas the house, which would leave everyone unconscious. If things went smoothly, we would be able to locate Eliza and leave through the front door before the handlers started to wake. We had a ten-minute window to make this happen.

"We'll see you on the other side," Mills said, her ponytail swaying as she turned back to the road. She drove off quickly and quietly.

Once Cody and I settled on the perimeter of KATO's security, Cody pushed his comm in. "Alpha team in position."

"Copy." It was Walter. He was running Command for this mission, which was one of the main reasons why I would be doing as little communicating with Command as possible. The two of us hadn't gotten along that great on our last missions. He didn't trust me, which made it difficult for me to trust him. He was supposedly the best tech, which was undoubtedly why he was assigned to a mission like this one.

"Beta team in position," Rachel said shortly after us.

"Command, we're waiting for your word," Cody said to Walter.

"Stand by," Walter said. The line went quiet for a moment. "Security system is disabled. You're clear to move in."

We'd each been given a pellet gun, equipped with pellets specially designed to pierce glass and release a knock-out gas. I felt good holding the gun—if I remembered correctly, my mother had developed something similar. I would bet this weapon was based on her technology.

"On my mark," Cody said. I took aim and waited for his signal before firing off my pellet. I had the upstairs, Rachel had the downstairs, and Nikki and Cody had the basement. "All right, we're on the count." We had to wait fifteen seconds for the gas to disperse, do its job, and dissipate. When the time had passed, Cody signaled us in. "We have ten minutes to get in, get the girl, and get out." If we were inside longer than that, the handlers were likely to wake up and catch us. "Let's move."

I took the lead, darting around the back of the house with Cody close behind me. Rachel and Nikki took the front. I kicked the door in. We quickly cleared the lower level of the house before meeting in the center. From there, Cody and I headed for the basement—where I was sure Eliza was most likely to be—while Rachel and Nikki searched the upper floors, looking for the handlers to make sure they stayed down.

It was decided that I would lead the way downstairs. Cody and I both had our guns out. He put his hand on the doorknob and met my eyes. I nodded once and he opened the door without hesitating. I gave a quick scan of the stairs and found them empty. We hurried down the stairs as quietly as we could.

"We've got eyes on both handlers," Nikki said in our ears.

The basement looked almost how I thought it would. It was big—as big as the house itself. But I knew right away something was wrong. At headquarters our space was almost completely empty. However, this room was littered with buckets, rags, plastic bags, needles, and metal tools with purposes I was sure I didn't want to imagine.

Despite the difference, I found memories surfacing. They slammed into me before I could prepare myself.

I was eleven, battling with another agent—a North Korean native code-named Centipede. The space was solid concrete with the occasional metal pole lying around the edge for handlers to use as punishment. I had challenged Chin Ho the day before. He'd given me a bruised jaw and cut my Gerex in half—it was enough for me to work out, but I was still shaking and struggling to keep up. Centipede landed a debilitating punch to my stomach and I doubled over. Had I not been experiencing some level of withdrawal I would have recovered. Centipede was my biggest competitor inside KATO and she took advantage. She swept my legs out from under me, knocking me to the ground, then grabbed my arm and forced me onto my stomach. Her knee was on my back and my arm twisted within centimeters of breaking.

Then the whistle blew. We were under strict orders regarding how far we should go with each other for each fight. Sometimes, it's kill or injure, but today it was only disable. Centipede held her position until another hand replaced hers on my wrist. My heart sped up. It was my handler. His knee pressed into my back hard—harder than Centipede was capable of. I could just barely get a breath in. I tried to turn to face him, but his free hand slammed my cheek into the floor. I was amazed it hadn't shattered.

"How could you bring me so much shame!" His breath was hot in my ear and it was taking everything I had to stay quiet. Any sign of pain or weakness would make this worse. He turned my arm just a little bit farther and a whimper snuck out of me. It was all he needed. He gave my arm a hard final twist.

The crack reverberated around the hollow room.

"Raven!" Cody's sharp voice pulled me back. I focused on him, swallowing the bile that had scorched my throat. I couldn't do this now. Not on a mission—especially one as important as this. "You good?" He looked mildly alarmed.

"Something's not right here," I said, taking in the room again. The tools, the clutter—it shouldn't be like this.

Cody's eyebrows knitted together. "How do you mean?"

"The training facilities at KATO are empty. Almost—hollow." The crack of my arm echoed in my mind. "I wouldn't expect it to be exactly the same. But it should be similar. There's more going on here."

His eyes hardened, but he didn't comment. "Let's find the girl and get out."

I bit my lip and nodded, all of this suddenly feeling even more urgent. I scanned the room, looking for a door. I was sure KATO had to be keeping the girls down here. Even though they were in the middle of nowhere, they wouldn't risk anyone seeing and potentially questioning what was really happening in this house. Then I saw the small doorknob coming out of the wall in the corner. I approached it slowly. "You have another pellet?" I asked.

Cody switched guns. "I do."

If I had to guess, the room the trainees were kept in was built like a bomb shelter. There weren't any windows or any signs of life outside the room. It was the middle of the night, so it was a safe bet the girls were asleep, but we needed to be sure they stayed that way. I got closer to the door and found a small keyhole under the knob. I pushed my comm in. "Echo, Onyx," I said to Nikki and Rachel, "do you guys see any keys around?"

"Yeah," Nikki said. "One of the handlers has a set. I'll meet you at the stairs."

I rushed to the basement steps and Nikki tossed them down to me. I caught the keys and hurried back to Cody, who still had his pellet gun out. I caught his eye briefly, preparing him. I unlocked the door and yanked it open in one fluid motion. Cody shot the pellet inside, and I shut the door even more sharply than I had opened it. I kept my hands on it, holding the door in place for the fifteen seconds we needed. When time was up I pulled it back open, and Cody and I both went inside without any hesitation. I searched the room.

There were about twelve girls lying on the floor, asleep. My stomach turned knowing all too well that right now, knocked out, they were probably in the deepest sleep they'd had since they started KATO's training program. I scanned each face quickly, trying not to think about the girls we were leaving behind. I found Eliza. She was the farthest from the door. Her long dark hair was spread out around her. I caught a glimpse of her burn scar on her neck.

"There," I said to Cody, gesturing to her. He nodded, and scooped her off the floor. She looked thin—too thin. KATO may be the prime example of irresponsibility but they didn't use starvation as a tactic. It was counterproductive. They needed their agents strong and able to fight. If they wanted to deprive them of anything, it was the Gerex.

The basement door banged open and Cody and I both froze. Before I could check in with Rachel and Nikki, one of the handlers came thundering downstairs. Cody and I both reacted, instinctively moving to the hollow space under the stairs. I put myself in front of Cody and Eliza, leaning protectively back into them, and speaking so softly I was sure even the alert KATO operative wouldn't hear. "I'll deal with him, you get her out of here."

Cody gave a single sharp nod, not questioning or challenging. I picked my moment carefully, waiting until the handler was fully down the stairs. He had his gun out and his back to us. I charged at him, taking him completely by surprise. We didn't want a gunfight— the goal was to get Eliza out. I rammed the handler into the wall before he could react, his gun clattering to the floor. Out of the corner of my eye, I saw Cody on the move. He called quickly for an extraction as I sideswiped the KATO handler's knees. He didn't get the chance to brace himself before his head crashed into the side of the bottom stair, knocking him out.

I hurried up the steps, glancing back just long enough to confirm that he stayed on the ground.

"Echo, Onyx, I thought the handlers were down," I said into the comm. I was already running toward them. It couldn't be good if one had gotten away from them.

"They are," Nikki said as I hit the first floor of the house. "We're staring right at them." A feeling of dread spread through me as I tore up the rest of the stairs. I found Nikki and Rachel in the biggest room, which seemed to be the main office.

They did, in fact, have two bodies in front of them. Bodies that were starting to stir. The first face meant nothing to me, but the second one made my heart stop. I searched for his right hand, my eyes resting on the ugly burn scar on the webbing. "We need to get out of here. *Now.*"

They both looked at me with questions written all over their faces, but they didn't need to be told twice. The three of us headed out the front door. KATO would know someone had been here, but hopefully it would take some time before they knew it was the IDA.

We hurried down the path to our getaway car. Cody and Eliza were in the front with Agent Parker, which left Rachel, Nikki, and me the backseat. Rachel jumped in first with me right behind her, leaving Nikki to bring up the rear.

"How is she doing?" I asked Cody as we started to drive.

I looked at Eliza, who was still unconscious but propped up against him. "She seems okay," he said, scanning her face. I sank into my seat. The adrenaline was starting to wear off and everything we found inside that house began to settle in my mind. I put all of my effort into fighting off the craving I knew would be coming. I rested my head against the back of the seat, and forced myself to take long, controlled breaths. Next to me, Nikki had covered my fist with her hand. She knew what was going on with me, and it helped knowing she was there.

"Jocelyn," Nikki said, with a note of concern in her voice. "Who was that?" I could feel every eye in the car on me.

I pinched the bridge of my nose, still sorting through what I had seen. "That was the director of KATO." My stomach churned. He had been the assistant director when I was there, but we had received intel that he had taken charge after our invasion. I exhaled evenly. I could have killed him tonight. *Should* I have killed him? I couldn't process anything when I saw him—all I could think to do was run.

The silence hung in the air until Nikki broke it. "He was meeting with one of the handlers."

"They were going over this together when they dropped," Rachel said, unzipping her sweatshirt. She pulled out a folder, and passed it to me.

It was Eliza's file. It was labeled as "Python"—her code name—not her given name. But this was different from the one Travis and I had back at the IDA.

The line under Eliza's picture was the part that bothered me the most.

Subject: 075 Project: 08562

My forehead tightened as I studied it. "I have no idea what that means," I said. "I've only ever heard us referred to as agents or trainees." Or a few other choice words we didn't need to get into. I studied the file for another beat. I was starting to develop a theory.

"We're about ten minutes out," Parker said. I looked to Nikki, to tell her my suspicions, but I never got the chance. I turned my head just in time to see an airborne projectile hurling toward the car.

Chapter Five

CENTIPEDE

W e were spinning through the air before I could get a word out. The missile hit the ground, exploding fifty feet from us, and the shock waves sent us tumbling. We took a final turn before skidding to a stop, the tires somehow finding their way to the ground.

"Is everyone okay?" Cody asked, surveying the front seat and turning back to us. His eyes found Rachel first, who nodded. My attention was on Nikki. She was unconscious, her head was bleeding, and her arm was bent in an unnatural angle.

"Nikki's not," I said, completely failing to keep the panic out of my voice.

"Don't move her." Rachel leaned over me, feeling for her neck. "Her head's banged up, but her pulse is strong. We need to get her spine stabilized."

"Our options are pretty limited here," Cody said, assessing the situation. Next to him in the front seat, the driver was calling for the second extraction car and a backboard.

Then I remembered what had happened right before the car flipped. I looked frantically out the window, and I saw someone coming closer. "We have another problem," I said.

A girl was jogging toward us. Once she was close enough, I realized I knew her. It was Centipede.

My muscles stiffened. Centipede and I had quickly become rivals at KATO. She had been the only one who could ever challenge me. I didn't know where she was coming from tonight. She wasn't in the safe house—I would have noticed. But that was a problem for later.

Nikki was hurt, and Eliza was unconscious. A car was at least a minute out. We wouldn't get away. Centipede would kill the others on sight, but I was sure she wouldn't kill me. After everything I'd done, KATO would want me back alive. They'd want me to talk and they'd want me tortured. They'd want me to pay. I suspected that was the only reason she didn't try to do more damage to the car—she needed to make sure I didn't die.

"I have a plan," I said. I found Eliza's folder at my feet and pressed it into Rachel's hands. "I know who this is. I can hold her off. When the car comes, you get Nikki and Eliza and you get out of here." I paused to meet each of their eyes, making sure they understood. "Get them on the plane and safe, then come back for me."

Cody gave me a skeptical look. "I don't think so," he said. "I don't like the idea of leaving you alone with this."

"I can handle it," I said. My voice was firm and commanding, but I felt myself getting defensive. "She's a KATO agent and I've fought her before. I know how to deal with her."

I glanced at Rachel, assuming that, in this case, she would be on my side. My plan got her and the others out, leaving only myself at risk. I was surprised to see she didn't seem any more convinced than Cody. The only difference was that she didn't say anything.

Centipede was getting closer and I was losing my patience. "This is the best plan," I said. "I know what I'm getting into."

I looked at each of them. Cody's lips were pursed, but he sighed. "Don't get yourself killed."

I climbed over Nikki, kicked the bent door open, and ran toward Centipede, prepared to meet her head-on before she got anywhere near the others.

She came to a stop when she realized who I was and broke out into the truest smile I had ever seen on her face. "Well," she said, "you are making my job easy."

I narrowed my eyes. "I doubt that very much."

She arched her eyebrows at me, shrugging. "I was sent to bring you back, and here you are coming to me. It doesn't get too much easier." So I was right, she wasn't in the house. This was a mission for her. She smiled wider and there was a gluttonous look in her eye. I was sure she was thinking about the extra Gerex she'd get as a reward for bringing me back to headquarters.

I circled her. Her attention was on me and I wanted to keep it that way. I didn't want her seeing what was going on in the car behind me. And this way, I would know how long I had to hold her off for. I noticed her hand slip behind her back, and I knew she had some kind of weapon. If she couldn't kill me, it had to be a tranquilizer. I reacted before she had the opportunity, grabbing her hand and twisting her arm upward. I was just quick enough to pull the tranquilizer gun out of her back holster, but then she surprised me. She twirled herself around, ducked under my arm, and reached for the tranq gun with her other hand. She grabbed my wrist, trying to pull it, and me, closer to her. She had my hands twisted up, then kneed me hard in the stomach. I doubled over, dropping the gun. I got myself together enough to kick it far away from both of us. I would not go back to KATO—especially not like that. Not without a fight.

Centipede spun away from the gun, balling her fists and putting them in front of her face, ready to go. I knew she would never turn her back on me, even if it *was* to get a weapon. She would never give me the chance to pull a gun on her. I hadn't killed anyone—at least not that I knew of—since I started at the IDA. It was something I was proud of. But Centipede didn't know that. And the truth was, if I had to choose between letting her live and going back to KATO, I was sure I'd find it in me to pull the trigger. This wasn't like Chin Ho. She didn't raise me.

I kept my hands up, not daring to reach for my gun. Making a move directed at anything but Centipede would give her the upper hand. She came at me, attempting another hit to my stomach, but I pivoted away from her. I did my best to protect my left shoulder. It ached slightly, but it was manageable. I needed to keep it that way. I didn't want her to find out I had a weakness. She threw a punch at my face and I got in one to her chest. It knocked the wind out of her, but slowed her down for only a second. We kept dueling. And the longer it went on, the more I realized I didn't have the upper hand that I used to. I didn't feel nearly as quick or as sharp as I should have. I had lost all awareness of what was going on with the others. I couldn't afford to split my attention. I also lost track of how much time had passed, and I felt myself starting to fade. I didn't know how much longer I could keep up with her.

Just as I was about to cave I heard a car come up right behind me. Centipede took another swing at me and I dodged to the right.

Just as I did, a bullet spiraled past my shoulder from behind. It was on course for Centipede, but she saw it coming and hit the ground.

"Raven, let's go!" It was Cody. He was in the backseat of the car, waiting with the door open. I took advantage of the fact that Centipede was still on the ground, and ran toward the car without looking back. I was a foot from the door when I felt the sting on my right ear.

I didn't slow down to assess what had happened. I knew Centipede was running for me. I dived forward, just barely making it to the car.

"Whoa," Cody said, pulling me inside and closing the door as the car sped off.

"I think she hit me." I felt my ear as I tried to catch my breath. Cody's face stiffened. "Tranquilizer," I said, trying not to panic. I may have avoided KATO, but I still couldn't afford to be tranqed. Dr. March had warned against putting any kind of drug in my system. We didn't know how my body would react if we did.

The realization spread across Cody's face as he leaned closer to the top of my ear, trying to get a better look. "There's no puncture," he said. "I think the body of the dart grazed you." He pulled back to scan my face. "How do you feel?"

I breathed through my nose, trying to sort through the emotion, adrenaline, and the beginnings of a craving to assess myself. Relief flooded through me. "I think I'm okay."

Cody collapsed into his seat, and I thought back over everything we had seen since we'd landed in Russia, struggling to keep myself in check.

. . .

A field medic was working on both Nikki and Eliza by the time Cody and I got on the plane. They were each lying on one of the benches toward the back of the small cabin. Rachel was sitting across from Nikki, watching the medic closely. The engine was already running when Cody and I boarded so we took off quickly.

"Nikki's stable," Rachel said the second she saw us, "but she has a head injury and a broken arm."

"Has she woken up at all?" Cody asked, taking a seat next to Rachel. I stayed standing, craning my neck, trying to get a better look at Nikki, but the medic blocked my view.

"No, not yet." Her voice dipped a fraction and she pulled her arms in, like she was trying to rein in her emotions.

"What about Eliza?" I asked.

Rachel made eye contact with me for a moment before breaking it. "They're keeping her unconscious until we get back to the IDA."

I nodded; that was probably the safest thing. We were in no condition to explain anything to her while we were in the air. I also suspected, based on what I'd seen in that house and the file Rachel and Nikki had recovered, that there was more physical damage done to her than even I had expected. She was better off waiting for Dr. March.

I finally sat down on the bench behind Nikki. I put my back against the wall and pulled my knees into my chest. The mission continued to play in my head on loop. The house full of girls we had to leave behind, how bad Eliza looked, and the *director* of KATO lying on the ground. Then Centipede.

I bit my lip hard. Facing her didn't feel like a reckless move, but it was definitely a miscalculation. I'd underestimated Centipede and overestimated myself. I didn't factor in that she was on Gerex and I wasn't. If she had actually been trying to kill me, I was sure I wouldn't have walked away from that fight.

I felt the craving strengthen and did what I could to focus on breathing. This mission was creeping under my skin, making it hard to fight off, especially since my mind was trying desperately to go back further. Back to my time at KATO and the other instances the two of us had squared off. But I wouldn't let myself go there. I'd freed myself from them. Now all that mattered was moving forward.

A bag of ice appeared in front of my face and I lifted my chin to find Cody feet from me.

"Your jaw isn't looking so good." He pressed the bag into my hands.

"Thanks," I said, embracing the numbing cold that came with it.

He nodded, then sat down across the aisle, facing me and watching me closely. "You're unreal," he said, a smile playing at his lips. "And I mean that in the best way. Walking into a fight like that—" He shook his head. "I don't know if it was the smartest thing to do, but we all wouldn't have gotten away if you hadn't."

I pressed into the wall, leaning my head back and focusing on the ceiling. "I did what needed to be done." That was how I always operated.

Cody didn't say anything for a while. He was quiet for so long that I looked up to see if he was still there. He was, and he was studying me like I was the toughest code he ever had to crack. Then he shook his head again and repeated, "You're unreal." There was a note of admiration that I didn't know what to do with.

He left me alone after that, and I spent rest of the flight working to keep myself under control.

Chapter Six

UNWELCOME FEEDBACK

I still felt edgy when I got back to the IDA, but more or less okay. Enough so that I headed for Simmonds's office first, instead of Dr. March's. I'd need an acupuncture treatment, but I was stable enough for a debrief and I wanted to get better at managing the cravings.

I was surprised to find Travis waiting in the lobby of the operations building when I got there. He was leaning against the wall with his arms crossed but straightened sharply when I opened the door.

"Hey," he said, approaching me eagerly. "I heard what happened. Are you okay?"

"Yeah," I said, rubbing my exposed right ear where the tranquilizer dart had grazed it. "Do you know anything about Nikki or Eliza?"

He fell into step next to me as I headed for the stairs. "Nikki's still unconscious. She's having some scans done, but the doctors say she's stable. They'll know more once the results come back."

I nodded, feeling a mixture of unease and relief—it wasn't good, but it could have been a lot worse. "And Eliza?"

"Dr. March was with her," he said. "I don't know too much more than that."

I nodded and massaged the back of my neck, trying to convince myself to relax.

"How's your shoulder?" he asked, shooting me a pointed look.

"It's all right," I said, rolling it. "Sore, but I've had worse."

Travis arched his eyebrows. "You know when you say that, given your past, it's not saying too much."

I smirked. "I'm not downplaying it. It hurts, but it's really not too bad. I was able to keep her to my right."

He eyed me, trying to work out if I was telling the truth. I must have passed the test, because he moved on. "Simmonds said I could sit in on your debrief, if it's okay with you."

"Of course it is." I turned the knob to Simmonds's office and started to step inside.

My focus was still on Travis, whose eyes widened the second the door opened. "There's one more thing I should tell you about—"

But he didn't get the chance. One very angry voice got my attention.

"What could you have possibly been thinking?"

My head snapped away from Travis to see my father, standing in the middle of Simmonds's office, his jaw locked tight. In the back of my mind it reminded me of when I was younger. I didn't remember him being angry often, but when he was, it was really bad. I think the last time was when I had taken my bike out without telling anyone and ended up in the street.

I shook my head a few times, trying to force my clouded brain to clear. He wasn't finished.

"How could you be so irresponsible?" His voice held a quiet tension that he seemed to be struggling to control.

I felt my guard go up and annoyance start to build in my chest. "What are you talking about?"

This question seemed to make him even more agitated. He started to answer, but Simmonds cut him off.

"Chris." His voice was sharp and authoritative. "Not only is this not the time, but it's not your place. She's *my* agent."

But my dad didn't even seem to hear him. "How could you take a risk that insane?" He was yelling now, eyes bulging. "That was so far off book! You could have gotten yourself killed! How could you even think about taking on an enemy agent by yourself?"

I rolled my shoulders back and drew myself up to my full height. "I know that agent," I said. "I discussed the options with my team. I knew what I was getting into."

"That mark on your ear tells a different story!" He seemed to get angrier the more the conversation went on. "You're lucky it wasn't a bullet!"

Travis took a step forward, so he was right next to me now. "Sir, you need to back off." He squared himself to my father, and while he wasn't yelling, his voice was firm.

But at this point, I was far too enraged to give Travis the floor. "It wasn't luck!" I snapped. Because while I had most definitely made a mistake, it wasn't the mistake he'd thought I'd made. "I knew she wouldn't kill me. KATO wants me alive."

"So if you lost, you'd be back with them?" His jaw flexed. "You're not in any position to make that type of decision."

"Actually, I was." I felt my stance stiffen. "*I* was the one in the field. And I don't have to defend *any* of my choices to you!" He had no business criticizing me. Especially when it came to KATO. "I was with them for *ten years* and you were nowhere to be found. You don't get to weigh in now!"

"That's enough!" Simmonds said, coming around from behind his desk. I was sure he'd tried to stop us several times before now, and I had been too focused on fighting back to notice. My father opened his mouth, ready to debate the issue further, but Simmonds didn't let him. "I have given you a lot of leeway here, but this is my department."

My dad's face started to redden. He wasn't ready to let this go, but I'd had more than enough.

"I need to go see Dr. March," I said to Simmonds. "I'll come back with Travis later. We can talk then."

He nodded once and I was gone without another word.

I made it as far as the stairwell before Travis caught up to me. "Joss, hang on."

I whipped around and took a step toward the stairs, my stomach a twist of emotions I couldn't identify. "Please let me go," I said. He leaned away, taken aback. I took a breath, calming myself enough to speak. "I need some space right now."

He gave me a concerned once-over, but after a moment, he nodded. I hurried up the stairs, leaving him and my angry father behind.

. . .

I stayed in the medical wing long after Dr. March had finished with the acupuncture treatment. I felt significantly more stable now, but I still wanted to hide.

I couldn't get my dad's angry red face out of my mind. What I had pulled off was nearly impossible. Once he might have been happy about it.

I found myself lost in a time when he was.

I went through a phase as a kid where I loved to throw darts—I'd gotten the idea from a game show on TV. I'd made my own sad darts out of crayons and a target from paper, which I taped to the wall in our basement. The darts wouldn't stick to the target, but I knew if I hit my mark. Then for my seventh birthday my parents got me a Velcro dart set. I played with it for three days straight and before long I was hitting the mark without too much effort.

"You can't be serious," my dad had said one day as he inspected the result of my latest game. One was dead center with the others not too far outside of it.

"What is it?" I asked him, confused.

"You've got really good aim, kid." He smiled at me, impressed. "Let's try something different. Do you think you can hit the outside ring instead of the bull's-eye?"

It took me a few tries to adjust, but eventually I had the six darts ringed around the edge of the target. "Wow." My dad shook his head in disbelief and I beamed. "All right, let's try something else."

He spent weeks modifying my game daily, having me either throw from farther away, shoot for a specific part of the target, or a combination of both.

After a few weeks, we moved the target outside so I could get even more space from it. My dad stuck the target to a tree. Then he had me throw a dart through the air—not at the target, but just to see how far

I could throw. Once he'd measured the distance and told me that was how far away I had to stand. He pressed a rock into the ground so I'd know the spot, and stood with his back to the target, before laying the darts out on the ground in front of him.

"Now, what you're going to do," he said, "is glance behind you and find the bull's-eye. Then, you're going to grab a dart, turn and throw, and hit your mark."

He demonstrated. He looked over his shoulder for less than a second, before reaching for a dart with his back still to the target. Then, in one easy motion he whipped around and let the dart sail through the air. It hit the bull's-eye dead-on.

I felt my eyes widen. "Daddy, that's too hard."

He laughed. "It's hard, but it's not too hard. Not if you practice."

I looked up at him. "Is that how come you can do it?"

He nodded. "That's how it happened. Lots of practice." I didn't know my parents were spies. They used to tell me that they protected people, and I never thought too much of it. It was my normal.

I tried to throw the dart just has he had, and I missed horribly to the left of the tree.

"It's all right," he said. "Keep trying."

I turned back around, steeling myself, and tried again. I still missed, but not by quite as much.

By the end of the day, I hadn't come close to the target. I would have felt defeated had my dad not pointed out that I had, in fact, made a lot of progress. Now the dart dropped just to the left of the tree instead of ending up on the other side of the yard. "You'll get it," he said. "Just keep working."

It took three weeks. Three weeks of spinning and twisting and *learning how to adapt—which felt like months to me at the time. But every day I got closer, which made me even more determined. Once I started hitting the target, I flat-out refused to be stopped. My dad missed a few days here and there, but he was with me for the most part, helping me nearly every step of the way.*

I stunned myself the day I finally pulled it off. I still remembered how quickly I'd moved, whirling around, letting the dart fly, and finding it stuck on the bull's-eye.

I stared at it for a moment, completely shocked. Then I started jumping. "I hit the target! I hit the target!"

My dad came up behind me, swept me off the ground and put me on his shoulders. He ran around the yard laughing. "You did it! You're a master marksman!" I felt like I was flying.

He was happy. We were both happy.

And now we weren't. Most definitely not today.

A knock on the door brought me back. I glanced at the clock on the wall and saw I'd been here for an hour. Dr. March stuck her head in. "Agent Elton is out here asking for you."

I pushed myself up. "You can let him in."

She stepped back so Travis could pass, then shut the door behind him.

I swung my legs over the side of the bed and Travis sat down on the mattress next to me. He nudged me with his shoulder. "You doing all right? You've been in here for a while."

I let out a heavy breath. "I'm fine," I said. "At least as far as the cravings are concerned."

"I'm sorry I didn't give you a heads-up about your dad," Travis said. "He was in the room monitoring the mission with me. I knew he wasn't thrilled with your play, but I didn't realize he was that angry. He hid it well."

"He's not an agent anymore," I said, kicking the bed frame in frustration. "What was he even doing there?"

Travis ran a hand along his jaw, seeming to be debating something. "I'm not sure if I'm supposed to tell you this—"

My eyes narrowed. "Whatever it is, you better start talking."

He was still hesitant, but I stared him down until he caved. "He's been reinstated."

I froze. "He—What?"

"I was surprised too," he said. "I don't know when it became official. I found out when he showed up in the command center." He watched me closely, trying to gauge my reaction. "From what I know, it's strictly in an observational/consult capacity. But Asia and Europe are his areas of specialty." Of course they are.

I pressed my fingers to my forehead before straightening. "All right, I'll deal with it." I felt annoyed, but there didn't seem to be anything I could do.

Travis gave my knee a reassuring pat. "It'll be fine." He sounded so sure. "You'll just need some time to get used to it. So will he."

I bit my tongue to keep all of my disagreements from escaping.

"Did you check on Nikki and Eliza?" I asked. I needed to talk about something else.

He nodded. "Nikki's still asleep and Dr. March has been working with Eliza." I suspected that would keep her busy for a while. Dr. March was the head of the medical team, but she wasn't the only doctor the IDA had. She was, however, the only doctor who treated me, because of my complex drug history. Naturally, she'd have a similar interest in Eliza.

"What was it like in there?" Travis asked. He was talking about the safe house. "How did she look?" His eyes were hard—prepared for the truth. But I wasn't certain I wanted to tell him.

"Are you sure you—"

"Jocelyn." His sharp determined tone stopped me dead. "I don't need you to protect me. Not from this." I didn't know if I was trying to protect him or myself. Probably both.

"Okay," I said, giving him one last chance to stop me. He didn't take it. "It's really bad." I didn't sugarcoat it. There was no point. "I think—" I hesitated. I hadn't voiced this theory yet and I was a little afraid to say it out loud. I had a good feeling I was right, but I desperately wished I wasn't. "I think it was a testing house."

His expression darkened. "I don't like the sound of that."

"Yeah," I said, standing to pace. "You shouldn't." I swallowed, giving myself a second before I explained. "As far as I've been led to believe, there are two safe houses that KATO uses to—experiment on agents."

"What do you mean, 'led to believe'?" Travis asked.

I shrugged. "It was something our handlers used to threaten us with. But I had never heard anything about it from the higher-ups, so I didn't give it much weight. I thought it was just another lie used to manipulate us," I said. "I guess it makes sense, though. The downside of kidnapping children and forcing them to fight is that not all of them are cut out for it."

"So instead of killing them, KATO experiments on them." The

amount of venom in Travis's voice could kill a person in seconds.

"Some of them, anyway." I shrugged. "My handler's threats were never specific, but he used to imply that these safe houses were how KATO found different techniques to torture their enemies and new techniques to keep the rest of us in line."

Travis's face sharpened. "*Them*."

I blinked. "What?"

"You said 'keep the rest of *us* in line.' But you're not one of them anymore."

I inhaled slowly through my nose. "Right. Old habit." I crossed my arms and made an attempt at a reassuring smile before continuing. "We can go over the details with Simmonds, but between the intel we had going in, everything I know about KATO, and the file Rachel and Nikki found in the house—which was in the hands of the director of KATO, by the way—I'm pretty positive she was being tested."

Travis's eyes widened. "The *director* of KATO was there? You're sure?"

I nodded. "I saw enough of his face, and I got a look at the scar on his hand. He got it giving a tolerance test to a new agent years ago. She surprised him and turned the hot poker on him. I heard it happen." I smiled for a moment, remembering how his screams carried down the hall. "She was my hero for about five minutes. Then he killed her."

Travis shook his head, disgusted. "This keeps getting worse."

"Yeah, tell me about it."

After a moment, he stood. "All right, we need to talk to Simmonds and figure out what our next move should be." I stepped toward the door, but Travis caught my arm. "Maybe you want to change first?"

He looked pointedly at my sweatshirt, and it was only then that I noticed it was covered with Nikki's blood.

I grimaced. "Good idea. I'll meet you there."

. . .

I stopped short when I stepped out of the stairwell onto my floor of the student housing building. My father was leaning against the wall beside my door. He straightened when he saw me coming. I drew a long slow breath, steeling myself before continuing toward him.

I walked past him to unlock my door. "I'm really not looking to be yelled at right now." I put all of my effort into fitting the key in the lock, purposefully avoiding him. "And I don't have time for it."

Out of the corner of my eye I saw him raise his hands in surrender. "I didn't come here to yell." His voice was surprisingly gentle after how fiercely he had spoken to me in Simmonds's office. "I'm sorry I yelled at all. I just want to talk."

I ground my teeth together to bury my frustration. "I don't have time for that either."

"Come on, kid." I froze. He used to call me "kid." It'd been ten years since I'd heard it. My insides were a mess of conflicting emotions I couldn't sort out, but I forced myself to face him. His expression was open and honest and slightly desperate. "I'm trying here."

I studied him for a long moment, weighing my options, before I stepped back to let him in my room. He paused close to me as he passed, meeting my eyes squarely and giving me no place else to look. "Thank you." He was more sincere than I could handle, and it took everything I had to nod.

I shut the door behind me, and for the third time in the past three days we were alone.

I perched myself on the edge of my bed, drumming my thumbs against my navy blue comforter, while he crossed his arms and leaned against my dresser, looking as anxious as ever.

We sat in silence for a while until my dad worked up the courage to break it.

"I've been reinstated." He watched me closely, trying to gauge my reaction. "I'll be consulting on Europe and Asia." I nodded steadily, but stayed quiet. "Which includes KATO."

"Yeah," I said, finally. "That part I figured out."

He squinted at me now, like I was a complex puzzle that needed solving. "I don't want to make this—uncomfortable."

I shrugged. "It's a little late for that."

He let out an ironic laugh. "I guess you're right."

I crossed my arms, pulling them in close. "Why did you do this?"

His eyes widened a fraction, and he looked mildly surprised. "Get reinstated?" I nodded. "You said you weren't leaving. That means I'm not either."

I took a moment to process what he was saying. "You're staying for me?"

His face softened. "Where else do you think I would go?"

I swallowed the bubble of emotion that had expanded in my throat. I'd been trying to avoid him since I found out he was alive, and he was staying for *me*. Maybe I could get used to the idea of him being around.

"You've been gone for seven years," I said. "How did you get your high clearances back so quickly?" A few months ago I had tried to access his personnel file but the clearance level was unusually high for a file as old as his. It meant he'd had to have access to some secure intel. The fact that he had been allowed to observe my mission into a KATO facility told me he hadn't just been reinstated, but he'd been restored to his elevated rank.

"I left the IDA in good standing," he said with a shrug. "Plus, Roy owed me. We've been friends for a long time. He knew you were alive when you showed up in the field four years ago, and he didn't try to track me down until now."

Deep down, I didn't think it would have mattered. Back then I was very much convinced that I could not be saved. At least this way he didn't have to see me in action. "Simmonds probably had his reasons."

"He did," my dad said. "They aren't good enough. I had a right to know you were alive."

I nodded slowly. He was here, he wanted to stay, and he was angry he wasn't here sooner.

"If you're going to be around, you can't holler at me like you did today," I said. "Not ever."

He bowed his head, looking slightly ashamed. "I know. Roy— Director Simmonds—he told me as much after you left."

I arched my eyebrows. "And you listened?"

He shrugged. "I might not be happy with him, but he's good at his job. He always has been. And ultimately, he's taken care of you." A smile tugged at the corner of his mouth. "He thinks very highly of you."

"I complete missions," I said. It didn't have to be anything more than that.

"Oh, yes. I saw that," my dad said, eyeing me skeptically. "So, do you always take crazy risks like squaring off solo against an enemy?"

"That wasn't crazy, it was calculated." He wasn't attacking me, but I couldn't help feeling a little defensive. "I knew what I was doing."

He tilted his head to the side, doubtfully. "She came pretty close to getting you."

"It was a lot closer than I thought it would be," I admitted. "I may have made a slight miscalculation, but I knew her well enough to recover."

He rubbed his hand across his forehead. "I think there's going to be a lot about you in the field that I'm going to hate."

"Probably," I said with a smile. "But it won't exactly be easy for me either. I'm not used to any of this." And him being around—it was a glaring reminder of KATO. No matter what he said or did, there would always be this hole between us that they had caused.

"You know," he said, after a moment, "if you ever want to talk about—"

"I don't." I didn't need him to finish his sentence. "And we're not there yet, anyway."

He seemed taken aback and even a little disappointed, but he covered it quickly. "Fair enough."

We both got quiet again. Suddenly it felt like any progress we'd made had been erased, and I was the one responsible.

"If you want," I said, hesitating, "Travis and I are meeting with Simmonds to discuss the mission."

He tilted his head a fraction. "Are you asking me to sit in?"

I nodded slowly. "If you want to."

He smiled. "I'd like that."

"Okay." I exhaled, and I didn't know if it was out of relief or fear. "Just give me a second to change."

. . .

Travis arched his eyebrows when my dad and I approached.

"We talked," I said, keeping my explanation limited. "He's going to join us for the meeting."

"All right," Travis said, still notably surprised. "That's good. We'll take any insight we can get." My dad nodded to him as we filed into Simmonds's office. He was waiting for us.

"Are we ready to try this again?" Simmonds asked, looking between me and my father.

My dad tipped his chin. "We are." Travis and I took the seats in front of Simmonds while my dad leaned against the wall to the right of the desk with his arms crossed.

"Now," Simmonds said. "Let's go over what we know and what you learned."

Travis and I took turns sharing the details of what we had worked out before the mission. Then I took over, explaining what had happened in Russia, while Travis added information based on what he had heard in the command room. My father stayed mercifully quiet.

However, we came to a grinding halt when I mentioned that KATO's director had been there.

"The *director* of KATO?" Simmonds asked. "In a safe house in Russia?"

I nodded. "He was the assistant director when I was there. I'm sure you saw the observational intelligence reports that indicate he's been promoted. Which would make sense. After our invasion I can't imagine that they would let the previous director live, let alone remain in charge."

"Yes, I've seen the reports on the change." Simmonds went to his computer and sent an image to one of the monitors behind him. "This is who we now have on file as the director. Kim Jin Su. Is this who you saw?"

The man in the picture had cold harsh eyes and a rigid jaw. A chill ran down my spine. The part I hadn't told anyone—the part I wasn't *planning* on telling anyone—was that he was the one in charge of suggesting and authorizing our more painful punishments. Handlers were allowed to withhold Gerex and inflict a certain amount of pain on their own. But anything that might involve a broken bone or take some time to heal had to be authorized to ensure that an upcoming mission wasn't jeopardized by internal matters. And while Chin Ho was always the one to deliver the authorized punishment, the assistant director sometimes enjoyed watching.

My father came closer to get a good look. My stomach roiled. Having him here made this even more difficult.

I focused on the image, swallowing hard. "That's him."

Simmonds's eyes jumped to my father, who was staring at the screen transfixed. There were too many emotions playing across his face for me to work out, but that alone was enough to tell me that there was a lot more to this than I realized.

"What is it?" I asked, looking between Simmonds and my father. "What do you know about him?"

My dad turned slowly to face me, and it was clear that the last thing he wanted to do was say what he was about to. "He—" His voice broke. He cleared his throat and tried again. "He's the one who took you."

Chapter Seven

COMMON ENEMY

I felt numb. My head was spinning and the only thing I could hear was my father's words echoing in my mind. I was vaguely aware of how tightly my hands were clenching the arms of the chair, which also seemed to be the only thing keeping me from curling into a ball. I stared straight ahead, trying to wrap my mind around everything.

Strangely enough, I hadn't thought much about the specific person who had taken me, but I remembered the whole event clearly. There were four of them on the assignment but only one went directly for me. He separated me from my mom and dragged me out the door. They all wore masks, so I never saw any of their faces. Everything that came after was so fast and so much worse that I never thought about that one agent who brought me into all of this. But I should have.

A solid grip on my left arm jarred me back to life. I blinked hard and turned abruptly to find Travis sitting on the edge of his seat with a firm hold on my forearm. "You back?"

I sucked in air and nodded, forcing my fingers to release the chair I was strangling. "Yeah." My throat was dry and my voice hoarse, but I didn't have it in me to care. "Yeah, I'm here."

Every eye was on me, but it was a long moment before anyone spoke. Or maybe it wasn't that long. Maybe it just felt that way.

It was Simmonds who finally broke the silence. "They never told you?"

I shook my head hard enough to rattle my brain. "And I never asked. I didn't think—" I felt a small tremor in my arm and clutched the chair tighter in an attempt to stabilize myself. I took a long slow breath, exhaling evenly, trying to get it together. "I didn't know anything."

"How much did you interact with him?" my dad asked.

I tried to ignore the tingling in my hands. He wasn't asking for details here. It was a question I could handle. "Not often, but more than the director. My handler was my primary contact."

My father's jaw clenched. "I think he was around you more than you realize." There was an edge to his voice. "After you and your mom were taken, I spent most of my time getting to know him. He had a pretty big interest in medical development." My heart rate picked up. We were getting too specific for my comfort level, but my father didn't seem to notice. "Seven years ago, our intel said you—and your mom—were his last field mission."

"That's still the case," Simmonds said. "At least as far as we know."

Ultimately, I wasn't the one KATO was after that day. My mom was. They wanted her to develop Gerex. And if I *was* his last mission, then I would have to believe that he was personally invested in the project.

My dad's eyes locked on me. "I've been reading up on the drug your mom developed," he said. I tensed. "They used it on *you*, didn't they?"

I drew a sharp breath through my nose. It wasn't a secret anymore, and I didn't want to lie, but I wasn't ready for him to know yet either. Still, I bit down hard on my lip and forced myself to nod, wishing I hadn't invited him here.

"So," Travis said, squeezing the hand that still rested on my arm, "the fact that he was in this safe house means this is as big as we thought it was." I shot him a grateful look for changing the subject.

My dad watched me for another few seconds, eyes hard, before refocusing on Simmonds.

"Maybe even bigger," Simmonds said. "Not only has he not been on a mission in ten years, but according to our databases, he's barely left North Korea in that time. The fact that he's taken a personal interest in this is greatly concerning."

I pressed my fingers to my temple, trying to think. "We need to talk to Eliza."

"I agree," Simmonds said. "She's being evaluated further by Dr. March and the medical team tomorrow. After that we'll have a better idea about how to approach her. Hopefully we'll get some answers. In the meantime, we're going to see if we can come up with more of Jin Su's travel history."

"You mean you haven't been tracking him?" my dad asked, eyebrows arched.

Simmonds's eyes locked on him. "We may be an elite agency, but he is a first-class operative. You know as well as I do that he has always been excellent at moving around the world undetected."

"But you think now that we have a confirmed sighting, we should get some intel on his activity," I said, seeing where he was going.

Simmonds nodded at me gratefully. "Precisely."

My dad looked mildly annoyed that I'd backed Simmonds, but he moved on. "What about that other agent who was there? The one you fought. You said you knew her."

"Yeah." I kept my voice as casual as possible. "She was there for me." I could feel all of them looking at me, but I kept my focus on Simmonds. I didn't want to discuss this with my father. "But that's not unexpected," I said, pushing us along. "What's more important is that if Eliza matters to them, they'll be coming for her too. She may even get priority over me."

Simmonds nodded. "You make a good point," he said. "We need to work out why she's so valuable."

The conversation didn't last too much longer. We finished going over what we had and were in agreement that our progress hinged on three things; what Eliza had to say, Jin Su's travel history, and working out the importance of the KATO files we already had access to. But for the time being, we had done all we could.

When I left the office I headed in the direction of student housing. Travis fell into step next to me, but stayed silent.

I glanced at him out of the corner of my eye once we'd made it outside and saw him giving me a very pointed look.

"What is it?" I asked, even though I was sure I didn't want to know.

"What's the story with the KATO agent you fought?"

I picked up the pace. "There's no story."

He rolled his eyes. "Please don't insult me. You changed the subject way too quickly back there. I know you. It means you're holding back."

"I really don't want to get into it," I said.

"Hey." He pulled me to a stop. "I thought we were past the point where you kept things from me." I ducked my head, trying to avoid his scrutiny. It may have gotten easier to talk to him about KATO, but that didn't mean it still wasn't hard. "Especially when it relates to a mission."

I pursed my lips. He had me there. And since there was a possibility she could pop up again, he really did deserve to know.

I sat down on the bench outside of the student dorms. Travis took the space next to me and waited patiently for me to start talking.

I needed a minute to get my tongue working. "She—Centipede—was the second best agent at KATO when I was there." I stayed focused on the tree in front of me, even though I could feel his gaze.

"So that must make her their new number one," he said, following.

I nodded. "It would appear so." I bit my lip, thinking back. "She got to KATO about a year after me. She was my age, and native to North Korea. I tried to befriend her." I tensed at the memory. "It was the first time I tried to do something like that. The agents that had been there before me never reached out and I was too afraid of them to initiate anything. KATO didn't want us working together and they punished us for being too friendly. Still, I thought it would be better with a friend." It sounded foolish. It *felt* foolish—even then. "I thought I'd have a shot with someone new."

"I take it that didn't work out well," he said.

"No." I bit back a laugh. "Not at all." I finally looked at him. His jaw was locked in anticipation of what was coming. I pushed on. "I didn't know that much about North Korean culture at that time. KATO had us trained and conditioned to compete with each other and to tell on each other if someone wasn't complying with their policies. I thought that was just how KATO worked. I didn't realize it extended to the entire country."

"So she knew you weren't supposed to be friendly and ratted you out." His voice was harsh.

"Yeah." I gripped the edge of the bench, thinking about what my handler had done to me as a result. Then I shook my head, refusing to let myself go there. "She was rewarded for turning me in. And over the years she became my biggest internal enemy. She wanted to be their top agent in the *worst* way, but I would never let that happen. My status was the only thing I had going for me in that place. I wasn't about to let anyone get ahead of me."

Travis's fist was clenched so tight his knuckles were white. "I *hate* them."

"Tell me about it," I said, sighing. "I was already on edge enough knowing that they're gunning for me. This really doesn't help."

His forehead creased. "You're *not* going back there," he said. "We've been over this."

I stared straight ahead and nodded, because I still didn't know how to tell him that this was so far outside of his control.

. . .

The door banged open, startling me out of a dead sleep. Men in masks poured into the room, guns out. My mom was next to me in seconds, pulling me close and dragging me to the closet. We barely made it a step from the bed. One of the men got to her, knocking her on the back of her head. She didn't pass out, but it was enough for her to lose her hold on me.

An agent grabbed me while the others went for my mom. His cold harsh eyes twinkled. Terror coursed through me like nothing I had ever known before. I moved instinctively back to my mom but he held me tight. I struggled against him, crying and screaming and battling to get to my mother, who was now facedown on the ground. He yanked me out the door and down the hall. I never stopped fighting.

I woke up sweating and panting, but for a change I wasn't shaking. It took me a moment to realize it was still the middle of the night. I found my control fairly quickly, but that didn't do much to chase away the nightmare. I rubbed my forehead, watching the images play in my mind. There were only four men there, but it seemed like so many more at the time. It felt—overpowering. Now it seemed so obvious that the person who had taken me had been Jin Su. I'd seen his eyes through the mask that night, and many times over the last ten years. But in the grand scheme of everything that had happened at KATO, the kidnapping itself seemed minor. My brain could only hold on to so many details. When I woke up in KATO a few hours after, I found my new handler, Chin Ho, watching me. I didn't remember if I'd been knocked out, or drugged, or if I'd just passed out. Training started immediately, and once it did, nothing else seemed to matter.

I pulled my knees to my chest and rested my head on the wall behind me. I may have managed to contain my craving, but there was no way I'd be able to fall back asleep after a dream like that.

. . .

It was six o'clock before I decided that I couldn't stand being in bed anymore. I headed over to the medical wing to check on Nikki and Eliza. Nikki had woken up. She had a concussion and a broken arm that would keep her out of the field for a while, but she was in good spirits and was expected to make a full recovery. She was being kept in the medical wing so the doctors could monitor her head injury. When I finished with Nikki, I tried to find Dr. March to ask about Eliza, but one of her staff members said she was busy with a patient.

My nightmare had made me restless, so I was particularly relieved when Simmonds paged me to his office shortly after breakfast. Both he and my father were waiting for me when I arrived.

"Do we have something on Jin Su?" I asked. If both of them were there, it had to be related to the director.

"No," Simmonds said. "This is about Eliza."

I straightened, glancing at my father for half a second before focusing on Simmonds. "How is she?"

"Her nutrition is lacking, but Dr. March is working on that," Simmonds said. "Our bigger concern right now is that she won't talk."

I shrugged, not at all surprised. "KATO has their agents well trained to keep their mouths shut." I rubbed the burn scar on the back of my neck. I saw my father watching me and dropped my hand, making sure my ponytail hid the mark.

Simmonds shook his head. "It's more than that," he said. "Our behavior experts are able to tell the difference between agents who won't talk and agents who are *afraid* to talk."

I nodded, seeing where he was going with this. "I'm sure she is afraid. Fear is the tactic they use most." My dad shifted against the wall and I looked at him just long enough to see a muscle in his cheek twitch. I gripped the back of the chair. I knew he'd be around for a certain amount of KATO-related discussions, but I had hoped they would be more current and less personally related to my past. I forced my attention back to Simmonds. "Let me talk to her."

A small smile stretched across Simmonds's lips. "I was hoping you would say that."

My heart beat a little bit faster, but I did my best to ignore it. I had been on her side of things. I would know better than anyone what questions to ask. "Is there anything I need to know?"

Simmonds leaned forward to read her file. "She's still on the Gerex for now. Dr. March is afraid to take her off of it until we know more about her situation."

I nodded, remembering my own detox. Coming off of it was almost as traumatic as being on it in the first place. She wasn't talking as it was. Taking her off the drug against her will wouldn't convince her to trust us.

"She also doesn't know her father is dead," he said. "One of the behavior specialists broached the subject with her, and the second his name came up she covered her ears and yelled until she was left alone."

"Okay." I exhaled evenly. I wouldn't be the person to break the news to her if I could help it. "When are we doing this?"

"We can go now," he said, standing. "I'll page Dr. March and let her know." Both he and my father moved toward the door and alarms went off in my head.

I grabbed my dad's arm, pulling him to a stop, then looked back to Simmonds. "Can we meet you there?"

He glanced uncertainly between the two of us, but nodded. "Very well."

I turned to my father as the door closed, but I found I couldn't meet his eyes.

"Hey, kid?" Now I looked at him, his face full of questions. "What's this about?"

I exhaled evenly, finding my strength. "I need you not to come to this."

He leaned away from me, confused. "What? Why?"

Because I was sure that once he'd learned some of the specifics of what I'd done, he'd push me for more, and I really didn't want to go there. I carried more guilt about my past than anyone should ever have to know, but that much I could manage. The part I couldn't handle was that, when it really came down to it, I didn't have any regrets. I did what I had to, and I would do it again. It was what convinced me that my heart was not as good as Travis seemed to think it was. The little girl who used to run around the living room—the girl my father was proud of—would have had regrets. I didn't want him to think of *her* doing the things I did. And I was fairly certain that if he knew all of this he would look at me in a way I wouldn't be able to handle.

But I kept my answer much more simple than that. "I need to say things to her. And I won't be able to say what I have to if you're there."

His brows drew together, and I could see him struggling. "All right," he said, though his voice sounded flat. "If that's what you want."

"It is." I worked to stay detached.

He nodded once and I did my best to ignore the hollowness in his eyes. "You should go," he said, turning away from me. "You don't want to keep Simmonds waiting."

I swallowed hard and backed out of the room.

. . .

My heart beat faster the closer I got to the medical wing. I had pushed my father out of my head and tried to focus on Eliza, but that only made the situation worse.

I was relieved to find Dr. March waiting for me. Her presence made me feel a fraction calmer even if she wasn't here to take care of *me* today.

"Are you ready for this?" she asked, looking at me out of the corner of her eye.

I tugged my hair. "I honestly don't know."

She squeezed my arm reassuringly. "We'll be right there if you need anything."

I couldn't decide if that made me feel better or worse. Dr. March led me to the back of the medical wing—farther back than I had ever been. She unlocked a room and showed me inside. It was an observation room.

Simmonds was already there as I expected, but I was thrown to also find Travis. I had assumed that I would be the only person in on this since I was the only one at the meeting.

Travis gripped the rail that ran along the bottom of the window, staring through the glass, transfixed. On the other side was Eliza. I stood next to him to get a better look.

She was in a hospital bed, but it wasn't like the others in the medical wing. Those were smaller, yet appeared to be more comfortable. This bed was longer and wider, but looked stiff. Eliza was either asleep or sedated, and from the looks of things, her ankles were chained to the bed. I whirled around to find Simmonds. "Why is she chained down? She isn't a prisoner."

"No, she's not," Simmonds agreed, keeping his voice even.

"She was a little—destructive—when she first woke up," Dr. March said, stepping forward. "It seems that as long as we limit her mobility, she's calm enough."

I looked between the two of them. It must have been clear how unconvinced I was, because Simmonds continued. "The ankle cuffs are padded, and digitally controlled, so we can release her from out here if we have to. She's perfectly fine."

I turned back to her, fighting the urge to debate the issue. The chains reminded me too much of KATO, but I had to remember that Eliza was different from me. She didn't ask for help. We were forcing it on her. And because of that, she had to be handled differently. Travis stood next to me, barely taking his eyes off of her.

"Is your father coming?" Simmonds asked, seeming to just realize I had come alone.

"No," I said. "I need to do this without him."

Simmonds held my eyes briefly, and I saw his understanding. Then his phone beeped. He scanned it and grimaced. "I need to address this. It'll only take a minute." He stepped out.

"I'm going to start to wake her up," Dr. March said, following Simmonds out of the room. A few seconds later she was on the other side of the glass with Eliza.

Travis bowed his head, looking away from the window for the first time since I'd entered.

"You don't have to be here," I said to him. He straightened to look at me, tension stretched across his face. "Your goal was to bring her back. You made that happen." A part of me badly wanted him to leave. Travis knew more about my time at KATO than anyone, but between my father showing up and KATO targeting me, I found myself feeling more exposed than ever. My stomach twisted at the thought of shedding another layer—even to him.

"I thought my goal was to get her back," Travis said. "I thought that would be enough—but look at her." He broke his eyes away from me. "I did that do her."

"You didn't—"

"She was my responsibility." His grip on the rail tightened. "I need to see this through." I swallowed my argument.

We watched Eliza in silence until March and Simmonds returned a couple minutes later.

"Okay," Dr. March said. "She hasn't said much at all. At least, not about anything that makes sense. She's been angry and harsh, but hasn't revealed anything important. We need you to get her talking. Based on her weight and muscle mass, it doesn't seem like they've been training her the same way they did with you. We'd like to know as much as possible, but at this point, just getting her to share *something* would be a victory."

I nodded, still not taking my eyes off of her. Her long dark brown hair hung around her face. I could tell from here that her eyes were bloodshot, and Dr. March was right—she looked way too thin to be an agent. I finally turned to face them. "Is there anything else you need?"

"Learning what happened to her is the priority," Simmonds said.

I took a long breath and headed for the door. "I'll see what I can find out."

I didn't look at anyone else as I stepped into the hallway.

There was a security guard in front of Eliza's room. Dr. March had her security card out, ready to swipe it against the sensor. The guard let us pass, and Dr. March stopped in front of the door, turning around to face me. "We have two guards on standby if you need them for some reason."

"Okay," I said, nodding, "but it shouldn't come to that."

She smiled and stepped aside, then I could see Eliza sitting at the bottom of her bed, the length of the mattress behind her. The restraints must have had plenty of give, because she had her legs crossed, her elbows resting on her knees, and her head in her hands. She looked calm and in control, but there was a fire just behind her eyes that suggested this was an act.

"Eliza," Dr. March said, speaking to her as if she were someone on the verge of a nervous breakdown. "Eliza, there's someone I want you to meet." Eliza didn't so much as glance in our direction, but Dr. March carried on anyway. "This is Jocelyn Steely."

Eliza finally turned her head to look at me. It was slow and calculated. Like she was a puppet being controlled. She studied me, but she didn't speak. Dr. March nodded in a way that told me this wasn't unusual, then took a step backward. "We'll be watching," she said, keeping her voice low so only I could hear. "If you need anything, direct your question to the window."

I nodded, but I couldn't take my eyes away from Eliza. Dr. March gave my shoulder one final squeeze then stepped back into the hallway. Even though she shut the door as gently as possible, it almost seemed to echo in the quiet of the room.

Eliza and I stared at each other for a moment, neither of us speaking.

She was the one to break the silence. "You're a traitor." There was a startling coldness to her voice that was unnerving.

I hadn't had enough time to think about what I was going to say here—but maybe that was a good thing. It kept me from psyching myself out.

"She's a traitor!" Eliza said again, this time to the mirrored window. So she knew we were being watched.

I pulled the lone chair in the corner closer, so I was sitting next to the bed but in her line of sight—purposefully putting my back to the window. The only thing that separated us was the bottom bed rail. I watched her evenly and worked to put all of this in perspective. This wasn't about me; this was about helping *her*.

"You're a *traitor!*" She shrieked the last word at me, as if she thought she was being ignored and hated it.

"Yeah," I said. "I figured that's what they'd say." I leaned a little bit closer to her. I couldn't be rattled by what she was saying. I had to connect with her. "But what exactly did I betray?"

Eliza's lip curled slightly at my question. "You know what." She spat the words at me, disgust marring her face. "You betrayed the directive. They had plans for you." I drew a sharp, unexpected breath. I knew they did. But hearing her say it got under my skin. Still, I forced myself calm. This was about *her*.

"What happened to you when they first brought you in?" I asked, my voice was casual enough, even though it was a loaded question.

She didn't answer, but I didn't need her to. "They took everything from you, right? They took your clothes, your jewelry—anything you had on you that had *any* meaning." The beginning of anything awful was always the worst, and the same was true for KATO. The first kill, first fight, first injection. When things got "normal" for me, it was because I'd learned to steel myself. "Do you remember that?"

Her face hardened, and this time when she spoke her voice had lost its icy edge, making her sound significantly younger than her fifteen years. "Of course."

"Do you remember the first time they broke your arm just to show you they could?" She pulled her left arm against her stomach, answering my question. I kept focused on her face so I didn't have to think too much about the first time it happened to me.

I pressed on. "Do you remember the first time they gave you Gerex?" She looked up at me sharply. "Do you remember how much it hurt? That feeling of fire spreading through your veins?"

"I only feel the fire without it," she said through her teeth. She was struggling against something inside her. I could see it all over her face.

"Now," I said. "But I'm talking about the first time. I know how badly you want it now, because I do too. But the first time they put a needle in my arm I didn't want it, and it didn't feel good—at least, not right away." I swallowed. "I will never forget how much it hurt that first time."

She stayed silent, but her breathing had heightened. It was ragged and shallow, and just barely in control. When I was sure I'd made my point, I moved on.

"Don't you think there's something wrong with a group that has to drug you just to keep you coming back to them?" I asked. "And we both know that's just the *tip* of what they did to their agents during 'training.'"

Again, she didn't say anything, but her face twisted in agitation. I saw her start to shake. I couldn't tell if it was out of fear or anger, but I knew I was getting to her. Now I needed to get her to trust me. I needed her to see I was on her side.

"I know everything they did to you, because they did it to me too." I glanced at her neck and saw her small burn scar peeking out from underneath her hair. "I know why you have that burn, and how long it took to make. I know about the scars from when they cut into your feet. And I also know they did something to you in that house. Something they didn't do to me."

Her eyes went hollow at that, and any humanity I'd uncovered went dark. "You don't know *anything*!" Eliza said. She jumped to her feet, pulling at the chains as she stood on the bed. I had to fight against the instinct to back away. She towered over me, scanning the room, and I could see her trying to find a way to get to me without hurting herself. She couldn't. "You don't know ANYTHING!"

Her voice rang through the room.

I waited to make sure she was finished. "Then why don't you tell me all about it?" I did my best to keep my voice calm.

But it didn't work. Whatever ground I may have gained, I lost by trying to get an answer out of her. She dropped back to the bed just as suddenly as she stood up. Her legs crossed again, only this time she pulled them too her chest. Her hands found her ears and she started shaking her head back and forth. She mumbled words I couldn't make out. I glanced back to the window, having no clue what to do. Dr. March was in the room and next to me in an instant. She swooped in on Eliza, pressing something into her vein. It wasn't Gerex—it calmed her too quickly—but it was similar enough that I had to look away. Eliza wasn't clean yet, and Dr. March didn't seem to have reservations about medicating her.

Once she had relaxed, Dr. March helped her to stretch out on the bed then tucked her in. I had a hard time leaving her. I didn't know what I was expecting, but it certainly wasn't a meltdown of that level.

"Come on," Dr. March said, pulling at my shoulder. "We should talk with the others." I tore my eyes away from Eliza and forced myself to follow.

Chapter Eight

A RISK WORTH TAKING

Talking with Eliza had rattled me, but I did my best to hide it. "That didn't go well," I said when Dr. March and I rejoined Travis and Simmonds in the observation room. Simmonds turned to me while Travis watched Eliza, deep in thought.

"You had her talking," Dr. March said. "That's something. We've had behavior specialists working with her and you had her attention longer than anyone."

"Does she always have this bad of a reaction?" Travis asked. Dr. March didn't answer, but held his gaze in a way that said plenty. I set her off.

I lowered my chin to study the floor. I would *hate* if someone dragged my past out of me like I had done to her.

"This is good," Dr. March said, seeming to know I needed to hear it.

I shook my head. "I pushed too hard."

"But you set her up for next time."

I cringed at the idea of having to do that again, but if I had made the most progress with her there was really no other choice. We needed her to get to a place where she really understood what they did to her so she would *want* to be here.

"She's—" Travis started, but cut himself off. His jaw locked and his attention was on Eliza. She was asleep and looking downright peaceful. "I don't know who that girl is." He looked to us. "When I was with her she was quiet, and observant. Now she's explosive."

Dr. March nodded thoughtfully. "Yes, based on the reports we had from when she was under our protection, I had gathered as much," she said. "I have to update her behavior specialists. Today was good progress. Hopefully we can get to the bottom of this soon." She gave his shoulder a maternal squeeze and headed for the door.

"I have a meeting to get to," Simmonds said. "Good work, Agent Steely."

I nodded, even though it didn't really feel like good work.

Travis sighed deeply when the door shut. I gave him a once-over. He seemed to be fighting to stay in control. "You should go to class," he said, straightening. "I need to go hit something."

That was a feeling I could relate to. "I'll meet you later in the mission prep room?"

"Yeah." He sounded relieved to have something else to focus on.

. . .

I found myself grateful to be sitting in Agent Lee's class that afternoon. Being surrounded by a roomful of people who didn't know—and didn't want to know—the details of my history was a welcome change of pace. The afternoon only got better when I got to Agent Harper's class. It was my first time in his room since I had strangled him. So far, I hadn't heard a word about the incident from anyone.

Harper proceeded to spend the entire class actively avoiding me.

About halfway through, Gwen spun around. "Look at him," she said with a smile. "He's terrified of you."

"Of course he is," Olivia said. "She found his weakness. The last thing he wants is Simmonds finding out what he's been doing."

"It's thanks to you that I even had that card to play," I said to Olivia. She gave me a small smile before turning back around. Gwen was right about her. She was a natural strategist. I couldn't imagine why she resisted it so much.

The class got even better when Sam slid his phone across the desk at me. It was a message from another tech specialist. My eyes darted to him. "Is this what I think it is?"

Sam smiled. "Tell Elton to meet us after class. We have some more files to look over."

I spent the next half hour biting my lip to keep from smiling. There was no guarantee that this would shed any more light on the situation, but after this morning I was desperate for even the possibility of progress.

. . .

I wasn't at all surprised to find Travis already in the mission prep room when Sam and I got there. I had sent him a message as we were leaving class, though I was sure he headed right there after his time in the training room anyway.

"All right," Sam said, taking a seat at the computer. "These should be pretty straightforward."

He pushed a button on his keyboard and sent some files to the monitors above him. Each was organized the same way as Eliza's—a name with a series of facts underneath, followed by large chunks of text. My eyes widened as the realization set in. "They're *all* KATO agent files." There had to be at least twenty. They were organized by code name. Some I recognized, but some I didn't. It wasn't too surprising that agent files would be grouped together, but what *was* surprising were the code names themselves. Hornet, Venom, Monarch—they were some of KATO's most elite agents, and I couldn't imagine why Eliza's file would be included. And Eliza's was different from all of them. The files in front of us continued with details written in sizable chunks of text, but Eliza's ended abruptly.

These files were also decoded and translated. Sam pulled up a file and zoomed in on the first box next to the agent's picture. "There are two things that pop as being nearly identical in each file. This is the first one."

It was a line I had decoded when I was working on Eliza's file. "That says they've labeled this agent as trained and loyal," I said.

"Yes, it does," Sam said with a smirk. "And by the way, they really missed the mark with you."

Travis looked at me sharply, and I tensed. I could feel his eyes searching my face, trying to read me.

"I have a file here?" I asked.

"You do," Sam said. He glanced up at me and seemed to know better than to pull it up.

I swallowed hard, thinking of everything that could be in that file. "I'll deal with that later." I put my attention back on the screen. "What's the other similarity?"

"The second thing is in the very last box." He pulled it up on the monitor. This was a box that hadn't completely made sense in Eliza's file even after I tried decoding it. It was also the only box that had more of a sentence than a simple word or phrase. "They all start out the same, but the last couple words are different."

The file on the screen read, *Executes trust with North Star.*

I leaned closer. "Those words are upper-level code words from something else, but I can't remember what." I stared at it harder, as if that would fix the problem, but it wasn't clicking.

"Hey, Sam," Travis said, his eyes glued to the screen. "Can you pull all the photos up?"

"Yeah, sure." He typed quickly, and a few seconds later the monitor was full of KATO agents.

I scanned each image, my throat constricting as I realized what Travis had picked up on. "Almost none of them are Korean."

"How common is this?" Travis asked. "Because aside from you, there are maybe one or two other KATO agents that the IDA knows of who came from another country."

"Nearly everyone I trained with at headquarters was Korean," I said. "I assumed it was the same across the agency." I pressed my hand to my forehead, annoyed that I had never considered the possibility. "I've heard some of these names before. I never thought they'd be anything other than Korean."

"We need to sort through these files," Travis said, taking a step back. "Sam, thank you. This is huge. Joss and I can take it from here."

"Are you sure?" Sam wilted slightly.

Travis nodded. "It's up to us to figure out how this all adds up."

"All right." Sam picked up his backpack, making no effort to hide his disappointment. "Let me know if you guys need anything else."

I waited to speak until it was just the two of us. "Do you have a plan?"

"I think we need to focus on the demographic information," Travis said. "You work on figuring out what those words are code for, and I'll go through and work on how the differences fit together. We can take inventory of the photos as we go. Hopefully, we'll find something that explains all of this."

We set to work. I went from one file to another. No two files had the same coded word, but several of them looked familiar. We were about an hour in when Travis broke my concentration.

"Joss." There was an edge to Travis's voice that made me nervous, and when I turned I saw I had a reason to be.

My picture was on his screen. It gave me chills to look at. My hair was down, curling every which way, completely out of control. The part that unsettled me the most was my eyes. They looked so—dead. I knew when this picture was taken. They were updated every year. This one was a couple weeks after I had shot Travis. It was right before I seriously started looking for a way out of KATO. When I was still trying to figure out if I had managed to get away with leaving Travis alive.

"Take it down," I said. "I'll go over it myself first."

"Jocelyn." His voice was soft and kind, and I couldn't stand to face him. "It's *me*."

"I know that." My tone was sharp. I couldn't do this today. Not after this morning with Eliza. "I'm asking you to take it down." I looked at him now, hoping that he understood. But he didn't. He seemed confused and almost hurt.

"But—"

"It's not about who you are. It's about what that is." I closed my eyes for a moment to steady myself. "I want to know what's in there first. And I've had enough sharing for today anyway."

The comprehension finally spread through his face. "All right. I get it."

"Thank you."

He nodded, and turned back to his computer. "You said Centipede was almost as good as you, right?"

"Yeah," I said. "Why?"

"Most of these agents are foreign, but a handful are Korean," he said. "If she was that good, why wouldn't she be one of them?"

I shrugged. "I'd imagine KATO still has other operations going on. If they sent me here, they'd need someone to replace me as their top retrieval specialist." And then I understood everything. KATO *sent* me here.

Travis tilted his head, reading me. "What is it?"

I stared at him, wide-eyed. "Pull my file back up."

"What?" His eyebrows knitted together, confused. "But I thought you said—"

"I know what I said." I rolled my chair over to him. "Pull it back up."

Judging from the look he was giving me, he thought I was insane. Still, he did what I asked. I found the last demographic box. It was what I expected. I pointed at the last word. "That's KATO's upper-level agency code for the IDA. That box means that they were sending me here."

Realization dawned on his face, and I could see he was following me.

My heart raced with a mixture of excitement and horror. "I'm not the only agent they had planted in an enemy agency."

"That's why each of these girls is a different nationality," Travis said.

I nodded. "I wouldn't be surprised if they've been kidnapping girls for years with this in mind. It's probably the reason they have different safe houses. They wanted to keep all of us as separate as possible. That way we wouldn't know the whole plan."

"How did the IDA miss this?" Travis asked.

I shrugged. "It's a big world, and the IDA is the only agency that has such a wide international interest."

Travis closed his eyes for a beat, seeing what I was getting at. "So we were the main concern. KATO made sure to keep their foreign agents away from us."

"My guess is the only foreign agents you saw were the ones who were too good *not* to put up against you," I said. "Which was also most likely the only reason you and I squared off so much."

Travis raked his fingers over his scalp. "So why is Eliza in this group, then?"

I tilted my head. "My best guess is that she was being prepped for England when they changed their minds for some reason. That's also probably when she was moved to the Russian house."

The more I talked, the darker Travis's face got. "We need to get all of this to Simmonds."

I was already halfway to the door.

Chapter Nine

EXPOSING DETAILS

My dad was leaving Simmonds's office when Travis and I got there. He looked annoyed but not angry, and I couldn't help but wonder what he and Simmonds had been talking about. He blinked when he saw me. I hadn't spoken to him since I asked him not to monitor my talk with Eliza.

"Jocelyn." He seemed a little unsure of me now, but nowhere near the uncertainty he'd had when we first met. He glanced between Travis and me. "Is everything okay?"

"We figured something out," I said. "You should stay."

His eyes lifted, and he stepped aside to let us in.

Travis and I moved toward Simmonds, with my dad a few paces behind us. "We worked out how the KATO files Sam pulled are connected," I said.

We caught them up on our latest discovery, including the varying nationalities of the agents in question. By the time we were finished, they were wearing identical grave expressions.

"How do you think they got inside these agencies?" my dad asked. He had migrated to his spot next to Simmonds's desk. "I reached out to our cooperating countries when you were taken. No one had any similar instances, and as far as I know, that's still the case." He looked to Simmonds. "Has anything changed?"

"No," Simmonds said. "And someone would have contacted us if it had. They would have wanted to establish a pattern."

My dad turned back to me. "None of these other agents had the connections you do."

"They were probably kidnapped for different reasons, like Eliza, or sold to KATO. Regardless, I'm positive KATO made sure their disappearances were well covered." I passed a flashdrive off to Simmonds with everything we'd been able to work out. "I would bet they got into other respective agencies the old-fashioned way: by building a history and a profile that would make them look like the ideal recruit. Then the agent would apply and enter through the traditional recruiting process." I ran a hand over my hair. "That's why we didn't think of it. Because the way they pushed me into the IDA was so unusual. They used my background in a way they can't do with anyone else."

"I'll contact our allies," Simmonds said. "We may not know the names they're using, but we have their pictures."

I nodded in agreement, but a part of me hated the plan. If we did that, each agency would take their agent captive, and KATO would know how much we'd worked out. Once that happened, we would never know what their endgame was, and there would be nothing to stop them from finding another approach. I exhaled heavily, irritated. It was so much easier to monitor intel when KATO still thought I was on their side. As afraid as I had been, the inside access I'd had made a huge difference.

I straightened sharply as a plan started to come together in my mind. It was incredibly risky, but if it worked we would have an advantage like nothing the IDA had ever known. I bit my lip, knowing once I put this out there, there would be no taking it back.

My dad's expression darkened. "I think I hate the look that's on your face right now."

I gave him a halfhearted apologetic smile. "I have an idea." An idea that he would most definitely dislike.

Next to me, Travis seemed to be holding his breath.

"Agent Steely," Simmonds said. "What are you thinking?"

I turned to Simmonds. "What if we don't tell anyone about them yet?" I said. I felt a swell of excitement and anxiety in my chest, but I didn't back down. "What if instead we turn some of them? We give them the chance to spy for *us*?"

The stunned silence that followed my proposal was exactly what I expected.

Travis was the first to find his voice. "You want to make more double agents?"

I nodded. "I can't possibly be the only person who would jump at the opportunity to escape KATO. It didn't seem possible before, but I did it. I can reach out to others."

"You're a success story," my dad said. There was a note of disbelief in his voice, which I was sure was due to the absurdity of this idea. But I could see a way to make this work.

"All of the solid information we've had has either come from me, or from our trip inside their headquarters. We need to keep that intel coming if we're going to stay on top of them. And if Jin Su is taking a personal interest in something, we need to put ourselves in the best position possible." The more I talked, the better this idea sounded. I hadn't felt truly ahead of KATO since they found out my identity. This would be the chance to fix that. "We have agent files with KATO's notes. We can go through each file and give them our own assessment, using my file as a baseline for what to look for."

"You make a compelling case." Simmonds dipped his head in a way that made me think he was actually considering this.

"But it's also *insane*," Travis said, as if he couldn't believe no else had pointed it out.

Simmonds conceded a nod. "It *is* a serious risk. But it could also result in an invaluable asset." I saw the spark of ambition in his eye. He had proven to be particularly motivated to take risks if it meant we could damage KATO. If I could draw that out of him, I'd have a chance at getting this approved.

"This could be the best opportunity for everyone." I spoke with more certainty. "I'm sure most of their agents are brainwashed, but I can't be the only one to have avoided their methods."

"If that's true, then what do they need us for?" Travis asked. "These agents are stationed in their home countries. They can turn to their own agencies." He was far from convinced about any of this, but at least he was asking questions.

"They won't, though." I faced Travis, not only to give him my full attention but also to keep my father out of my range of sight. "Not if these other girls didn't come from spy families like I did." I looked to Simmonds. "If you didn't know I was taken against my will, would you have been so inclined to believe me? Even knowing about the drug?"

Simmonds leaned away from me, considering. "That's not an easy question to answer."

"And that's exactly why none of these girls will take the chance," I said. "They won't risk that this could backfire. But if we find the right people and I can talk to them, there's a good possibility I can bring them over."

"How will you know they're not playing you?" my dad asked.

I glanced at him, thinking for a moment. "We offer them the one thing that would pull their loyalty to us," I said. "The chance to be Gerex-free."

Travis raised his eyebrows. "Do you think that will be enough? Because from the way you talk about it, it seems like it would take some serious commitment on their part."

"For the right agents, it will be. It was my one condition coming in here. We just need to find a couple whose files look like mine," I said. "And if we share what little we know about Eliza, that should sway them even more. They won't like knowing KATO's after more control."

"All right," my dad said. "If these agents know you're off the drug, why would they wait for us to help them? Why wouldn't they get themselves clean?" I tried to keep my face neutral. I tried not to be bothered that he was learning so much about my past.

"KATO wouldn't want them to know I'm off of it," I said. "As it is now, their control hinges on those girls believing they don't have an out. I left KATO with a Gerex supply. I'm sure they were led to believe I haven't run out yet." I tipped my head forward, hiding my eyes before I continued. "And it's not a detox that an agent is likely to stick with on their own. It would leave them too vulnerable for too long. I know *I* wouldn't have done it on my own even if I knew it was possible." There's no way I would have gotten through it without Dr. March. I couldn't imagine making a break from KATO and attempting to detox while they came after me.

My dad stayed quiet, and Travis was tense next to me. I breathed slowly through my nose, feeling like I'd shared more than I wanted to with my dad here, but I didn't see a way around it.

"All right," Simmonds said, breaking the silence. "Here's what we're going to do. Agent Steely, you and Elton are going to go through the files tonight, come up with a short list of possible agents and a plan. Get it to me by the morning. If it's detailed and thought out, I'll take it to the board for approval."

Travis looked at Simmonds sharply, but didn't speak.

"Thank you, sir," I said.

He put his hand up as if to hold off my excitement. "I'm not saying it's an option we should take. But your risks have paid off in the past. You've earned the right to have this on the table."

I dipped my head. "I appreciate that."

Simmonds nodded. "In the meantime, I'm going to need to let the other agencies know they have a mole. I'll do everything I can to convince them not to take these agents captive, at least for the time being," he said. "I'll tell them we may have something in the works that will rectify the problem in the long run, however, we cannot leave the enemy inside our cooperating agencies with them unaware."

"Okay," I said, nodding, "that's fair."

"The two of you can go," Simmonds said. "Check back with me in the morning with your plan. I should also have more details by then."

I thanked Simmonds again and left the office, my head reeling with possibilities.

. . .

I moved quickly to the mission prep room, fighting against the mixture of excitement and anxiety that was swirling through me. I took a seat and started opening agent files.

"Hang on a second." Travis grabbed the back of my chair, turning me to the side and taking a seat next to me. "Are you sure you know what you're getting into here?" His face was contracted in question and concern.

"As sure as I can be," I said, crossing my arms. "But it would be nice if you were a little more on board."

"Part of being your partner is making sure you don't put either of us—or the agency, for that matter—in a bad situation." He gave me an even look.

I slid backward to give myself some space. "You know how I feel about that place. Do you really think I would suggest this if I didn't think we could pull it off?"

"I think sometimes you take insane risks." He raised his eyebrows pointedly. "Especially where KATO is concerned."

"You're not wrong, but I'm not being reckless this time. I'm not rushing into anything." I kept my voice even, despite the fact that I felt increasingly desperate for him to see where I was coming from. "I'm willing to think this through and make a plan."

"There are other ways to find out what these agents know." He held my eyes and I couldn't look away. "Why are you pushing this angle so hard?"

"I've survived KATO because of intel," I said, my nails digging into my biceps. "I crawled around their ventilation shafts so I could learn as much as I could about their operations. Then when I came here, I played my part to keep them talking. And now I hardly know anything. If we do this the safe way and let these KATO operatives be taken by the agencies they've infiltrated, the most we'll get is a one-time intel dump. And that's if they talk at all." I rubbed the burn scar below my ear, remembering the lengths KATO would go to in order to keep their secrets. Travis didn't miss it. I dropped my arm and pushed on. "We need a steady stream of information if we're going to get serious about beating them. And we *need* to beat them."

Travis's eyes widened slightly as he seemed to realize something. "You don't feel safe here, do you?"

I bit my lip. The mixture of dread and delight that came when he noticed things like this still took me by surprise. "I feel more protected on this campus than I have in a long time," I said. "But I'm not *safe*. Not really. Now that they know where my loyalties lie, I won't be safe as long as they're out there. I'll be an easy target until we have a direct plan of action to combat them."

The concern in his face deepened. "All right," he said, his voice thick. "I'm with you as long as Simmonds is. Whatever you need."

I felt the tension in my neck and shoulders lessen, and I looked him square in the eye. "Thank you."

He nodded. "Let's see what we can come up with."

I pulled up my file first. I hadn't had a chance to really look at it yet. Letting Travis read it was unavoidable since we were using it to compare the other files to, but at the very least, I wanted to read it all on my own before I shared.

Travis glanced at my screen. "How's it look?"

"It's not too bad," I said, relieved. "It's like the others—more of an overall assessment of my time at KATO than a detailed history. It puts a lot of emphasis on what they believed my state of mind to be."

Travis came closer to read. He looked to me, giving me the chance to stop him, but I didn't. The file referenced some missions and actions, but the focus was on how I had responded to their brainwashing, punishments, and manipulations. They were pleased, overall.

"What does this mean?" Travis asked, pointing to a line. "Loyalty demonstrated by rapid behavior correction upon reprimand."

I swallowed, keeping my attention on the screen as I answered him. "It means that when they reprimanded me I fell in line immediately. At least as far as they knew. They thought I changed my behavior out of loyalty, and because I didn't want to anger them. But I really just got more careful about what I was doing."

"Like crawling around in the air ducts?" he asked.

I nodded. "Exactly." KATO had only caught me once, and punished me to the point that they were sure I'd never do it again. But I did. I was just more cautious about my approach.

Travis and I spent the next couple hours mapping out my file and pulling out every detail that KATO misread. I translated the meaning behind KATO's language for Travis. He didn't ask for specifics or stories once we really got into it. We had too much to get through.

After we had my file sorted out, we turned to the others. We sent them to the monitors on the wall behind the computers and prepared to go through them one by one.

"We can get rid of Venom right now," Travis said. That was a name I'd heard around headquarters. She was a straight assassin who had a reputation for being very good at her job. "I don't even need to read her file. She won't work."

I looked at him sharply. "Have you gone up against her?"

"No, but I know agents who have—including Cody." He shook

his head. "She is nothing like you. You used to be cold about your kills, but she *enjoys* them. That's the last person we need on this."

I took her file off the screen. "I think we can rule out Hornet and Raptor too." Travis shot me a questioning look. "They're known for going way too far on their assignments. KATO considers them to be very thorough. If that's the case, I think it's safe to assume that they're entrenched in KATO's mentality."

"What did they consider you?" he asked.

"Efficient." I pulled the two files down and looked at the fifteen we had left. "All right, let's try to narrow this down to no more than five possibilities that we can investigate further—if we're even that lucky."

We were in the prep room most of the night, first condensing the list of agents and then coming up with a plan of attack to pitch to Simmonds in the morning. We'd come down to four potentials: Lotus, Misty, Monarch, and Shadow.

Their files were similar to mine, but we planned to dig deeper, into both our databases and our allies', and build complete profiles before we made a move. While we had been working, I had realized that there was one more person we needed to get on board if this was going to work.

"I know who our first recruit has to be," I said to Travis after we more or less had a strategy figured out. "And I don't think you're going to like it." Hell, *I* didn't like it, but I also didn't see another way. Travis's eyes narrowed, waiting. "Centipede," I said.

He scanned my face, clearly waiting for some kind of punch line. "You can't be serious."

"She's been assigned to recapture me," I said. "I've been on one mission since KATO learned the truth and she found me. It's going to be really hard to talk to these agents and keep all of this away from KATO if she's on my tail. Even if she doesn't get to me, she'll still report back to KATO who I contact. And if she *does* turn, it could give us direct access to headquarters, which none of these agents can do."

He squinted at me, trying to understand. "Two days ago you told me a whole story about how she turned on you. What could possess you to think there is any way this would work?"

I chewed on my cheek. "I have something on her—or rather, I know KATO has something on her. And I think we can use it to our advantage." Travis looked skeptical, but he was listening attentively. "I overheard her handler talking not too long after she was brought in. Centipede was put in KATO, but the rest of her family was sent to a labor camp. Her handler said it was something he could use to make her fall in line quickly."

"So part of the reason she follows their orders is to protect her family," Travis said.

I nodded. "She got up to speed in KATO fast—really fast. I don't think she needed to be manipulated as much because she had more to fight for than most of us."

Travis leaned back in his chair. "But if that's true, then what makes you think you can her change her mind?"

"Look at who we're dealing with." I wheeled a little closer. "There's no way her family is still alive. Not after all of this time. The conditions in those camps are on KATO's level, and they're even less concerned about the health of their workers. But I doubt Centipede knows they're dead. If we push her to investigate, and she finds out KATO's been lying, there's a good chance she'll be pissed enough to take our offer."

Travis let out a puff of air. "Yeah," he said. "No matter how KATO she is, if that was what kept her focused, then exposing the truth may be enough—especially if you're offering her the out while it's still fresh." He tilted his head to the side. "But I still don't like it. We don't have data on her, and given your history—"

I held my hands up. "Hey, if you've got another way around it, I'm all in. I would much rather do this without her. But I don't have any other ideas."

He thought for a moment then grimaced in defeat. "All right, well, take this to Simmonds. If he signs off, we'll give it a shot."

I wasn't thrilled at the prospect of including Centipede, but having this plan made me feel a little bit more in control.

Chapter Ten

WORLD TRAVELER

We met with Simmonds early the next morning. He had talked with all of the cooperative agencies who had KATO moles and managed to convince them not to capture their operatives with the understanding that we were working toward a more permanent KATO solution. I knew it had to have been a hard sell, but he managed to pull it off. We also briefed him on our plan, including the short list of agents, and the situation with Centipede.

His eyes widened as we walked him through our planned approach for Centipede, but he let us explain. "I agree that this team will not succeed if she's tracking you," he said when we had finished, "but are you certain this will be enough to turn her?"

"Not *certain*," I said. "But I know it's the only thing that has a chance at working. And if she signs on, she'll have to give us crucial, verifiable intel to prove she's on our side. Crucial enough that KATO would never authorize her to mislead us with it. If she comes through we'll know we can move forward."

Simmonds looked to Travis. "What's your take on all of this?"

Travis shrugged. "I think it's a hell of a risk," he said. "But a well-planned one. I'd put it right up there with going into North Korea."

"It would be even more solid if I could give Centipede some kind of proof that her family is dead," I said. "I know the IDA can't get into KATO from here, but hacking citizen records shouldn't be as difficult. I can tell you that Centipede showed up at KATO on August twenty-third, a year after I was taken. I also learned that her family consisted of her grandparents, her mother, two younger sisters, and a younger brother. There can't have been many families like that, at that time, coming in one family member short."

"We do have a few back doors," Simmonds said, running a hand over his jaw. "All right," he said, after a long moment. "If the board signs off, we'll do what we can to get you some intel to help with turning Centipede. However, we'll only consider moving forward on this if you can win her over. The rest of your plan is as sound as something like this can be, and I believe the access this can give us to KATO is worth it."

"Thank you, sir." I felt the excitement course through me. This was happening.

Simmonds nodded. "You've been up most of the night. Take today to rest. I'll page you when I hear something."

. . .

I had spent a good portion of the day asleep, so when my pager went off close to seven that night I was alert and ready.

I hurried to get changed, then hustled over to the operations building. Since Travis lived off campus, I had beaten him to the office significantly. However, when he arrived he too looked sharp and ready to work.

Simmonds was alone in his office. "Your team's been approved," he said. "But we'll get to that later. I paged both of you because we've tracked Jin Su's travel prior to his stop at the safe house in Russia."

I tensed. I couldn't even appreciate the fact that we'd been approved. "You mean he didn't come directly from North Korea?" I pressed my heels into the ground to keep them from bouncing.

"It doesn't appear that he did."

Travis grimaced. "He's really good at finding his way around under the radar."

"He's better than even I had given him credit for," Simmonds said, pushing a button on his keyboard. A series of images appeared on the screens behind him. Most were of a building, but one of them showed Jin Su standing at the reception desk in a very impressive lobby. I ran my tongue over to the right corner of my gums where a molar used to be. I had always hated this man. He'd stood near me while Chin Ho ripped my tooth out of my mouth, taking great care to stay in my line of sight. It was as if he wanted to make sure I knew he had a hand in it. That was two years ago.

"Where were these images taken?" Travis asked, pulling me back to the operation. I dragged my eyes away from the screens to pay attention to Simmonds.

"He's in a biological research lab in Austria," Simmonds said. "This is the only confirmation we have that he was there at all."

"I imagine KATO wiped every other trace of him." I forced my fingers to uncoil and pressed my hands against my legs, hating that this man still made me anxious—even now. "It's amazing this picture got through."

"In more ways than you realize," Simmonds said. He zoomed in on the image. "He must have wanted to keep this under wraps, because he didn't resort to KATO's usual fear tactics. He went in the front door and signed in, like any normal visitor."

Travis's eyes squinted, studying the picture. "We have a clear shot of the visitor log."

I arched an eyebrow as I saw what he was getting at. "So we can see exactly who he was meeting with." I couldn't make out the first name, but the last name, Fiser, was as clear as could be.

"And it gets even better," Simmonds said. "The company's cyber security is extensive and impressive. I imagine that's part of the reason why KATO couldn't completely erase the evidence of Jin Su's visit. It's nearly impossible to get into the system from a distance, and the security increases the deeper you move into the building. The only details we were able to pull were from the lobby. However, knowing who he was meeting with gave us a huge advantage."

I slid to the edge of my seat. "What do we know about him?"

"According to our tech department, Dr. Eli Fiser is an immunology expert. He's written numerous papers about how the human immune system works. We couldn't get past the security to pull any details from his office computer, but we were able to get into his personal email." Simmonds put another image on the screen behind him. It was an email from Fiser to a friend. I started reading as Simmonds continued. "Based on this, and other, similar emails, we're lead to believe that Fiser creates audio recordings of everything that is said in his office each day."

My eyes snapped back to Simmonds. "We can't possibly be that lucky." I was afraid to believe it—to get too excited.

"We believe that we are," Simmonds said with a small smile. "It seems that Fiser does an awful lot of thinking out loud. He's found this to be the best way to capture his thoughts."

I turned to Travis, who seemed just as eager as I was. "Does the fact that I'm here mean my field suspension has been lifted?" he asked.

"It does." Simmonds nodded. "I'm sending the two of you after the file."

He hatched the plan quickly. It was fairly straightforward. According to Fiser's calendar, he had lunch appointments out of the building every day this week. The plan was for me to break into the office and copy the audio file for the day in question, while Travis kept watch. Travis would be scheduled for the first appointment after lunch. He'd arrive early, giving me enough time to get in, and get out. Travis would be right outside the door in case Fiser, or anyone else, made an unexpected appearance.

"As far as your team is concerned, you've been approved for Centipede, and if she turns, no more than two others." Simmonds pulled a small metal case off the floor and slid it across the table. "These are satellite phones." I flipped open the case. They were compact, square, and silver. There were four of them. One for each of my potential recruits and myself.

The approval came with a long list of contingencies, such as that we had to keep them out of headquarters and thoroughly vet any intel they might provide. Nothing we wouldn't have done anyway, but the board still felt it was worth noting.

"All of this hinges on Centipede." He slid a letter-size envelope across the desk. "Here's the intel you asked for. If that isn't enough to make her turn, all of this is off the table. And if she doesn't show up at all, we'll have to reevaluate the situation."

"I understand," I said, tucking the envelope into the inside pocket of my sweatshirt. It went without saying that I was apprehensive about this, but I was starting to feel like I had some semblance of control of the situation.

"Walter will be on comms for this assignment," Simmonds said. I grimaced, but stayed quiet. As much as I hated it, Walter was the best tech expert. If the security system was as complicated as Simmonds said, he was probably who we needed. Since Sam was still a student, I couldn't ask for him on every assignment. "Once you're in the building, Walter'll be able to use your tablets to tap into security and keep you off their radar. You'll have to copy the file yourselves."

"We leave tonight?" Travis asked, standing.

Simmonds nodded. "As soon as Dr. March clears you."

Chapter Eleven

OPERATION CENTIPEDE

Travis and I made it through our medical clearances quickly. We were flying through the night, so we both forced ourselves to sleep for most of the trip, waking only as the plane started to descend.

"You know what you're going to say if Centipede's here?" he asked.

I nodded. I'd looked over the intel Simmonds had given me. It was photos of Centipede's family—dead. "I'm ready for her. And I don't doubt she'll be here." After all, I was her mission.

"If she shows up and we're separated, get word to me on comms," Travis said.

"I will. Trust me." I wasn't looking forward to being alone with her. After the way our last fight had gone, I wasn't so sure I could beat her on my own. "You deal with Walter as much as possible, okay?" I asked as I worked my earbud in. I'd work with Walter if I had to, but the more Travis talked to him, the better it would be.

Travis chuckled. "Yeah, I've got you covered."

The IDA had arranged for a car on the ground. Travis drove while I rode in the trunk. He would be parking the car in the garage so I could use it to access the building, giving us the cover we'd need to get in and out unseen. The plan was for me to use the air ducts to get to Dr. Fiser's office. Once Travis was inside, Walter would be able to access building security, which would give us a blueprint. He would then forward those plans to my tablet so I could navigate to the office. Travis popped the trunk before he headed in. I was waiting on two signals. One from Walter that he had ahold of the security cameras, which would set me in motion. The second sign would come from Travis that he was stationed outside the office. Once I had confirmation the room was empty, I would move in.

I could hear Travis signing in at the front desk. Shortly after, Walter gave me my cue. I eased the trunk open and did a quick scan, making sure no one was around. Then I rolled out and landed on my feet, staying low. It was the middle of the day, so we had a few hours until the garage saw a lot of action. Still, I wasn't taking any chances.

"There should be an elevator to your left," Walter said. "It's set to stop on the first floor unless you have an ID card. If you hold your tablet up against it, I can get you around that." I did as he asked and gave him the go-ahead.

"You're all clear," Travis said. "His office is on the tenth floor. There are six offices in the area and a small waiting room. That's where I am now, so I'm right outside if you need me."

"Copy," I said as the light next to the card reader on the elevator flashed green. I pushed the button for the tenth floor.

"Once the doors open, there's a supply closet immediately to your right," Walter said. "You can pick up the ducts there."

I passed a few researchers as I stepped off the elevator. They looked at me curiously, but I smiled at them and it seemed to calm any fears they may have had. The hallway was quiet otherwise, making it easy for me to duck into the supply closet. The vent was high, and narrower than I was used to. Luckily I could still fit through. I followed the tablet map until I found myself above Fiser's office. "I'm ready to land," I said into the comms. "Scorpion, are we still all clear?"

"Copy, Raven," Travis said. "You're good to go."

I made quick work of opening the vent, which was hinged at the bottom, and dropping into the room. I landed right next to the desk. It was a small, square, congested space. Lining the other three walls were shelves with books crammed in and stacked in every direction. The desk itself was covered with papers and even more books to the point that I had to dig to find the keyboard.

I plugged my tablet into the computer and pushed in my comm. "Command, I need you to crack his password." A few seconds later, the screen flickered and I was in. First, I checked to make sure he wasn't currently recording his office—he wasn't. Then I quickly located his notes folder and found all of the audio notes he had recorded during the past year. I scanned the end of the list, easily locating the date we needed. I plugged the flashdrive in and started the copy.

Since it was an audio file, it took longer than I would have liked. I had about a minute left on the transfer when I heard Travis's voice in my head—but he wasn't talking to me. "I'm waiting on him, actually," Travis said. "Is he in his office? I was told he would still be at lunch."

"He is," a male voice said. "This is a routine security sweep."

"Stall him," I hissed into my comm. If I took the flashdrive out now, it would interrupt the transfer. We wouldn't have enough time to start all over and get the copy before Fiser returned. Travis kept talking but I was running out of time. I quickly turned off the monitor and covered the keyboard with papers but left the flashdrive plugged in so the transfer continued. I hoisted myself back into the vent and pulled the grate closed, just barely getting it in place before the door opened. The room looked exactly as it should, save for the blinking flashdrive.

I slid deeper into the vent to stay out of sight, which also meant I couldn't see the guard myself. I could hear his footsteps around the perimeter—or at least as close to the perimeter as he could get. He lingered in the office for another ten seconds before I heard the door shut. I edged closer to the vent, still not daring to jump out until I heard from Travis. But I could see the drive. The light blinked for another three seconds before going dark. The transfer had finished.

"He's gone," Travis said. "But Fiser's back from lunch, and he's headed my way."

"I'm wrapping up," I said, dropping out of the vent for the second time. I grabbed the flashdrive swiftly, then turned on the monitor, locked his computer, and checked to make sure everything was where I'd found it. I was locking the vent back in place when I heard Travis talking to Fiser, doing his best to keep him in the hall until I was out of the way. I made it to the elevator as Travis started to lose him.

"I'm clear," I said to Travis. "I'll see you at the extraction."

Travis started bumbling his excuses to Fiser, apologizing, saying he must've gotten his times mixed up and would reschedule. He needed to ditch Fiser and sign out at the front desk to avoid raising any red flags. I beat him to the garage easily.

We were almost out. I had made it halfway to the car when everything changed.

I heard movement behind me only a millisecond before the gun pressed against the base of my skull.

I froze. I felt a hand on my holster, removing my gun and tossing it aside. The clatter echoed through the confined garage, but there wasn't any indication that anyone had heard a sound. It was Centipede. There was no one else it could be. I knew Travis was already on his way. I'd just have to hold her off until he got here.

"You can't kill me," I said, keeping my voice even. "So why don't you put that thing away?" I turned around slowly. Centipede didn't stop me, but she didn't lower the weapon either. Her lips twisted into a condescending smirk, and I had a hard time not punching her for that alone.

"Who said there were bullets in this gun?" she asked. My heart picked up a beat, but I didn't dare give her the satisfaction of asking a question. She provided the answer anyway. "Darts." She tilted her head to the side and I could see she was holding something back. "Full of Gerex."

I went stony. Something in my face must have betrayed me because her smile got even more twisted.

"I heard you're off of it now," she said. "Is that true?" Again I didn't answer. I was shocked that she knew. I breathed through my nose, trying to stay calm. I had to focus on why I came here—though that was awfully hard to do with a gun full of Gerex in my face. "You probably don't want this, then." She was wrong. I *did* want it. I just knew better.

"If you shoot that, you won't walk out of here," I said. It was the only thing I could think to say. The only thing I thought would matter to her. Once I got that drug in my system, she wouldn't stand a chance against me. I didn't want to kill her, but I would to save myself from them. Her face hardened and she took a step forward. I needed to feel her out before I gave too much away. "What if I told you there was a way you could get off of it too. Would you be interested?" I watched her face intently, trying to gauge her reaction. Her eyes widened barely even a fraction, but I caught it. I'd surprised her.

She recovered quickly, narrowing her face and squashing any hint of curiosity I'd stirred. "You have nothing to offer me."

She pulled the trigger, and if I hadn't been KATO-trained I would never have gotten out of the way. I crashed into the ground, feeling the relief and disappointment of dodging the dart. I swung a leg in the air, kicking the gun just hard enough to knock it out of her hand, while also preventing it from traveling too far. I wanted it for myself. The gun fell in between us, but Centipede charged at me instead of going for the weapon. I spun away from her, giving myself an extra beat to find my feet. I had learned last time that I couldn't beat her in a fight—not without the Gerex. However, half the reason she came so close to defeating me before was because she knew me as well as I knew her. She knew what to expect. To beat her this time, I'd have to fight my instincts. If they said kick, I threw a punch. If they said to block, I ducked, avoiding her attack completely. It turned out to be surprisingly effective. I had her off-balance within a couple of punches. A quick sweeping kick to her legs took her down.

I spun away, grabbing the Gerex gun and pointing it at her. Instead of inciting fear, as a normal gun would have, I saw the excitement dancing in her eyes. It occurred to me this might have been crueler than holding an actual gun. I was dangling what I was sure was a powerful dose of Gerex right in front of her face and refusing to pull the trigger.

She stared up at me, wide-eyed and desperate. I felt my hand start to shake with a craving and I shoved it aside. Instead, I put all of my energy into talking with a steady voice. "I can offer you an out."

Now she laughed. "I'm the one hunting *you*."

"And yet, look who's holding the gun." I tried not to think about exactly what I was holding and instead focused on the power it gave me. I tipped my head to the side. "I've always been better than you. So why don't you try shutting your mouth and listening to what I have to say."

She glowered at me but for a change stayed silent.

"We have intel," I said. "Intel that would affect you and every other agent in KATO. I promise you, you will care about it."

Her eyes flashed and I saw the anger building. "These are *lies*."

"They're not." My voice was firm and in control. I had her gun and I had her attention, which meant I had the upper hand. "Now that my cover is blown, we need someone on the inside. You have access to headquarters. If you help me, I can help you."

"I will *never* help a traitor like you." There was poison in her voice.

The elevator dinged behind me before I could answer. I dared to glance back, praying it wouldn't be a civilian.

It was Travis. His stance stiffened the instant he saw me with a gun in my hand. A car was blocking Centipede from his line of sight, but he drew his weapon instinctively. Travis walked slowly around the car and he didn't even blink when he saw who was standing in front of me. "You good here?" he asked.

"Yeah," I said. "So far."

He nodded evenly, but didn't lower his gun.

I turned back to Centipede, and Travis stepped behind me, prepared to shoot if he had to.

"What's wrong?" Centipede asked, smirking. "You can't take care of yourself anymore?"

I bit my tongue, refusing to take her bait. "I'm offering you the chance to escape."

"And why would I leave the greatest country in the world for *you*?" She was referring to North Korea. One thing I'd learned quickly inside KATO was that they truly believed they were living in the best country the world had ever seen. Eventually I learned the whole country believed that—or at least they pretended to. North Korea was filled with lies and propaganda created by the people in charge and its residents were isolated and afraid enough to go along with it.

I looked Centipede dead in the eyes. "You've seen enough of the world to know you've been lied to." Her eyes hardened, but only for a second. It was enough to push me forward. "And if they lied to you about that, what makes you think you haven't been lied to about *other* things?"

She shifted away from me, getting instantly defensive. Her instincts were good enough to be afraid. "What are you talking about?"

"I know about your family," I said. Her face contorted in confusion that quickly gave way to anger. I kept talking before she could collect her thoughts. "They're why you fight so hard at KATO, right? They were put in a labor camp and KATO told you if you don't perform, they'll kill your family."

She leveled me with a glare that most certainly would have

killed me if she had the ability. "You don't. Know what. You're talking about."

"You and I both know there's no way they're still alive," I said. "Not after all this time." She was ready to attack me, armed or not. I was pretty sure the fact that Travis was still covering me was the only thing keeping her in place. "Do you really want to work for the people who killed your family and lied about it?"

The look on her face told me in no uncertain terms that she was absolutely livid.

Suddenly Walter was in my ear, squawking that the clock was almost up on the cameras.

"You've got to wrap this up," Travis said, his eyes still locked on Centipede.

I fished out the envelope and one of the satellite phones Simmonds had given me and stepped toward her. "Take these." I pressed the items into her hand. "Open the envelope alone. You have twenty-four hours to call me and change your mind. If I don't hear from you, we'll pretend this never happened." I did my best to act like she wasn't holding the future of my operation in her hand.

"I'm not leaving here without you," she said, standing straighter.

I twirled the Gerex gun in my hand as if it didn't faze me. "I have your weapon and my partner has a bullet on you." Travis raised his gun a tick higher. "Do you really think you can find a way to bring me in alive before he puts you down?"

"And I'm supposed to believe that you'll let me live?" There was a hint of panic in her voice. I doubt Travis even noticed it, but I'd spent a lot of time with Centipede. I'd learned to pick up on the slightest hint of weakness.

"Yes," I said. "This time, we both walk away. And if I don't hear from you, it'll be the only time."

Her face tightened as she studied me, trying to get a read on the situation. "I will *never* call you," she said. Then she spun on her heel and left the garage. Her neck twitched as if it were a struggle to keep from looking back at us.

Chapter Twelve

STRUGGLING THROUGH

Travis and I didn't speak on the ride to the airstrip. I was too distracted by the gun in my lap to start a conversation. I turned it over, studying it. I was *holding* Gerex. It was sitting in my hands. And it was after a mission, which had always been a trigger. Once we got on the plane I could go to the bathroom and—

No. I couldn't do that. Not after everything.

I lifted the gun up, feeling the weight of it. I couldn't tell if it felt heavier or lighter than a normal gun. Maybe it was both? Was that possible?

I followed Travis onto the plane. He yanked the door shut behind us, checked in with the pilot, then came back to me. "Why didn't you call me when she showed up, like we talked about?" he asked.

"You were already on your way." My voice sounded distant and my focus was on my hands. I was still transfixed by what I was holding. Travis didn't know there was anything special about it. I didn't have to tell him. Even if I didn't use it now, I could get it inside the IDA like this. "You need to take this gun from me," I said finally, working to keep my voice from spiking.

"What?" He eyed me uncertainly. "Why don't you put it down on your own?"

I took a long slow breath, summoning the courage to find the words again. "Please. I need you to take it."

"Jocelyn—"

My eyes locked on him and I tightened my hold on the gun. "*Travis.*" I was only vaguely aware that my breathing had gotten heavier. "It's loaded with Gerex darts and I can't let go."

He visibly swallowed and after a long painful moment, he pried the gun out of my hand.

Once he had, he disappeared toward the front of the plane. I didn't know where he'd put it, or what he had done with the drug inside. I felt my hand start to shake, but overall, I was surprisingly steady, considering what I had just been holding. I slid into one of the benches, leaning forward to rest my head on the seat in front of me. The pressure on my forehead felt soothing somehow.

When Travis came back, he sat down next to me. He twisted in the seat so he was facing me, his head tucked so it was level with mine. "How are you doing?"

I stayed hunched over, gripping the edge of the bench, working to keep myself stable. "I think okay." It was easier to battle through the craving now that I wasn't holding the drug.

I felt his hand on my knee and I appreciated the extra security. "There's supposed to be an acupuncture kit on board. Do you want me to get it?" Dr. March had taught him the basics before we'd gone to North Korea.

I shook my head. "It's not that bad. I want to start getting through these on my own."

He sighed, and I was sure he disagreed, but he didn't push the issue. "If you're sure." He shifted away from me, and I knew he was going to leave—to give me space.

My hand darted out and grabbed his the second he stood. Because I didn't want space. His presence helped more than I could describe, and in a way I didn't fully understand. I kept my head down and focused on breathing. I didn't want to see his expression. He sat back down without a word, an inch closer than he had been before. He knew exactly what I needed.

. . .

"How are you feeling?" Travis asked when we landed.

I took a slow deep breath, assessing myself. "Better."

He gave me a once-over, his face full of doubt. "You still don't look that great." I bit my lip, but I didn't disagree. I wasn't shaking, but my insides were a twisted mess. "Go to Dr. March," he said. "I'll meet you in Simmonds's office." He gave me a pointed look and I knew this wasn't an argument I was going to win.

While I settled in for my treatment, I asked Dr. March for an update on Eliza.

She looked dismayed. "She's been acting out a great deal since you spoke with her, so we've had to keep her sedated more frequently lately."

"Acting out how?"

"She's been very resistant to her behavior specialists," Dr. March said. "She even went as far as punching one of them. She also tried to pull her hair out, which a specialist believes was to avoid a conversation."

"Do you think she *wants* to be sedated?" I asked, sitting up slightly.

She shrugged. "That's one theory, but we don't know enough to say anything for sure right now." I opened my mouth to say more, but she put a hand on my shoulder to quiet me. "Let me worry about her, okay? You have more than enough on your plate."

She slid the first needle into my ear and I took a deep breath, doing my best to relax.

I headed to Simmonds's office when I was finished in the medical wing. Travis and my father were the only people there when I arrived. They stopped talking when I entered and I was afraid to even ask what they were discussing.

I took a seat next to Travis and glanced up at my father, who was again standing against the wall. "I didn't see you before we left."

"Yeah." He rubbed the back of his neck uncomfortably. "Roy and I didn't see eye to eye on a couple things."

"About our assignment?"

My dad shook his head. "No, I didn't even know about that until after you were gone." There was a bite to his voice that suggested this was another point of tension. "But it sounded like you guys did great."

Simmonds arrived before we could discuss the situation further. "Good," he said, "you're all here." He spared my father half a glance as he took his seat. "Let's get right to it." He was gruffer than usual. I guessed this was somehow related to whatever had kept my dad away before our mission. Travis and I both seemed to sense that the quicker we moved through this, the better.

We took turns walking them through our assignment.

"She knew you were off the Gerex?" Simmonds asked, his eyebrows raised.

"Yes," I said, "but I suspect she's the only agent who knows. If the wrong agent found out, they could make a break for it. As far as they were concerned, Centipede could be trusted because they were also holding her family over her."

"Which you took away from them," my dad said. "So it more or less went according to plan."

I shrugged. "As much as could be expected, anyway. She still walked away without a hard yes, but the fact that she let me walk away at all means she won't go back to KATO with any of this. She can't spill our secrets without getting herself in trouble. I gave her a twenty-four-hour window to contact me, so we won't know anything more until that time's up."

Simmonds nodded, taking this in. "All right, then. We'll keep this in motion for now." I relaxed slightly, relieved to still have a shot at this. "I'll have an analyst go over the file you brought back and page the both of you when we have details to discuss." It was a clear dismissal, and Travis and I didn't need to be told twice.

Chapter Thirteen

NEW ALLY

I was exhausted but couldn't sleep. I knew I wouldn't be able to until time ran out on Centipede's clock. Despite her answer, I still hoped she would come around. Instead I laid in my bed, studying the ceiling and thinking back on the interactions I'd had with Centipede over the years. I had learned my lesson after she ratted me out to the handlers. No one at KATO could be trusted. That was the instant that life in KATO became about protecting myself, even at the expense of the others.

It had been sixteen hours since we'd left Austria, and I had all but written her off, when the satellite phone lit up. I stared at it for a moment, not daring to believe that she could truly be reaching out.

"Hello?" I held my breath as I waited for an answer, praying this wasn't a trap and that I wouldn't hear a KATO handler on the other end.

There was a long pause and my heartbeat filled the silence. I'd lost track of how long I'd been waiting when a voice finally spoke. "I'm not agreeing to anything, but I want to hear your offer." It was Centipede.

She had called. There was still a long way to go, but this was the first step I needed. "Did you open the envelope?"

"You wouldn't be talking to me if I didn't." Her voice was harsh, and I suspected it was to mask the pain. My stomach churned. I knew what it was like to find out someone had killed your family, but I didn't have to live with the visual evidence.

"Do you know how long they lied to you?" I asked. I'd imagine she could guess ages based on photos. It's what I would have done once I got past the initial shock. I'd study every angle.

"What difference does it make?" Centipede snapped.

"It doesn't." I knew better than to push her. It was big enough that she called.

Again there was silence, so much of it that I thought she may have hung up on me. Then I heard her breath. It was rattled and coming in sharp bursts. She wasn't crying. She was having trouble breathing. It wasn't the first time I'd heard her breathe like that.

Centipede and I stood facing each other on opposite sides of the training room, preparing ourselves for an exercise. We were twelve. In the center of the floor was a gun. The goal was to beat your opponent to the gun and put a bullet in her. We were to shoot to injure, not kill. There was one bullet in the gun. Successfully complete the training exercise and you got an extra quarter dose of Gerex. Shoot and miss, and both agents lost Gerex for twenty-four hours. Get shot, and lose a day's worth of Gerex, plus additional punishments.

Chin Ho blew the whistle and set us both in motion. Centipede made a mistake from the start. She went for the gun. I, however, went for her. I grabbed her arm as she reached for the weapon and flipped her onto the ground. Then in one motion I swept the gun off the ground, pivoted, and fired a bullet into her leg.

My aim was perfect.

She cried out in pain as I tossed the gun aside. Centipede was dragged out of the room almost immediately, but I wasn't thinking about her anymore. I was paying attention to my handler, who had pulled a needle and a vial out of his pocket.

I didn't see Centipede again until much later. The other agents and I were already stretched out on the floor for the night when she was brought back to us. I watched her struggle across the room in the dark. She settled herself in the corner, and I lay awake, listening to her ragged breathing.

"They hurt you, didn't they?" I asked into the phone.

Her breath rattled again. "It was the second time I came back without you." She sounded tired now. I could understand why. Existing in KATO was exhausting on its own. On top of that, Centipede had spent years thinking she was fighting for her family, only to find out she was fighting for nothing.

"You said in Austria you had intel that would affect every KATO agent," she said, seeming suddenly more assertive—as if she realized she had exposed her weakness. "What is it?"

"I'm not sharing the details until you give me information on KATO that I can verify," I said. She started to talk over me. I raised my voice so it was louder. "For now, I'll tell you this much." She quieted long enough to listen. "Our intel suggests that they are looking to add to the power they have over their agents."

Another long pause. "How do they plan to do this?" There was a hard angry edge to her voice. She had plenty to be angry about where KATO was concerned, and I intended to use it to my advantage.

"I've told you enough," I said. "Now I need to be sure that you're not playing us."

There was more silence on her end. I was sure she was considering backing out. But then she spoke. "KATO knows your location. I tracked you from Korea five weeks ago."

Now I was the one breathing hard. I wanted her to be lying, but in my gut I knew she wasn't. It made too much sense. "That's how you've been able to find me in the field," I said. "You've been tracking me from headquarters."

"We haven't cracked your security yet. That's why we're still on the outside," she said, continuing as if she hadn't just dropped a massive bomb. "We know the signs for when a perimeter check is about to occur and how to avoid it. One agent is permanently outside the IDA. I'm there when you are, and I leave when you do. I report directly back to KATO each time I leave to follow you. They restock my Gerex every time I come back."

It explained everything. Since KATO had another agent stationed at the IDA, they would be aware when Centipede left to tail me. Like a typical KATO mission, she had to keep up with me on her own, without any help from them. She reported back to KATO each time she left the base because if she failed, they would want to know why. For us, this was a gift. It explained how, despite being followed, we were able to get to Eliza. KATO didn't know where we were headed until it was too late.

My mind was spinning. I had to get to Simmonds. He needed to know. "Where are you right now?"

"On a plane coming to you."

"Okay, we'll look into all of this and get back to you," I said. "For now, keep that phone on you. I have it silenced so it won't call attention. Check it often and call me back ASAP if you see that I called."

"Don't expect me to wait for too long," she said. Then she hung up.

I hurried across campus to the operations building. We had gotten back from Austria early in the afternoon. It was evening now, but Simmonds would still be in his office. The door was locked, which was a sign that Simmonds was in the middle of something. Normally I would have waited for him to finish, but this was too important. I pushed the button next to the door, buzzing repeatedly. The door unlocked with a click. There were about ten people stationed at various points around the office. Simmonds took one look at my face and cleared the room with the exception of my father, who had also been in on the meeting.

I quickly relayed the conversation I had just had, keeping Centipede's punishment to myself.

"They know how to detect our perimeter checks?" my dad asked when I had finished.

I nodded. "According to Centipede. She's on her way back here now. She also said there's an agent permanently stationed outside the IDA."

"KATO agents don't work together," Simmonds said, looking to me for an explanation.

"They're not working *together*," I said. "They were each given a separate assignment. One to watch me and one to watch the IDA. They're aware of each other, but that's it."

"We'll investigate this," Simmonds said, standing and heading to the back door of his office, which I believed led to the command rooms. "Stay by your pager. I'll want to speak to you when we know more."

He left me to see myself out.

. . .

I killed time in the cafeteria, getting some food. I wasn't all that hungry, but I hadn't eaten since we'd gotten back and I needed something to do. I sat at a table by myself, stirring my soup as my mind ran through the events of the last hour.

KATO was here. That was the only thing I had been able to think about since I left Simmonds's office.

I was so completely lost in thought that I hadn't noticed Travis until he took the seat across from me. Unlike me, however, he didn't have any food. He looked a little irritated, but I had no idea why.

"Simmonds just briefed me," he said. "How could you not tell me Centipede contacted you?"

I pinched the bridge of my nose. I didn't call him. It didn't even occur to me. "I'm sorry," I said. "I wasn't thinking—at all." I was frustrated with myself. "Did Simmonds—tell you what she said?"

His face softened. "They are not as close as you think they are."

"They're *here*." I tried not to sound rattled, but my voice dipped enough for Travis to notice. I swallowed hard. "I knew I wasn't safe from KATO, but I wasn't prepared for them to be this close."

He squeezed my hand. "They're locked outside. And we don't know anything for sure."

I shook my head hard. "I should have known. Especially once Centipede started showing up. I let my guard down too much."

"You didn't." He was intense and insistent. "You were injured. You—"

"She's been across the fucking street!" I hissed at him, my voice soft enough that only he could hear. "She's been right outside my window for over a month."

I tried to pull my hand out of his grasp but he held on tighter. Travis leaned over the table, meeting my eyes and ensuring I couldn't look anywhere else. "If this *does* check out, we're in a position to handle it. The IDA has plans in place."

I exhaled heavily. "You're right. I know you're right, but—"

"It's KATO," he finished for me. "I get it. But for now, we're ahead of them again."

. . .

Both my and Travis's pagers went off as we left the cafeteria. "This isn't good news," I said.

Travis tilted his head to the side. "You don't know that."

"We've only known about this threat for a few hours," I said. "It would take days to confirm no suspicious activity. The fact that we're getting paged now means they found something."

Simmonds and my father were ready for us, their expressions serious. It was enough of a confirmation to turn my stomach.

"They've got someone watching us, don't they?" I asked, lowering myself into a chair.

"They do," Simmonds said, spreading a series of surveillance photos across the desk for both of us to see.

It was the sidewalk across from the IDA's campus. I scanned the images, looking for something that stood out. I found it in seconds. There was one person in each image who had her face covered, but in a different way each time. Sometimes it was with a hat, or a hood. Other times with a book or a map. The stance was the same in each photo, though, so I was sure it was the same person. There was one close-up profile image that gave a clear view of the girl's neck. A burn scar. She was most definitely KATO. According to Centipede, they knew how to pick up on our security checks, so I suspected the different disguises were to keep from alerting the guards monitoring the exterior cameras.

"They've also got a camera here," my dad said, pointing to a telephone pole on the corner. "I found something similar across from each entrance."

"How did we get the pictures without tipping them off?" I asked.

My dad shrugged. "We knew they had to be ground level since they seemed to be able to monitor only our comings and goings. So instead of doing a formal security check, I went scouting."

I raised an eyebrow at him. "*You?*"

Despite the situation, he cracked a smile. "I actually used to be a pretty good spy."

"Right," I said. "Of course." Even with everything I knew about my father's history, I had a hard time picturing *this* version of him doing fieldwork. Even if it was just outside the IDA's walls.

Next to me, Travis studied the photos. "So, Centipede was telling the truth." He looked up at me. "At least you have a reason to trust her."

"Yeah," I said, "though I think I'd rather she'd have been lying."

"Centipede's story will, of course, require more investigating," Simmonds said, moving us along. "But I'm prepared to trust it for the time being. KATO is not patient enough to sit on our location if they have the option to make a move. The fact that they're across the street tells me they don't have the intel to invade."

"They also can't blow us up or do anything destructive without running the risk of killing me or Eliza," I said. "As long as one of us is in the building, everyone should be more or less safe."

"I'm inclined to agree," Simmonds said.

"You know Centipede better than anyone," my dad said. "Do you truly believe this intel can be trusted?"

I nodded. "I do. It makes too much sense, and there is no way that KATO would ever be okay with this information getting out. She would be in a lot of trouble if it got back to them that she gave us a heads-up. I still don't know yet if we can trust her to stick with us in the long run, but she's pretty angry KATO lied about her family. So for now I believe she's on our side."

"Very well, then," Simmonds said.

Travis shifted forward. "Are we initiating relocation?"

Simmonds nodded. "I already have the student supervisors on standby."

"How many phases are we talking?" my dad asked.

Simmonds ran a hand along his chin, considering. "We'll start with three for now, with a contingency plan to expedite if needed."

I glanced between the three of them, trying to keep up. "What exactly is happening now?"

"We have several plans in place to relocate the IDA if the situation calls for it," Simmonds said. "Each plan has a number of phases, depending on the severity of the threat. The first phase is always the relocation of the students to a temporary secure site until we can establish a new permanent base. I'll be initiating that right away. In this case, our next phase will be relocation of our intel, followed by relocation of active personnel."

"And our watchdogs won't notice any of this?" I asked.

"The point is to carry on as if we don't know they're watching," my dad said. "There are underground tunnels that can get the students, and eventually us, to the airport undetected. As long as they're just sitting there, we proceed as normal. Then we disappear before they even realize the campus is deserted. In the meantime, we'll have people monitoring the situation now that we know what we're looking at. If anything changes in their patterns, we'll speed up our process."

"I have to call Centipede back and let her know this checked out," I said, standing. "And she's going to want some intel if she's going to stay with us."

"That's understandable," Simmonds said. "But give her as little as possible, and see what else you can get out of her while you're at it. Specifically if any of the other agents know you're off the Gerex."

I nodded. "Absolutely."

"Do you need anything from us?" Travis asked.

Simmonds shook his head. "Not right now. But we should have analysis on the audio the two of you recovered on your last assignment very soon. I'll page you when I hear something."

. . .

I called Centipede when I got back to my room. She picked up right away. "Did you get confirmation?" she asked.

"We did," I said. "And I have a couple more questions for you." She stayed quiet and I took that as a sign to continue. "You know I'm off the Gerex. Does every KATO agent know? Or just you?"

She snorted. "Do you really think they'd want everyone to know something like that?" She didn't wait for an answer. "I was the one tasked with tracking you, so I was the only one they told. I was ordered to secrecy."

I relaxed, relieved to have been right. "Do you know if I'm the only agent KATO sent out for an extended assignment?"

"What?" she asked. "How would I know that?" I started to change the subject, but she cut me off. "I think it's time for you to give me something. How is KATO going to add to the power they have over us?"

I bit my lip before I spoke, debating how to keep her satisfied without sharing too much. "I was in Russia to retrieve a KATO operative based on intel we had that suggested she was the key to the future of KATO's training and control." She already knew where I was and that an agent was taken. I was trying to expand on intel she already had. "We don't know too much more than that right now, but I've seen enough of the situation to know the threat is real."

"What makes her so important?" I heard the eagerness in her voice, which was good. It meant I had her hooked in more ways than one.

"We're working on it," I said. "But in the meantime, I have locations for other KATO agents who might be able to help us get some intel."

"You really think you can pull other agents away from them? Away from the Gerex?"

"I pulled you away, didn't I?" I asked.

"Not everyone has family secrets you can use," she said.

I sighed, exasperated. We were getting farther from the point. "Centipede, are you in or not?"

There was a small growl of frustration on her end. "Call when you have something new." And then she hung up on me for the second time that day.

Chapter Fourteen

PARTIAL DATA

I woke up the next morning to find my tablet lit up next to my bed. I grabbed it and saw a video call from Sam coming through.

"It's about time, KATO girl," he said. "I've been calling for hours. Even Gwen and Olivia got tired of waiting."

"I thought you guys were supposed to be on the move?" I asked.

"We were. You should have seen the production Agent Harper made out of *that*." He shook his head, mildly annoyed. "We landed a couple hours ago. I'm not supposed to say where, though."

"I see you've already got your computer system up and running." I was not at all surprised to see that had been a priority.

"That's the main purpose of my call," he said with a smirk. "Just because I'm not on the base doesn't mean I can't help. My resources may be limited, but, well, we both know how good I am."

I laughed. "Yeah, I'll keep that in mind."

"I'm serious," he said. "I may not be able to do as much, but I can help."

"I know you can, Sam." I smiled, appreciating that I had someone on my side. "Thank you."

"That's what I'm here for," he said. "Try to stay out of trouble while I'm gone."

I rolled my eyes. "I could say the same to you."

"I'm locked away with Agent Lee and Agent Harper. How could I possibly get into trouble?" he asked, with a mischievous glint in his eye.

I laughed as he disconnected. It wouldn't be nearly as interesting without him around.

The impact of the relocation was obvious as soon as I left my room. With the students gone, I was most certainly the only person living in the student housing building. It felt strangely hollow. In fact, most of the campus seemed eerily quiet. The number of active agents had outweighed the students from the time I had started with the IDA, but since the students lived on campus they seemed to account for a lot of the general hustle and bustle. It was something I hadn't noticed until they'd been removed. It was also strange to find my afternoons were suddenly free. Though with everything that had been set in motion in the past few days, I doubted I'd have any problem filling the time.

Simmonds confirmed this theory quickly. I was halfway through breakfast when my pager went off. This was almost certainly about the audio we'd recovered.

I was already waiting outside of Simmonds's office when Travis arrived.

"Did you see any KATO agents lurking outside?" I asked him.

He shook his head. "No, but I tried not to look too hard." He didn't want to give us away.

After about ten minutes, the door to Simmonds's office opened. Older tactical and administrative agents poured out of the room.

They were grouped in twos and threes and all seemed to be in the middle of one intense conversation or another.

I looked to Travis. "Is this about the relocation?"

"Probably," he said. "But I've never been a part of one before so I can't say for sure."

Simmonds was at his desk, paging through files. He looked up when we entered. "Did you make contact with Centipede last night?"

"I did," I said, sitting on the edge of a chair. My father hurried in with a folder. "She confirmed that she's the only one who knows that I'm off the Gerex. She also doesn't seem to have any intel on KATO's current plan. At least not right now."

"Well," my dad said, dropping the folder on the desk, "at the very least, we can officially corroborate her story. I ran the girl we caught watching us through facial recognition." He opened the folder and laid out the images from the previous day along with an IDA profile. "We don't have too much on her, but we can confirm her involvement in KATO assignments."

I nodded. "This is good." At least, as good as it could be. It meant I could give Centipede a little bit of a longer leash in the future.

"I'm assuming you also needed us for something else?" Travis asked.

"Yes," Simmonds said, turning back to his own files. "We did get something from Austria, but it turned out KATO was more prepared for Fiser's office than we thought. It would seem that only half of the conversation was recorded."

"Which half?" my dad asked.

"The second part."

Travis sat up straighter. "Can we hear it?"

"I have it right here." Simmonds clicked on his screen and the four of us quieted.

It was silent for several seconds, then we heard a voice.

"In theory, it could be harvested and modified similar to how the smallpox vaccine was created." That had to be Dr. Fiser. He continued. "But this is all theory. I'd have to see the sample if you want a more specific answer. This isn't a situation science has ever had a reason to explore."

"Your theory is all I'm asking for." My heart pounded on instinct. It was definitely Jin Su. I rolled my shoulders, trying to shake off the fear. "This is all I needed to know."

I heard footsteps next. They were moving away from the microphone. Probably Jin Su heading for the door. Then he stopped. "Not a word to anyone about this. Or I may find good use for your daughters."

I swallowed hard, breathing through my nose to keep the bile from rising past my throat, and thinking of all of the things he could do to back his threat.

On the recording, the door had finally closed, and Fiser started to pant. Simmonds turned it off once the hyperventilation set in.

The office was dead silent. I stared straight ahead, not daring to look at any of them, but when I spoke, I couldn't keep my voice from shaking. "He went from this meeting directly to Russia." To *Eliza*. Simmonds stared at his computer screen, seeming to be lost in thought. Next to me, Travis was hunched over, his head in his hands. "Is there any evidence of something wrong with her?" I asked.

Simmonds shook his head. "According to Dr. March, Eliza's as healthy as can be expected in her situation."

I ground my teeth together. It had to be related to her. But right now, it didn't seem to add up.

"Can I tell you what part I *really* didn't like?" my dad asked. He seemed calm enough, but I noticed tension in his stance. I focused on him, waiting for him to continue. "We may not know what he asked, but that answer we heard was *very* specific. Which means it had to start with a specific question."

I was trying to see his point, but Travis got there first. "People only ask specific questions when they've already asked the general ones." He looked briefly at each of us. "Specific comes when they're close to figuring something out."

I ran a hand over my hair. We needed to know what happened to Eliza.

"Okay," Simmonds said, after another long moment. "Here's what we're going to do. Jocelyn, you are going to talk to Eliza again."

I exhaled evenly through my nose remembering how the last time went. "Are you sure about that? Dr. March told me she hasn't been doing that great since I talked to her."

Simmonds nodded. "You pulled something out of her. We desperately need to know how she fits into all of this, and if anyone is going to get her to share, it appears that person would be you."

I held his eyes. I wasn't thrilled at the prospect of trying this again, especially if I had triggered her more destructive behavior. But he was right—we needed her to talk. "When do you want to do this?"

"This afternoon," Simmonds said.

"What do you need from me?" Travis asked.

"Elton, I'm sending you to England. You're going to find out everything you can about Eliza before she was kidnapped. As far as we know, she doesn't have any family left, but talk to anyone else who may have known her. Her friends, her teachers, and especially her doctors. We need to know what about her led Jin Su to an immunology specialist."

Travis nodded. "Absolutely, sir. When do I leave?"

"After we talk with Eliza," Simmonds said. "That way you'll have the most up-to-date information."

"You don't want me on that too?" I asked.

Simmonds shook his head. "It's a one-person job, and Elton's been there before," he said. "I'll meet both of you and Dr. March in the medical wing later today."

I nodded reluctantly and followed Travis out of the office. I was slightly surprised to find my father was right behind me.

Travis glanced at him. "I'll meet you in the prep room," he said. "We still have more background to gather on the potential recruits."

"Yeah, I'll be right there." I watched him into the stairwell before turning to face my dad.

"Listen, kid," he said. "I'd like to be there this afternoon. If that's all right."

I bit down on my lip, remembering everything about my past that had come up the last time I'd talked with Eliza. "Actually, can you not be?"

He looked startled and hurt. He opened and closed his mouth a couple times before finding the right words. "I thought we were doing better."

"We are." My voice sounded broken. "But we're not there yet."

"You said that before, but it doesn't seem like anything's changed," he said. "Why is that?"

I shook my head.

"Come on, kid. Throw me a bone."

I took a breath. If I had learned anything since I got out of KATO it was that sometimes I had to trust, even if I wasn't sure I was ready. I knew I couldn't give him—or anyone—the specifics they wanted. But, again, he was trying. He stared at me intently, but I gazed past him when I started talking. "Because I did things—" I cut myself off. I couldn't do this. "Forget it," I said. "I don't want to talk about it."

I looked at him to gauge his reaction. There was a sadness in his face I couldn't handle and I shifted away from him, taking a step toward the stairs. "Wait," he said, reaching for my wrist, "just hold on a minute." He pulled me back and I didn't fight him. I was shaking, but if he noticed, he didn't say anything. I stared straight ahead, waiting for him to talk. "Jocelyn." I faced him, and saw his expression was open, and completely without judgment. "You did what you had to because *I* left you in there."

I started shaking my head. "That's not—"

"*Yes.*" He held my eyes, determined to make me believe him. I saw a pain and sadness so raw it hurt to look at. "That's what happened. So you have nothing to be ashamed of."

I looked away from him now and whispered, "If I were you I would have thought I was dead too."

He squeezed my wrist just a little bit tighter and when I looked back at him, his eyes were shut. "That doesn't matter." He seemed to be trying to calm himself down. He opened his eyes once he got control. "You can hold on to your story for as long as you want. But if you want to talk about it, you can tell me. I have no place to judge anything." Suddenly, it was hard to swallow—hard to breathe. I felt the sting of tears in my eyes and I couldn't explain where they had come from. I needed to get out of there.

"I have to go—sort through some files." I pulled out of his grasp and was down the stairs before he could stop me again.

. . .

I massaged my neck as I entered the mission prep room, trying to make myself relax. Travis turned enough to study me out of the corner of his eye.

"What was that about?" he asked as I sat down at the computer next to him.

I shook my head. "He wanted to watch my conversation with Eliza later." I put my attention on powering up the computer.

"And you said no?" His tone made me freeze. It sounded as if he thought I should have said yes. I turned my head slowly in his direction.

"I'm not ready for him to know what happened at KATO," I said.

"He's heard enough to have an idea what goes on in there."

I swiveled my chair, giving Travis my full attention. "It's hard to talk about KATO to begin with, but with him around it almost feels suffocating."

"You tell me things," Travis said.

"When you drag it out of me," I said, wrapping a curl around my finger.

He tipped his chin, conceding my point. "But still. You tell me."

"You didn't know me before," I said. "He knows who I was, and now he's getting to know who I am. Sure, maybe he can guess the details of what happened in between, but guessing and knowing are two different things." I put my attention on my arm, which I was shifting uncomfortably on the table. "I don't want him to know what I did and I don't want him to know what was done to me. Because I don't want him to think about that eight-year-old girl going through it all every time he sees me. I don't want him to picture how different I could have been." I bit my lip, stuffing the unexpected emotion back in its place, and giving myself a moment to breathe. "I want him here, and I want him to know me now, but I don't want him to know how I got this way."

Travis was quiet for a long time and it forced me to look up at him. His face was laced with pain, but his eyes were understanding. "I know you're not asking me for advice, but you lost ten years with him. You can't pretend that time didn't exist."

I swallowed hard. "It's not a good story to share."

"No, it's not," Travis agreed. "But it's *your* story."

I shook my head. "I'm not ready for him to know."

Travis held my eyes and seemed to be in the middle of some kind of internal debate, but eventually he nodded. "It's something you should think about."

"Right," I said, turning back to my computer as Travis did the same. "Because we don't have enough on our minds as it is."

"If it helps," he said, not looking away from his screen. "I don't think you'd be *that* different if KATO hadn't taken you."

I arched an eyebrow in disbelief. "Really?"

"Yeah." He smirked. "I'm pretty sure you'd be stubborn and reckless no matter who raised you."

Now I glared at him. "I should have killed you when I had the chance."

He laughed hard and I fought off a smile.

"Hey," he said when he'd calmed down. He waited until I faced him again to continue. "I also think you'd be just as much of a fighter and just as fierce." His expression was serious now—so serious it jarred me. "Those aren't qualities you got from KATO, they're the reasons you were able to endure them." I drew a sharp breath and an energy I'd never experienced swirled in my chest. "I'm not trying to push you. I know better than that. But you should know you have *nothing* to hide from anyone."

My mouth seemed incapable of working, but I felt myself nodding. Travis smiled lightly, almost as if he understood, before turning back to the task at hand.

Chapter Fifteen

INNER KATO

Travis and I spent the rest of the morning going through the files of the agents who had made our short list. We worked slowly, taking in one agent at a time, discussing and analyzing every note KATO had put in their files.

By the time we arrived at the medical wing that afternoon, my insides were churning. Between the intel on the audio files, the talk I'd had with my father, and the conversation I was about to have with Eliza, I felt completely on edge.

I took a minute in the hallway, working to center myself. "You good?" Travis said, glancing at me.

"Yeah," I said, though I wasn't sure I believed myself. "I'm just—preparing."

Dr. March was waiting in the observation room when Travis and I finally crossed the threshold. Eliza was again sedated. Dr. March said it was the only drug Eliza was getting, aside from the Gerex, which the IDA had on hand since I'd arrived four and a half months ago.

I'd left KATO with a four-month supply and had barely used any of it, so we had some time to get her to come around. But the sooner we could get through to her, the better.

Once Simmonds showed up, Dr. March put me in the room with

Eliza and started easing her off the sedative. "If she wakes up with you here, you might be able to get her talking before she's fully awake," Dr. March said. "Given her willpower, I'm not sure this will work, but we've tried everything else."

So I sat next to Eliza, again with my back to the observation window. It wasn't long before Eliza's eyes fluttered open. Her gaze locked on me, and she jumped up—or jumped as much as she could. Her feet were still tethered to the rail. She scrambled to the foot of the bed, clutching the guardrail behind her. It was strange. She seemed like she was afraid of me this time. "Why are you back?" she asked. She was shaking now and I couldn't figure out why.

I slid my chair closer to her and she flinched like she was back in KATO. I suddenly understood. I knew the panic in her face because I had felt it too. "You dreamed about them, didn't you?"

"What?" Her voice broke. "No." She shook her head hard—harder than she should have. I was sure I was right.

"I dream about them too," I said, hesitating only slightly. "Sometimes I wake up certain I'm back there, strapped to a table, waiting for my handler to pull my fingernails out."

Her pupils dilated a fraction. She was breathing hard and still held the rail with a death grip, but her face seemed to soften.

"What did you dream about?" I asked. I needed to get her sharing. If she would just say *something* I'd have a shot at getting more out of her.

Eliza's breathing got heavier, and she started shaking her head even harder than before. It was moving fast—too fast. Back and forth and back and forth. I was afraid she was going to get whiplash. I shifted to sit on the edge of her bed, then touched her arm, hoping it would calm her down, but it had the opposite effect. Her shriek ripped through the room. "Don't touch me!"

I held my hands up and slid back into my chair. I watched her for a few seconds, and she did the same to me. I breathed slow and steady through my nose, trying to figure out what to do next. I needed a minute to think. I had tried to be understanding, but it didn't work. She didn't want to be here, so she was combative. But I was sure she didn't want to be at KATO at first either. They had managed to convince her otherwise. I had an idea. An idea I *hated*, but I couldn't seem to keep myself from speaking.

"This needs to stop." My voice was so icy and cold it scared even me. She sniffled, but stared at me, wide-eyed. I had her attention. "We are asking you questions and you need to start *complying*." Comply. It was a word KATO agents used a lot when they spoke English to me. We always had to *comply*. Eliza's face went white and I knew they had used the same word on her. I felt sick, not only because of what I was doing, but because it was working.

She let go of the rail and I knew why. Showing fear was showing weakness. It was the kind of thing agents would be punished for. "These secrets are not yours to keep," I said, standing. She cowered, pressing her back into the rail. I put my face inches from hers. "You need to *comply*!" She was shaking hard now, her head bowed, muttering "Misty" over and over again like a prayer. I knew that name. We had a file on it.

"*Speak!*" I roared at her, and it put her over the edge.

She shook her head furiously again, but with purpose. When she spoke, her voice broke. "I ca—I can't."

Something inside me snapped. The next thing I knew I heard

Eliza shriek followed by a loud crash. I blinked and realized the chair I had been sitting in was now on the other side of the room, broken in pieces.

I had done that. I wasn't even aware I'd thought about throwing the chair. I just acted.

I reacted like a KATO handler would. We needed her to talk, and I was suddenly prepared to do whatever it took.

My arms vibrated as my stomach churned violently. The craving I triggered combined with my own fear, humiliation, and anger was more than I could handle. I felt like I was in a fog.

I didn't notice Dr. March was in the room until her arm was around me. Eliza was once again sedated in her bed. When did that happen?

"Come on," Dr. March muttered in my ear as she pulled me forward. I noticed we were moving slowly, and then I realized it was because my legs were shaking.

She steered me down the hall and into the first open room.

"I'm sorry," I said. "I didn't mean—I thought she might respond to KATO tactics, but I didn't mean to go that far." I could barely get the words out.

She pulled me in closer, and sat us both on the bed. "Don't worry about that right now."

"Please—" I struggled to get the words out, but I needed her to know. "Please don't tell my father."

Her forehead crinkled, but she didn't question me. "All right," she said. "If that's what you want."

I nodded as the shaking got worse. No matter what Travis had said, I wasn't ready for him to know this part of me.

"You'll be okay," she whispered in my ear. "You're *always* okay in the end."

I folded deeper into her. At moments like this it was hard to believe that I would *ever* be all right. After a few minutes, she shifted away from me and eased me down onto the bed. I felt a hint of relief when she slid the needles into my ear, though it became pretty apparent that the acupuncture alone wasn't going to get it done. She started aromatherapy, and eventually my craving began to pass. I sank into the pillows, my eyes shut tight, embracing the calm that settled over me.

Dr. March ran a hand over my hair. "Take all the time you need." She didn't leave like she usually did. She pulled her chair over so she was sitting near my head. She put her hand on my forehead, massaging it gently. I felt myself relaxing even more. It only took a few more seconds for my mind to find a way to shut down.

. . .

The door banged open, startling me and the other fifteen agents in the room alert. It was Jin Su, and he wasn't alone. My heart stopped the second I saw Chin Ho. I wasn't the only agent he was responsible for, but I was sure he had come for me.

I was fourteen and I had just returned from my second mission. I had failed miserably. I was tasked with assassinating a Japanese weapons expert's family and stealing his technology, but I couldn't do it. My first mission had been to kill a young Indian princess. I'd completed that assignment and it still haunted me weeks later. When the time had come to pull the trigger on this second mission I just—couldn't. I had rehearsed my story a thousand times on the way to my extraction. I said that they weren't home—that I couldn't find them anywhere. I was taken off Gerex immediately for my failure, which I was expecting. But if both my handler and Jin Su were here, it could only mean one thing—they knew I lied.

They each grabbed one of my arms, and hauled me out of the room. They squeezed me tight—too tight, but between the pain of the Gerex withdrawal that had set in and the fear of what was coming, I barely felt it.

"I'm sorry," I said. "It won't happen again, I promise!" I sounded desperate and I didn't care—I was desperate. I repeated those phrases over and over as if it would somehow save me, but they didn't even acknowledge I was talking.

They dragged me into a small room and dropped me hard on my knees. I knew where I was once I saw the blood on the floor. This was the execution room.

Jin Su stepped back, positioning himself in front of the wall in a military stance, staring evenly. Chin Ho had come behind me. Then I felt the barrel of a gun pressed against my skull. My heart pounded with fear and absolute certainty that this would be the end of me.

"You have proven to be a great disappointment," Jin Su said. "This upsets me personally." His cold voice cut through my thoughts, adding to my fear. My limbs had tingled themselves numb, and I struggled to keep from showing how afraid I was, as if hiding my weakness could save me.

Chin Ho leaned over so his voice was in my ear. "You have brought me great shame. I expected better. KATO deserves better."

I felt the gun shift and I knew this was it. My heart kicked up, *pounding so hard it echoed through my body. Jin Su was all I could see. He would be the last thing I would ever see.*

I squeezed my eyes shut, and the tears rolled down my face. I couldn't hide the terror anymore and at this point it didn't matter. I waited for the bang.

But there was a click instead.

Time stood still as my ragged breathing filled the room. I felt the gun leave my head, but I didn't dare to believe that I was safe.

"You were very lucky Jin Su was merciful," Chin Ho said. "Thank him."

I couldn't think—I couldn't process anything that had just happened. I didn't act fast enough. Chin Ho yanked the back of my hair. "Thank him!"

I forced the words out, though I was sure they were incoherent. Jin Su nodded nonetheless and turned to the door. He stopped just short of it. "Next time there will be bullets," he said. "You will not get another chance to comply."

When I woke, it wasn't with the usual jolt into reality. Instead, I felt heavy, especially my eyes. It was like they were weighted down as my mind replayed the dream. But it wasn't a dream—not really. It was a memory. It was one of my most fearful moments at KATO. The combination of hearing Jin Su's voice and how the talk with Eliza had gone must have brought it out in me. I fought off a shudder when I remembered how I'd ended up in the medical wing in the first place.

It took all of my energy just to find a way to pry my eyes open. Dr. March wasn't sitting next to me anymore, but someone was. Actually, it was two people: Nikki and Travis.

Nikki smiled when she saw I was awake, her broken arm resting in her lap. "Good morning, sleepyhead—or I guess I should say good afternoon."

I rubbed my eyelids and pulled myself up so I could sit with my back against the pillows. The clock on the wall told me it was after four. I'd slept for hours. "Where's Dr. March?"

"I think she needed to check on some people." Nikki shifted up on to the bed, sitting with her back against the bottom rail, facing me. "She signed me out about an hour ago and said you and Travis were in here. Though no one will tell me what happened."

I exhaled slowly and the anxiety the dream had created faded into relief. "I—had a bad reaction to something."

Travis's eyes narrowed, but he stayed quiet. Nikki looked between the two of us, picking up on the tension. "I'm getting a sense there's a lot more to the story than that."

I shook my head, still trying to wrap my mind around what had happened.

Out of the corner of my eye I saw Travis look at Nikki and tip his head to the door.

"Right," Nikki said. "Well, I've been stuck in the medical wing since we got back from Russia, so I'm going to go for a run—or something." She paused just short of the door. "Find me if you need anything. My arm'll keep me out of the field, but I'm not concussed anymore, so my brain is yours if you need it."

I smiled at her. "Thanks, Nikki."

The door fell shut and then it was just me and Travis.

"Don't blow this off," he said the second we were alone.

"I'm not," I said, sitting up straighter. "I promise I'm not. I just—"

I pinched the bridge of my nose, trying to think. "I didn't see this coming."

Travis pulled the chair even closer, so he was right next to the bed.

I blinked, remembering something. "You're supposed to be on your way to England."

"I'm going, but I wanted to make sure you were okay first." He gave me a hard look. "Joss, what happened?"

"I don't know," I said, thinking back over the past few hours. "It started out as half of an idea. I knew KATO scared her, so I thought maybe I could use their conditioning to our advantage." I squeezed my temples, like I could push out the memories. "I *knew* it was a bad idea the second it crossed my mind, but I couldn't seem to stop myself." I swallowed hard. "KATO trained us to do whatever is necessary to get what we need. Being around her, and thinking about them just—pulled it out of me."

"She's okay," Travis said. "She was asleep when I left."

I tucked my knees into my chest. "That doesn't mean I didn't screw up her mind." I blinked and saw the broken chair on the ground. I still couldn't remember throwing it. "They're still in my head." My voice broke. I closed my eyes and rubbed the space between them, trying to get the image of Jin Su out of my mind. "They still have a hold on me."

The bed shifted and I felt Travis's hands on my shins. I blinked and saw his face a foot from mine. "They *do not* have a hold on you. If they did, we wouldn't be doing this." He dropped a file on to the bed next to him. It was an agent file.

"Misty." I'd almost forgotten. Eliza had said her name.

Travis sat back so I could spread the file out between us. "I read over it while you were asleep. It looks like she and Eliza were in the Indian safe house together. Their time didn't overlap for very long."

"She was the one KATO took when she was on her way to the orphanage, right?" I asked.

Travis nodded. "Yeah, her parents were politicians in Italy. They died in a car accident and left her behind. She didn't have any other family."

That was probably why she was picked. Her parents' status made her situation newsworthy, which meant KATO would have had access to it. They were in the market for an Italian, and she was the perfect target. Her disappearance had gotten a lot of attention at first, but as time moved on, the story died down. And without any family to push the issue, Misty faded into a tragic memory.

"Her agent file is pretty close to mine," I said, scanning over the more significant details again. She was currently stationed in the Italian intelligence agency, AISE. "In some ways she was even better than me." She had some slipups with her behavior, but all of her offenses were fairly mild and scattered throughout her time at KATO. Her weaknesses were in the more physical aspects of the job. She seemed to have kept up just enough to stay alive, but she took more than her fair share of hits.

"Don't you think that's a concern?" Travis asked. "Maybe her behavior was so good because she really is that brainwashed."

I shook my head. "I don't think so. I think she did the same thing I did—she told her handler what he wanted to hear and limited her mistakes. All of these offenses are so small and scattered, I wouldn't be surprised if at least some of them were on purpose."

"Do you think she should be the next recruit?"

I nodded. "Not only does she fit the profile, but if she has some kind of connection to Eliza, I could use it to pull her to our side."

The door opened, interrupting our discussion.

"Oh good," Dr. March said, smiling from the threshold. "You're up." Travis slid off the bed so Dr. March could get to me. "How are you feeling?"

"I'm all right," I said, which was more or less true, now that Travis had reminded me of our bigger victory. "I'm more concerned about Eliza. I'm sorry I lost it."

"It's okay." Dr. March tilted her head to the side, her eyes soft. "You seem to have this idea in your head that you're supposed to automatically get over everything they taught you. But you're not. It takes time."

"That's what I keep saying," Travis said.

I shook my head dismissively. "Not in this case. I know better."

"That doesn't mean your instincts go away," Dr. March said. "You're still artificially hardwired to win at all costs."

I bit my lip, letting her words sink in. I didn't put any thought into my actions; I only knew we needed her to talk. It felt desperate—similar to how I felt when I went on an assignment for KATO.

Regardless, I didn't want to talk about it anymore, so I returned to the more pressing issue at hand. "How's Eliza?"

Dr. March hesitated. "She's—different."

My senses heightened. "In a bad way?"

Dr. March shrugged a shoulder. "I don't know. It could mean that you're getting through to her." My stomach flipped at the idea of trying that approach again. "Aside from her periodic outbursts, she used to be fairly quiet. Now she keeps saying 'misty' over and over."

I glanced at Travis. "That's a lead we're working. Misty is another agent."

Dr. March's eyes widened a fraction. "That's excellent." She checked my pupils with a small flashlight. "You're clear to leave. I'll get word to you if Eliza says anything else that might be helpful."

I thanked her and turned back to Travis once she was gone. "We need to move on this," I said. "She's another one who probably won't accept our offer right away. The sooner we start this process, the sooner we get her talking."

"I can ask Simmonds to push the England assignment," Travis said. "You and I can stop there on our way back."

I shook my head. "All of this is connected. We need to know about Eliza's history just as much as we need Misty on our side," I said. "You go to England, and I'll go to Italy."

His eyes went wide. "There is no way you're recruiting a KATO asset on your own."

"I won't be alone," I said, smirking. "Centipede will be with me." Travis's expression narrowed and I rolled my eyes. "Obviously I'll bring IDA backup too. But Centipede really is coming. There's no point in recruiting these agents if we're not going to use them."

He put his hands on his hips. "I should be in on this."

"And I would rather if you were," I said. "But Simmonds is right. You were on Eliza's team a year and a half ago. You'll know where to look in England. I can handle the girls. We're as prepared as we can be. It'll probably go smoother with backup in the shadows anyway. Misty might be more open to this if it's coming from me and another KATO agent."

His lips pressed together tightly, considering. "All right," he said, "it's a solid plan. Just promise me you won't be reckless."

I smiled. "Don't worry. I've gotten better about that."

He snorted. "Yeah, I guess we'll see."

. . .

I went to Simmonds with my plan right from the medical wing. He studied Misty's file closely as I sat across from him. He glanced up at me periodically as he read. "You've never heard of her?" he asked when he was finished.

I shook my head. "I only knew the agents who were based out of headquarters. I picked up a few others when I was eavesdropping, but only if they were exceptional. Misty never came up."

Simmonds put the file down and furrowed his eyebrows. "If she's not that special, are you sure she's the best option?"

"I suspect I haven't heard of her because her fighting skills aren't as strong," I said. "She's a retrieval specialist. I think she's good at getting in and out unnoticed, and I think that's also how she stayed alive in KATO. Between that and her connection to Eliza, she could be an asset."

He ran a hand along his jawline, considering. "You said she's based in Italy?"

"She is."

"I'll touch base with the Italians and have them provide an address for you," Simmonds said. A weight lifted. He was signing off. "They were particularly motivated to cooperate once they realized who it was KATO planted in their agency. I'll let them know how we handled the situation with you. If you get Misty on board, you can tell her that they will help maintain her cover, but she'll report to us from now on."

"Thank you, sir," I said. "I'd also like to bring Centipede with me for this. I think it will help me win Misty over if I have another KATO agent on my side."

He looked a little uneasy, but he nodded. "All right, here's what we'll do. You and Centipede will meet with Misty on your own, but I'm sending Mathers and Hawthorne to cover you."

"Okay," I said. I wasn't sure how I felt about the two of them—or more specifically, Rachel—being involved in this, but I'd been prepared for it. "But it's better if these girls think I'm alone. We're still the enemy to them and if I keep showing up with extra IDA agents, we're going to scare them off."

"I can agree to that," Simmonds said. I nodded my thanks and stood, preparing to leave. "There's one more issue we need to talk about." I sat back down. "Now that you're really going forward with this team, we need to discuss the funding. The IDA doesn't have the budget for something like this, and with all the risks involved, the board isn't willing to take on the financial responsibility. So, if you want to keep this running, you're going to have to fund this program yourself."

My brows drew together. "How exactly do I do that?" I had heard bits and pieces about how the agency got its money, but I'd never had a full explanation.

"Half of the IDA's budget comes from supporting countries. However, in order to remain independent from any single country, we take on the responsibility for the other half ourselves," Simmonds explained. "This means that the only way our supporting countries can tell us what to do is if several of them are on the same page, in which case, there would be a good reason for us to listen to them. We get the remainder of our funding by using our systems to track missing items—and occasionally people—that have a sizable reward attached to their finding."

I nodded, understanding. "So, if a sculpture was stolen and has a hundred-thousand-dollar reward, the IDA would find and return the sculpture and put the reward money toward the budget."

"Exactly," he said.

"So, if I'm doing this, I have to track down my own stolen artifact," I said, seeing where he was going with this.

Simmonds nodded. "I've located an item in Turkey with a reward big enough to meet your needs. If it goes well with Misty, you can make that retrieval after you've finished in Italy."

I nodded. "That seems manageable." After everything I'd done for KATO and the IDA, stealing back a piece of art didn't seem too overwhelming. "But I want Centipede and Misty with me—if she signs on." Simmonds's expression hardened, and I saw the "no" sitting on his tongue. "We need some kind of trial run," I said. "And this is as low-risk as we're going to get. If they turn on us, or it falls through, then the worst that happens is we don't get the money."

"You make a valid point," he said. "But I still want Mathers and Hawthorne with you."

"They can be in the area," I conceded. "But I don't want them close. It needs to be the three of us. It's not a true test if they have guns to their heads." If I was being honest, the idea of being alone with two KATO agents and no backup made my stomach turn. But I was as certain as I could be that I had Centipede hooked. This would never work if I was afraid to be alone with them. "I can handle it."

Simmonds considered me, weighing his options. "All right. If that's how you want it. But you need to understand something." He leaned forward over his desk, his face stone serious. "If you get taken again, there will be no rescue team. That was a one-time operation, and that was only successful because it was preplanned. We don't have the intel or resources to pull it off again."

I breathed slowly, which did nothing to calm my pounding heart. "I understand."

It terrified me, but I wasn't about to back down. I couldn't see a more effective way to hurt KATO, and I would not be the reason this didn't go through.

"You'll keep your comm in, and it'll be open the whole time." This wasn't a suggestion or a point of negotiation. "I want to know what's going on."

I didn't argue. I wanted him to know what was happening too.

Chapter Sixteen

OPERATION MISTY

I waited until I was back at my room to contact Centipede. She didn't pick up, but she called back quickly.

"Do you have something?" she asked the second I answered.

"We need to meet in Italy," I said. "There's a KATO agent stationed there who knows more about the girl we have."

"How will that help?"

"She has a connection to Eliza, and we think she might be able to tell us what KATO did to her." I paced my room, half afraid something might have happened to make her change her mind.

"Eliza?" Centipede asked.

I shook my head, forgetting that no one at KATO knew her by that name. "The girl we took from Russia. KATO called her Python."

There was a long pause and I was starting to hate that I couldn't see her face. "Who is this agent and why is she in Italy?" she asked.

I relaxed. "Her code name is Misty and KATO has her planted in Italian intelligence."

"They what?" Her voice was sharp. I realized how this must sound to her. KATO was very good at telling us only what we needed to know to complete any given mission. We never had any sense of the larger operation. If she was assigned to me, I was sure she had to know that my mission had been to infiltrate the IDA. Now she had just learned KATO had a second agent in an enemy agency, which meant for the first time, she was starting to get an idea of how widespread they were becoming.

"I think you heard me just fine," I said.

"Leave as you normally would and I'll follow you to Italy," Centipede said. She didn't wait to hear where to meet me.

. . .

I didn't see Cody and Rachel until we were on the plane. I had left through the front gate as always, but I had Simmonds send the two of them through the tunnels. Since I knew Centipede was watching, I wanted to make sure she thought I was alone.

Rachel was an exceptionally skilled sniper, which would come in handy for an assignment like this. She caught my eye briefly when she and Cody boarded, giving me a small nod in what I imagined was supposed to be a greeting. She dropped down in the seat across from me and cut right to the chase. "I'll be stationed on the building across the street and Cody will be on the ground if you need backup. What else do we need to know?"

I noticed her leg bouncing ever so slightly. She was anxious and trying to hide it. I rubbed my palms on my lap, burying how uneasy I was starting to feel too. Maybe this was a terrible idea. But Centipede was on her way, we were in the air, and they were both looking at me, waiting for some kind of instruction.

So I swallowed my anxiety and pushed on. "All I need is for you to keep your distance. If the plan I have in place is going to work, it's crucial not to scare her off."

Cody arched an eyebrow. "From what I hear, you're one of KATO's top targets. I have a hard time believing anything short of a grenade would scare them off if they decide to come at you."

"I have Centipede hooked," I said. I met each of their eyes, trying to reassure them. And I was as sure about that as I could be. "I can use her to convince Misty, but if they find out I brought armed backup, they'll be after all of us."

Rachel gave me a very even look. "KATO's tried to kill me before. It didn't take." Her tone was pointed, but not harsh. I took a breath, knowing I was in no position to comment. Cody touched Rachel's arm briefly. She shot him a withering look, but fell silent.

"We'll give you the space you need on the ground," Cody said, redirecting the conversation. "But if it looks or sounds like things are going south, I'm coming for you."

I shook my head. "You only need to step in if I end up unconscious. But I won't let that happen."

Rachel tilted her head in my direction. "You really need to stop trying to talk us out of backing you," she said. "If you keep it up, I might just let you win."

"Don't be a noodle," Cody said to her. Rachel rolled her eyes and Cody turned back to me. "She's kidding." Though I wasn't entirely sure she was. "We'll stay out of your way as much as possible. And if it works out, we'll find our own way to Turkey so you can have the plane. We'll meet you on board after the mission."

"Okay," I said, "thank you."

I spent the rest of the flight preparing to be potentially outnumbered by the enemy.

. . .

I sent Centipede meeting coordinates before we landed. Rachel and Cody had the address and moved into position. I was meeting Centipede on the corner outside Misty's. That gave us the advantage of approaching the situation together, and allowed me to keep the specifics to myself until we got to the location. I wanted to put myself in a position of power as much as possible.

"Raven, I've got eyes on you," Rachel said in my ear. I nodded once so she would know I'd heard her. It was early in the day, but we knew Misty should be home. Simmonds reached out to the agency she was stationed with to confirm her location.

She lived on a quiet narrow street that could have easily passed for an alley. I leaned against the building while I waited for Centipede to show up. When she did, it was as if she'd appeared out of thin air.

She looked around her in every direction, and I knew she was checking for anyone who might jump out and ambush her. After two visual sweeps of the surrounding area, she seemed to decide we were alone. I noticed the bruising around her neck. That had to have been her punishment for coming back without me. They strangled her— probably within an inch of her life and probably more than once.

Centipede followed my eyes and pulled the collar of her jacket up, hiding the bruises as much as possible. "Let's get inside."

"This way," I said, leading her down the street. We stopped at the third door, and Centipede did another sweep of our surroundings. I clenched my teeth together, praying Cody and Rachel were hidden enough.

"Let me do the talking, okay?"

She arched an eyebrow at me. "Then why am I here?"

"To show a united front," I said. "And when we finish here, we have another stop to make."

I knocked before she could ask any more questions. The door opened sharply, pulling Centipede's attention back to what was happening in front of her.

I knew this was Misty from her picture. Her hair was pin-straight and her eyes unusually round, which made her seem much younger than her nineteen years. She took one look at me and swung her fist at my face.

I ducked it easily. KATO's files were right; she may have been a strong enough fighter to still be alive, but she was no match for me. She went in for another hit and I caught her fist before she could make contact. "I'm not here to fight you," I said.

She pulled her arm back again, but Centipede promptly punched her in the face.

Misty staggered backward. I caught her, getting a good hold of her arms so she couldn't attack either of us. She tried anyway.

"Hey, calm down." I talked in her ear as gently as I could. I backed her away from the door and Centipede closed it quickly.

Misty still struggled, speaking through gritted teeth. "I'm supposed to bring you in! You're a traitor!"

I tightened my hold. "Yeah, well I suspect you wish you were too."

She stopped fighting me then, freezing up instantly. "I don't know what you're talking about."

"I think you do. And I think it's something we should discuss," I said. "If I let you go, you need to promise not to run. Between the two of us, you won't get far." Her jaw was set in defiance, but she nodded.

Centipede straightened when I released Misty, ready to attack if necessary. Misty did a quick assessment of her situation, trying to see if she could make a break for it. She seemed to quickly decide she didn't stand a chance.

"Is there someplace we can talk?' I asked.

Misty nodded. "In here," she said. She led us down a narrow hallway and into a harsh, bare kitchen.

"Sit down," I said, gesturing at the small, scratched square table in the center of the room. She hesitated, but eventually did as I asked. She went to touch her face, but pulled her arm back sharply the instant her fingers brushed her right cheekbone. That was where she'd been punched.

I grabbed a rag off the countertop that looked more or less clean and crossed to the fridge. "Did you have to punch her?" I muttered to Centipede as I passed.

Centipede shrugged. "Your way wasn't working."

I bit my tongue and opened the freezer. I was glad to find Misty had ice, at the very least. I wrapped the rag around a few cubes and handed it to her. "Put that on your eye."

I sat down across from Misty, while Centipede remained standing, leaning against the countertop behind her.

Misty held the ice to her face, her eyes glued on me. "I don't know what you heard," she said. "But you have a very wrong impression."

"I don't think I do," I said. "In fact, I think you're smarter than everyone at KATO combined. Smart enough to trick them into believing their brainwashing worked on you." I watched her face closely. Her expression remained neutral but her eyes tightened. I was onto her. "I know that tactic well. I did the same thing. But you did it better."

Her fist was balled and I noticed her arm shaking slightly. I was sure it was out of fear. I'd exposed a secret she had closely guarded her entire time in KATO. "What do you want from me?"

"I want you to help us." I laid out my plan for her, limiting myself to the basics for now—that I wanted to put together a team of people inside KATO to help give the IDA an advantage.

"If you help us, in exchange, we can get you away from them," I said. "We can also get you off the Gerex."

Her expression sharpened at that. "You can?"

I nodded. "I'm off of it."

Her forehead tightened in confusion. "That's possible?"

"Yes," I said. "It's not easy, but it's worth it."

She looked back to Centipede. "Are you IDA?"

"No," Centipede said, pulling her arms in close.

"She's KATO," I said. "Her code name is Centipede." Misty's eyes widened a fraction in recognition, while Centipede shifted uncomfortably.

Misty turned back to me. "I can't do what you're asking."

"You haven't heard everything I have to say." I chewed on my tongue. I couldn't lose her. She was the perfect candidate.

"I don't need to." She angled her head to look me square in the eyes. "I'm not as strong as the other agents, but I found a way to keep myself alive in that place. What you're asking me to do—if I get caught—" She shook her head. "If you want to help me get out, then help me get out. But I cannot spy for you," she said. "I cannot take that risk."

"The IDA won't help you unless you prove to them that you can be trusted," I said. "That means making an enemy out of KATO."

"Then I can't help you."

"I think you can."

Behind Misty, Centipede rolled her eyes. "This is a waste of time."

I scowled at her long enough to make my point, then turned back to Misty. I pulled out my tablet, found Eliza's picture, and pushed it across the table. "Do you know her?"

She looked up at me sharply. "What happened to her?" I was taken aback by the amount of pure concern in her voice. By rule, KATO agents didn't trust or care about each other.

"Tell me what you know about her first," I said. "Then I'll tell you what I can."

She glared at me, annoyed that I'd lured her into a trap. "All right," she said, after a moment. "But this is all the help you're getting from me." I gestured for her to continue. "She was placed in my training house a few months before I was assigned here. I had an unexpected complication on a mission, so I was taken off Gerex for forty-eight hours. Python was brought in somewhere in the middle of that." I noticed Centipede stiffen. Misty looked down at the photo. "She saw I was in pain and she'd hold my hand, and try to help. I knew I shouldn't let her, but I was out of it, and it was nice to have someone there."

"She was new at that point," I said. "She didn't know the rules."

Misty nodded. "Exactly. I thought once she learned them she

would pull away, like we all did, but Python didn't. We kept our friendship a secret, and I tried to teach her how to survive in KATO. How to tell them what they wanted to hear. But she was too much of a fighter and she refused to let them believe they had her. She resisted them and took her punishments head-on."

Eliza had come into the agency older, which was probably why she was more determined to resist their cruelty. I did my best not to let myself imagine what her life had been like. "Can you tell me why she's special to them?" I asked.

Misty's forehead crinkled. "She isn't special. At least, she wasn't while I was there. They treated her just like everyone else." Her eyes narrowed in confusion. "What aren't you telling me?"

I laced my fingers together, giving her a beat to prepare. "We found intel that suggests Python is important to KATO, so we located her and went after her. She's at the IDA now."

Her eyebrows shot up. "Really?"

I nodded. "We pulled her out of a house in Russia. We believe it was a test house, and we're pretty positive she was used for some kind of medical experiment."

"They what?" Misty's expression hardened. "What's wrong with her?"

I shrugged a shoulder. "We don't know yet. But she's not the fighter you talked about—at least, she's not fighting *them* anymore. She's afraid, and she's doing exactly what KATO would want her to do." I fought off a shudder thinking back to how our last conversation had gone. "She's barely talking, but most of the time when she does, she's saying your name."

Misty's eyes lifted, and I understood why. Kindness between agents was rare. The fact that they had maintained a friendship at all was a miracle.

"This is why we need your help," I said. "KATO's planning something massive. They've got agents planted around the world, and now they did something to Eliza—to Python—that we have reason to believe they want to do to everyone else. You're in a position to do something to stop them."

She held my eyes and for a moment I thought she was in. Then she shook her head. "I *can't*. Not after all this time. I've survived this long by staying as efficient and unnoticed as possible. What you're asking—there's too much to risk."

I leaned over the table, determined to make her understand. "We don't know what they did to Python, but if they use it on everyone, you won't be able to avoid it. You can't outsmart medicine."

"I won't tell them you came here," she said, standing. "But I cannot give you what you want."

I had one more card to play. "AISE knows you're KATO. They also know who you were before KATO took you, and they want to help. But if you won't agree to work with us—if they think you're loyal to KATO—I honestly don't know what they'll do to you." I hadn't wanted to force her into this, but I couldn't leave here without her knowing that much.

There was a flash of hope in her eye, but it fizzled out in seconds. "I'd rather be their enemy than KATO's."

I bit my tongue and dug one of the phones out of my pocket and slid it across the table. "The offer stands if you change your mind."

She was the perfect candidate for this team. She resisted them, she wanted to get away, and she'd had a friendship with another KATO agent. Plus, she was smart enough to keep herself alive with subpar skills. I had to believe at some point she'd come around. "Is there anything I can say to Eliza? Something so she'll know I've talked to you?"

Misty thought for a moment. "As much as I tried to get her not to fight them, a part of me liked that she did. No one put up a fight like Python." She swallowed. Centipede stood rigid behind her, and I caught a small tremble in her chin. "Before I was relocated, I told her not to let them take her light. Tell her that and she'll know."

"Thank you." I looked her right in the eye, hoping she understood how much this meant. Misty nodded. "Call me if you change your mind."

"I won't," she said as I stood.

"You might." I glanced at Centipede. Her arms were crossed and her hands gripped her biceps. "Let's go."

I didn't get what I wanted from this stop—at last not yet—but I had something I could use with Eliza. For now, that would have to be enough.

Chapter Seventeen

UNEXPECTED VENOM

Centipede needed an extra push to leave Misty's house.

"You didn't make her agree," she said when we were outside.

"I didn't make you agree either," I reminded her. "It's a lot to take in."

"She could go back and tell KATO everything." She was trying to be calm but I saw a touch of panic in her eyes.

I shook my head. "She won't. What she said today was consistent with her file. She is successful in KATO because she keeps her head down."

She crossed her arms. "I don't like it. You need to go back in there and—"

"Hey." I cut her off completely. "I'm glad you're so invested, but this is my operation. You don't tell me how to run it." Centipede glared at me, and seemed to be searching her brain for a leg to stand on, but she didn't have one. "The way I see it, you have two options. You can either fall in line or take your chances with KATO."

She breathed hard through her nose and I knew what she was thinking. The damage had been done and she was too far in to back out.

"Now, we have one more stop to make," I said. "If you have questions I can answer them on the plane."

I started walking again, and this time she silently fell into step next to me.

. . .

Centipede didn't say another word during our walk to the plane. I spent the time trying to keep the situation in perspective. She was the only one who still reported directly back to KATO headquarters. She didn't have the safety of a cover agency to hide behind, which put her even more at risk than I had been. She was bound to push back on occasion.

"Where are we going?" she asked, the second we were on the plane.

I looked over the mission file Simmonds had sent with me. "We need to retrieve a painting," I said. "It's being kept in a warehouse in Turkey."

Her eyebrows furrowed. "Why do *we* have to do it?"

"Because it's a low-risk mission and we need practice," I said. I left out the monetary importance. I didn't want her to know how the IDA got its funding.

She looked around the plane, taking in every detail. It was nicer than the planes KATO usually used, though the interior wasn't all that special. I passed the mission file to her so she could see. "We're going in together."

She looked at me sharply, and I understood why. This was entirely new to her. It was how I had felt the first time I went on a mission with Travis as a partner. Since it was just the two of us, I would be the one calling the shots. Which meant I could ease her into this. We would each have our own job, similar to how KATO worked. To Centipede, it would still feel like the solo missions she was used to, but both of our assignments were dependent on each other.

I tipped the folder down so I could see it too. She was looking at the rough blueprints. "There's a room here." I pointed to the left of the page. "That's where the sellers operate out of. It's going to be your job to keep them from finding me in the room next door." That was where that painting would be kept. "I'll come in through the roof."

"I'll get the painting," Centipede said. There was no way I was letting her anywhere near the IDA's money—especially not when she sounded so eager.

"The painting is mine." I glanced at her out of the corner of my eye. "Unless you can't handle a couple of art thieves."

She rolled her eyes. "Of course I can handle them."

"Good," I said, shifting away from her. "Because if we can't work together here, we'll never stop KATO."

She breathed through her nose, and I could see she was trying to wrap her head around this.

"I don't want to go back to them," she said. Her voice broke in a way I'd never heard from her. I met her eyes and I was taken aback by the pain and determination they held. "You know, it's worse for me than it ever was for you."

This wasn't a debate I wanted to have. "It was hard for both of us."

"It was." She nodded. "But I was a Korean who was beaten repeatedly by an American. It was harder for me."

I blinked. I hadn't thought about it like that before.

"How long have you been off the Gerex?" she asked, sitting back.

She was hesitant but genuinely curious. I rubbed the crease of my elbow, giving myself a beat before I answered. "It's been four months, three weeks, and five days. And I can figure out the seconds if you really want to know."

She swallowed visibly. "How does it feel?"

"Amazing." I thought about all of the times I'd gone running to my handler, desperate for the drug, knowing he held all the power. It really did feel fantastic to know no one controlled me like that. Then those thoughts were replaced by the shaking and the extreme uncontrollable need that still filled me on a semi-regular basis. "And also terrible."

She watched me carefully, taking in every detail. "Do you miss it?"

I remembered how it felt to have the needle break my skin and feel that incredible rush—

I snapped my head away from her, focusing on the sky outside the window on my left. I refused to let myself go there, but I knew my silence said everything.

. . .

Centipede and I moved in on the warehouse together. I had a harness on, prepared to rappel down from the skylight. Centipede was going in the front door. According to the IDA, this location was a warehouse for an underground art auction. Everything in this place was stolen, though most didn't have rewards attached to them. The auction was slated for the next night, and the operators of this venue were staying on the premises until all of the merchandise was purchased and claimed.

"You know what you have to do, right?" I asked Centipede before we separated.

"These are low-level art thieves." She glanced at me out of the corner of her eye. "I can keep them occupied for five minutes."

I took a step way from her. "Give me three minutes to get in position, then make your approach."

"I *know*." We'd gone over this five times before we got off the plane, but I wanted to make sure she knew what she was doing. "You better hurry up." She tapped the watch I had given her. It was already running, counting down my three-minute prep.

I narrowed my eyes at her, but headed toward the fire escape on the side of the building. It was the middle of the day by now, but the area we were in was practically deserted. Reaching the roof undetected wouldn't be a problem.

There were five skylights along the top of the warehouse. Three of them showed no signs of art or people. One showed three people inside, who had to be the sellers. The last skylight gave way to the collection. All of the art was boarded up, making it impossible to distinguish one painting from the other. I pulled out my tablet and plugged the dimensions of the artwork into a program, then let the tablet scan the room. It located the painting in seconds.

It was off to the side, propped up against the wall—the smallest of the three that rested there.

I jumped back over to the office and saw the three occupants were involved in a tense discussion. I caught a glimpse of Centipede through the door window. She hadn't acted on them yet, which I found impressive. As long as they were occupying themselves, there was no reason to interfere.

I went back to the collection room, eased the skylight open and hooked my rope to the edge. I lowered myself down quietly, paying attention to the voices in the next room, which were getting louder and louder. I released the rope, quickly moving to the painting the tablet had singled out. My fingers had just brushed the board protecting the painting when a sound a few paces away made me freeze.

I began to turn around, but I hadn't gotten more than half a step when a hand twisted my arm behind my back. While the force was enough to bring me to my knees, it was the needle against my neck that made my heart stop.

"You have been a *very* bad agent." The voice was female, with a thick Turkish accent. She released my arm and circled around me, dragging the needle along my collarbone. I forced myself not to react when I saw her. Her face was round and framed with wavy hair that looked largely unkempt. She cocked her head to the side, similar to how a dog might if it saw something curious.

I knew her. Her code name was Venom and she was a KATO agent stationed in Turkey's National Intelligence Agency. We had her file back at the IDA. She wasn't based out of headquarters, but I'd heard her name tossed around at lot. She was the first person we ruled out for this team, at Travis's request, because of how much delight she seemed to get out of her assassinations. In the back of my mind, I knew she was in this country, but we would only be on the ground for less than an hour. I had no reason to believe she would have found us so quickly.

"You're Venom," I said. Because I had to say something.

An ugly smile snaked across her dry cracked lips. She was pleased to be known. "And you are Viper." She trailed the needle back up my neck, before letting it come to rest just to the right of my windpipe. "There are people who are looking for you."

My heart raced as the needle bent my skin. "How did you find me?"

"You are in my territory. I am always on watch." She added a little pressure to the needle on my neck. "I want to kill you, but they say I can't." She looked genuinely disappointed, and even a little irritated by this. "They say I should give you the Gerex instead. I'm to give it to you until you are unconscious, then I will bring you to them and be rewarded."

My heart pounded furiously. Everything I'd heard about Venom told me she was more than a little unstable, and now she had Gerex at my neck. And she wasn't just talking about getting me hooked again. She was talking about an overdose. I tried to fight off the sheer panic that was forcing its way into my mind, but I was losing.

This was it. This would be how I'd go back to KATO, and I'd be higher than I could handle.

I had been trying to contain my KATO memories, but in that moment, every single one flashed before my eyes. The burn on my neck, the fingernails they yanked, the teeth pulled. The bruises on Centipede's neck would be a kindness compared to the treatment I would receive. I was certain I would beg to be taken to the execution room just to escape it. I had one fleeting desperate wish that it was Travis in the other room, not Centipede. But I squashed it. Because that wasn't real. Venom in front of me with Gerex—that was.

I considered leaning into the needle, letting it break my skin, and accepting the only advantage that would come with going back to KATO. Then I heard the voices in the next room getting louder. It snapped me back into focus. I couldn't give in this easily—not with Centipede right next door. I brought her into this, and she was my responsibility.

Venom leered over me. Her body seemed to be made up of nothing but angles. Her finger found the top of the syringe and I pushed myself to find my voice.

"Hang on!" My words were rough and panicked but enough to stop her.

She squinted at me, looking very confused. "Why do you want me to wait?"

I raised my chin enough to look her in the eye. As much as I hated it, I only had one card to play here, and I was pretty sure I had an in.

"You don't like that you have to listen to KATO, do you?" Between Travis's reaction and what I'd heard, I was convinced Venom didn't have a problem with KATO's morals. But moments ago I had seen a discrepancy between her and the agency. She didn't want to drug me right now. She wanted to kill me. It was KATO who said she couldn't.

"It is not my choice." She moved to make the final push, but I spoke faster. The voices in the other room had turned to shouts and I tried not to look at the door behind Venom or think about what Centipede might have gotten into.

"What if it was your choice?" Her eyes slid from her task to focus on me. I kept talking. "I have a way for you to get outside of KATO's control."

She lessened the pressure, but only slightly, then scrutinized my face intently. "You are not lying." She sounded mildly surprised to realize this.

"No, I'm not," I said. "I did it. I can help you do it too, but you'd have to help me in return."

She took the needle off my skin and took a step back. It was then that I realized my hands were shaking. I thought about attacking her, but in that instant, I wasn't sure I could beat her. She watched me thoughtfully. "But KATO could catch me doing this, yes?" she asked.

"They could," I said. "Which is why you'd have to be careful with what you say to them and when you talk to us. We can also get your Turkish agency to help with a cover."

"And if this works I can be free of them?" The hopeful note in her voice would have been heartbreaking if she weren't holding my future in between her fingertips.

"Yes." I glanced at the needle in her hand. "You know how you feel like you can't live without Gerex?" She nodded. "Well, you can," I said. "I do."

Her eyes narrowed on me, her expression crossed between wonder and disbelief. "You do not take the drug?"

"No," I said. "I haven't for a few months now. It takes some time, though, and it's not something you should do on your own." Outside the room, I heard doors opening and closing. Then the voices were angrier and closer than ever. We were running out of time.

She jerked her head to the side, which I noticed was a habit, and watched me, her face scrunched in contemplation. "Yes, I will do it." She put the needle away. "I do not like listening to them. I wish to kill whoever I want." The voices outside stopped.

Then the door opened and Venom whirled around as Centipede came charging through. Both girls reached for their guns, and I jumped in between them.

"Hold on," I said, my arms outstretched. "We're on the same team." I made quick introductions. Venom didn't seem at all fazed by her new teammate. Centipede, however, was less than thrilled about the latest development.

"Aren't you supposed to be watching the room?" I asked, doing my best to get rid of her before she said something that would undercut all the work I had done to save myself.

"They're dead," she said with a shrug.

I gapped at her. "You *killed* them? All of them?"

"They were headed this way." She spoke as if this explained everything. I stared at her in mild disbelief. No matter how long I had been in KATO, I *always* avoided killing someone unless I absolutely had to. Yet she'd done it so easily.

"I do not understand," Venom said. "It sounds like she did good."

I took a long slow breath. Everything about this assignment had gone completely off the rails. "We don't kill people unless we have no other choice."

Centipede rolled her eyes. "We'll see how well that works now that she's on board."

Venom smiled, seeming to be very much under the impression

that this was a compliment. Then her face dropped. She craned her neck around in both directions with an unnatural range of motion. "We must leave now."

"Your agency already knows the truth about you. I'll have my director reach out and update them on your status." I reached in my back pocket and pulled out the last satellite phone. In my hurry to get out of the IDA, I'd grabbed the case with both spare phones instead of only taking one for Misty. Now I was glad I did. "This is for you," I said, holding it out for her. "I'll use it to contact you if we need to talk or meet. You can also call me if you need something."

She took the phone and studied it for a moment, before looking abruptly back up at me. "If you call I will answer."

"Good," I said, forcing a smile.

"Now we must go." Venom bowed to both of us as she backed out of the room. "You will be seeing more of me."

Once we were alone, Centipede rounded on me. Her face was hard and angry and maybe even a little afraid. "You brought *her* in? There's something wrong with her!"

The fact that this was coming from Centipede spoke volumes, but it was too late. Venom was on board. My heart was still pounding furiously from how close I had come to going back to KATO. "I didn't have a choice," I said. "I was in a jam and I saw an opportunity."

She snorted. "I hope you know what you're doing."

Yeah. I did too.

I lifted the painting off the ground and headed for the door. "I'll be in touch when I have something more," I said. This was where Centipede and I were separating.

She nodded tightly, and I saw a touch of tension in her face. She'd be going back to KATO empty-handed again. It wouldn't be enough to kick her off my case—KATO knew how good I was and if she couldn't catch me, no one else would. But there was undoubtedly a more severe punishment waiting for her when she returned.

Chapter Eighteen

PROGRESS

I was relieved when I got back to the plane and found Cody and Rachel waiting to take off. I passed the painting off to Cody as I struggled up the steps. I'd managed to keep the craving under wraps in the warehouse because I had to—my life depended on it. But now, that control was slipping.

"We got here not long before you did," Cody said. "It sounded like things got dicey."

I collapsed on one of the benches, shaking my head. I didn't have any words. The mission was catching up to me, and I could fully appreciate just how disastrous it had become. I had been entirely too close to returning to KATO—a fact that had left me shaking. Plus, now I had *Venom* on my anti-KATO team. I believed—at least for now—that she wouldn't go back to KATO. She seemed to hate everything about their control, but I had no way of knowing how loyal she would be to us. My stomach churned. This whole thing had gotten out of hand fast.

I replayed the mission, pausing when I remembered the needle on my neck. I had been *so* wonderfully close. If I had just let her push down on the syringe—

I shuddered, hating everything about this feeling—about how I could feel good for resisting, but frustrated for the same reason. My forehead was damp and I knew I was in for a very long flight.

I forced myself to sit up straight, as if I would feel better by simply pretending I was okay. It didn't work. I'd barely gotten myself upright before my body started curling in on itself. I stopped fighting and let myself hug my legs to my chest. Over the tops of my knees I saw that Cody and Rachel were both watching me from the other side of the plane with varying expressions of concern.

Cody glanced at Rachel, shooting her an expectant look. When she didn't move, he nudged her.

She sighed. "Yeah, okay."

I gripped my arms tighter as I watched her walk to a cabinet in the front of the plane and come back with a hard black case. She sat down in front of me and busied herself with digging through the bag, taking care not to look me in the eye when she talked. "Dr. March showed me what you need," she said. I noticed then that she was pulling out acupuncture needles. "It's around the ears, right?"

I nodded as I forced my legs straight. I didn't want to accept her help. After seeing how much I had hurt her, it didn't seem right. But it wouldn't be the first time, and I was so very desperate.

I closed my eyes, letting myself believe I was already back at the IDA and that this was Dr. March. The needles slid into my skin and before long, I started to feel some relief. It took longer to set in than it normally did, but each minute seemed easier than the last. I could hear Cody and Rachel talking quietly, but I was too out of it to understand what they were saying. It wasn't long before I had fallen asleep.

. . .

Physically, I felt much better when we landed, but I still couldn't get my mind off of how messed up everything had become. I started going back over every detail for the tenth time, preparing myself for the conversation I was going to have with Simmonds—and most likely my father—once I was back at the base. Now that I'd had some sleep I could see all the potential ramifications of what had happened in Turkey. It went without saying that a screwup like that could cost me my team. I needed them to believe this wasn't a mistake. Though it might be a hard sell, considering how close I'd come to being taken.

I still felt the needle and saw Venom's twisted smile as she prepared to knock me out. Then I blinked and I was back in KATO, water flowing over my mouth while I choked and struggled to breathe. I shook my head, trying to get rid of the thoughts. I had never been waterboarded at KATO, but I had seen it done to others. I'd been next to Jin Su when it happened. He stood with his arms crossed, looking thoroughly pleased with himself. I shuddered.

I massaged my temples, willing my mind blank, but there didn't seem to be anything I could do to turn it off.

"Hey." Cody waved a hand in front of my face, bringing me back to the present. He stepped back to stand with Rachel, who was near the door, ready to disembark. "You coming?"

I was about to stand when my pocket buzzed. My satellite phone was ringing. Misty's number flashed on the screen. "You guys go ahead," I said. "I have to take this." I waited until I was alone to answer.

"I'll help you," she said when I picked up.

I smiled into the phone. "What changed your mind?"

"I kept my head down all this time—I played my part, hoping that someday I'd get an opportunity to escape." I heard her swallow. "This isn't as clean as I want it to be, but I don't know if I'm going to get another chance."

"Okay," I said. "The director of the IDA will contact AISE so they know what's going on. They'll give you fake stories to pass back to KATO and make sure you look busy, but you'll be working with us from now on."

She drew a shaky breath. "Are you sure that will work?"

"It worked for me," I said. "If they hadn't called me back to head-quarters, I'd still be feeding them lies. And I had a personal connection to my agency. You don't, so they shouldn't expect you to do the same thing."

"All right," she said. Her voice was strong, but I noticed the touch of fear. I didn't blame her.

"I'll contact you when I have more."

I let out a sigh of relief when I hung up. At least now I could go to Simmonds with some good news.

. . .

An IDA agent was waiting for me at the gate. She took the painting, assuring me it would make it to the proper place, then said Director Simmonds was waiting for me in his office. There was no mistaking the fact that this was an immediate summons, and my excitement in winning over Misty faded quickly.

I gnawed on my cheek the whole way up to his office, thinking through the mission yet again. There wasn't anything I could have done differently, not the way the events had unfolded. Obviously, it would have been better if Venom never showed up, or if I'd thought to be aware of her. But she did and I hadn't. I did the best with the tools I had at hand.

"What the hell was that?" A voice cut through my thoughts. I startled and realized that not only had I made it to Simmonds's door, but Travis was there too. He was eyeing at me with so much anger that it was remarkable I hadn't felt it coming down the hall. "*Venom*? She was the first person we ruled out! What would possess you to bring her on board?"

"What, have you just been standing there, waiting for me?" I asked.

"You better believe I've been waiting." The anger radiated off of him, and my nerves were too shot to deal with it right then. Not while he had this attitude. "She's a straight assassin! And she *likes* it!"

"I know what she is," I fired back. "Do you even know what happened?"

"Of course I do. I was briefed."

I took a long breath through my nose, trying to keep myself in check. He was briefed. Which meant he didn't hear anything that happened firsthand. He had no idea that I'd had a syringe full of Gerex pressed against the vein in my neck. He had no clue how close I'd come to being taken. He didn't understand how essential that move had been. And to think, at the time, he was the person I had wanted there. "You don't know the whole story."

His face started to turn red at that. "I know you invited a crazy, careless assassin onto a team associated with the IDA. The one thing you needed to do was follow the plan! This has to be one of your most reckless—"

"No!" I spoke loud enough for my voice to carry down the hall. "You don't get to call me that. Not because of this. I'm not happy with how it turned out either, but I didn't have a choice."

"You need to get rid of her," Travis said. "Or shut down this whole operation. You can't move forward like this."

"Whoa." I held my hands up in front of me. "I am not giving up because one small piece isn't exactly what we planned."

"It's more than a small piece," he hissed. "Centipede was risky enough—this is suicidal!"

"I found her hook!" I argued. "She's just as invested as any of the others, and I'm not throwing all of this work and intel away because of something you decided!"

He still had a lot more to say, but luckily, the door to Simmonds's office opened, sparing me any more of this conversation. My dad stood at the threshold.

"Jocelyn." He sounded relieved. "I was coming to look for you."

I pushed past Travis and went into the office. He followed me.

I found myself breathing heavy. I closed my eyes, trying to shut everyone out. I just needed thirty seconds to myself.

"Agent Steely." I pried my eyelids open and focused on Simmonds. His expression was firm but not unkind. "You should sit."

I lowered into the seat behind me. Travis took the chair on my left, and my dad settled against the wall.

"What happened out there?" my dad asked. "We heard through the comms, but it felt like we were missing something." There was a note of genuine curiosity in his voice—like he truly wanted to understand. It was enough to take away some of my tension. I told them what happened, laying the whole thing out.

"She had the needle to your neck?" Simmonds asked. That was what they couldn't pick up through the comms. Travis was still next to me, and while he seemed to have calmed some, I still felt his anger. My dad's eyes were reduced to slits.

I nodded. "If she'd injected me—" I swallowed, thinking about what would have happened. "Gerex was tightly controlled at KATO, and when we were in the field, we were motivated enough to avoid withdrawal to pace ourselves. I've only seen an overdose once, but it was enough to know that two back-to-back injections of a full dose would have knocked me out in less than three minutes." An agent had tried to escape and her handler loaded her up. It looked like too much Gerex was just as bad as not enough—possibly even worse. She screamed for about five minutes before she passed out, and it took her days to recover.

"So to stay away from KATO," my dad said, "you offered her a chance to leave too."

I nodded. "I saw a sign that she disagreed with them—or at least that she doesn't like how they control her. It gave me a window in."

"The amount of damage she could do," Travis said, seeming to finally find his voice. I turned to face him. He seemed less angry, but no more supportive.

"It's not what I wanted," I said. "But it's what we're working with now. She's on board enough to keep our secret from KATO. And for now she seems to be listening to me."

"Exactly." Travis pointed at my words. "For *now*. She went from drugging you to siding with you in under five minutes. Who knows how long that will last—if she's even telling the truth." He turned to Simmonds. "Sir, this feels out of control." I fought the urge to snap at him. He stopped just short of saying Simmonds should dismantle the team.

I couldn't let that happen. While it was true that there would always be a chance that these girls would be found or that I would lose their loyalty, he wasn't with me when Misty called. He didn't hear how much this meant to her. He wasn't around when Centipede admitted that she didn't want to go back to KATO, and he didn't see the look on Venom's face when I told her she didn't have to be controlled by them anymore. They may be scared, and KATO may still have a certain amount of power over them, but they were invested. They deserved an opportunity to escape. I wasn't going to let this team slip away.

"It's not out of control." My tone was confident, yet dismissive. The last mission *had* gotten derailed significantly, but I was sure I could recover. I turned back to Simmonds, because he needed to understand. I didn't like the uneasy look on his face, but I refused to let this fall apart because of one unexpected variable—no matter how big it was. "Regardless of the complications, I came home with intel, a source of funding, and three KATO agents willing to work with us. They may have a lot to learn, but so did I. And I'd had *years* to prepare myself. We just need a little more time."

"Tell me more about the intel," Simmonds said. He seemed willing to listen, but still not overly convinced.

"Misty had plenty to share," I said, speaking quickly. "Eliza was close with her. She didn't know what happened to her, but I think I can use their relationship to get Eliza talking. She said Eliza used to be a defiant fighter. What ever KATO did to her took that away."

Simmonds looked disappointed, and I knew he was expecting more, but I believed it was enough. If Eliza was close enough to Misty to be muttering her name, I was sure I had plenty to work with. Despite his hesitance, Simmonds nodded. "I'll give it a chance," he said. "Because we don't have any other leads."

I risked a glance at Travis. "We didn't learn anything in England?"

"No," Travis said. He pulled his eyes away from mine and bowed his head in defeat. "There isn't any paper evidence of her anywhere. No school records or medical records. I came across some old teachers and friends, but they're all under the impression that the Fosters moved. Though no one could tell me where. It's like she disappeared and no one questioned anything."

I pressed my lips together. "KATO made her a ghost."

"They're really good at that," my dad said. There was a distance in his eyes that suggested his mind was somewhere else. He blinked back to reality and looked to me. "Anything more you can get out of her would be helpful."

I nodded and stood. "I'll talk to her first thing in the morning." I wanted my mind sharp when we spoke, not fried and worn as it was now.

Travis beat me out the door, and I took off to follow him. I still had a thing or two to discuss with him, especially now that he knew the details of the mission.

"Agent Steely," Simmonds said, stopping me just short of the door. "This will be your only opportunity. If your intel doesn't lead to some kind of insight, we may have to find a more concrete approach."

My jaw clenched, and I felt the weight of the entire situation fall to the pit of my stomach. "I understand." I turned to leave, but my dad caught my eye. I held his gaze for a moment. My next talk with Eliza wouldn't be about me. It would be about her and Misty. I didn't have to get into anything that happened in my past, or anything I'd done. "You should come tomorrow," I said to him. His brows arched in surprise. "If you want."

He nodded slowly, as if he didn't quite believe he had heard me correctly. "I wouldn't miss it."

I gave him a small smile, then hurried into the hall after Travis.

. . .

I caught up with Travis just outside the operations building. He was stalking across the courtyard, headed for the training facility. Without the students around, areas like this were regularly empty these days.

"Do you see why I made that call now?" I asked him. I was seconds away from going back to KATO. He had to understand.

He pivoted to a stop in front of the training facility. "Yes," he said. "I understand why you brought her in. What I don't understand is why you won't fix it."

I grabbed him. "I can't fix it! If I cut her out, she goes to KATO with everything." I arched an eyebrow. "Unless you're suggesting I kill her."

"I'm *suggesting*," he said through gritted teeth, "that you shut this whole thing down."

"This isn't the first time a mission hasn't gone as planned," I said. "It shouldn't be that big of a deal."

"Usually when missions go wrong they don't involve handing an unvetted enemy access to the IDA! And this one in particular has given us every reason to believe she can't be trusted." The vein in his neck started to throb. "If you have a different way to get rid of her and modify the plan, I'm all ears, but that's not what you're talking about right now."

"She knows too much!" I couldn't hide my frustration anymore.

"Which is exactly why you need to end the whole thing."

"No." I shook my head. "Not after all the work we put into this! The intel is too good to waste, and all of the girls are on board— including Venom. I'm not throwing that all away because you're panicking."

"This isn't panicking. This is being smart!"

"It's playing it safe," I said. "And we won't beat KATO that way."

"You won't beat KATO at all. You'll be high in their basement." I felt like he'd just slapped me, but I didn't let it show. Because yes, that was my greatest fear, but I wouldn't let that fear get in the way of bringing them down.

"I know the risks." I spoke slowly to keep my anger in check. "And I've got it under control."

He laughed in disbelief. "Then you know what? If you're so sure, I'll let you take it from here." He yanked the door to the training facility open and left me without looking back.

I stood there for a few minutes in shock. He couldn't possibly have just quit the operation. Was that even something he was allowed to do?

I hurried inside once my brain started working again. I needed him to hear me out, but I realized very quickly that wouldn't be happening now. The afternoon workout was in full swing, and the last thing that would help this situation would be a fight in front of every active agent in the IDA. I spotted Travis easily, pounding a punching bag on the other side of the room. He almost never used a punching bag.

"What's up with him?" I glanced to my left and saw Nikki had sidled up next to me.

"He's really angry with me," I said.

"Were you wrong?" she asked.

I shook my head. "He doesn't agree with my approach to something."

Nikki grimaced. "He can be such a noodle sometimes. Give him time. He'll get over it."

"I don't know about that." I looked at her out of the corner of my eye. "I think he took himself off the assignment we were working on together."

Her head snapped in my direction, eyes wide with disbelief. "He couldn't have meant it."

"It sounded like he did." I bit my lip. "Is he allowed to do something like that?"

"Well, he can ask for anything he wants, but Simmonds would still have to agree to it," she said. "He'll cool down before it gets to that point. I'm sure it's not as bad as you think."

I looked back to Travis, who was taking his anger out on the bag, and I hoped Nikki was right.

Chapter Nineteen

THE LAST PIECE

I gave up on trying to talk to Travis. He wasn't receptive to what I had to say, so there didn't seem to be any point. I had a hard time sleeping that night, which resulted in me being the first one to the observation room the next morning. I thought over everything Misty had told me as I watched Eliza through the glass. She sat crossed-legged at the bottom of the bed, her back resting against the rail.

I breathed slowly through my nose as I studied her. She looked calm, but I was sure it was an act.

I only managed fifteen minutes of peace before the door opened behind me. My dad walked in with a cup of coffee in each hand. He held one out for me. "I usually stop on my way here," he said. "I thought you might like one."

I eyed it wearily. "Coffee's probably not a good idea for me." I didn't really know whether caffeine would affect me, but it wasn't worth the risk.

"It's herbal tea," he said. I arched an eyebrow at that and he smiled lightly.

"Thank you." I tried not to act too shocked as I took it from him.

He nodded once. "You're welcome."

My dad had said Simmonds had given him the basics of my life since I'd come to the IDA. I guessed that included the side effects of living without Gerex.

I looked back to Eliza as I took a sip, embracing the way the tea scalded my throat. I needed this to work. I'd pulled three KATO agents into this mess. I couldn't let it all be for nothing.

"You're worried," he said. It was an observation, not a question.

I closed my eyes for a beat. "I really need her to talk."

"She will." There wasn't a trace of doubt in his voice.

I wanted to ask him how he knew, how he could be so sure—but the door opened before I could.

Simmonds and Travis entered, ending whatever moment my dad and I were having. Travis looked at me but didn't speak. I swallowed, hating this place we were in. But I didn't know what to say to fix it.

I put my focus back on Eliza as we waited for Dr. March. Eliza tugged at the chains that held her in place. She seemed pleasantly curious about them. I thought about the girl Misty had described. That girl had fire and fight—enough to openly square off against a KATO handler. The girl in front of me just looked lost.

Dr. March met my eyes when she came in. "Whenever you're ready." Her gaze was steady and firm. After the last exchange, I knew she was uneasy about what this might trigger. But I wasn't worried about myself. Not this time. I knew more about Eliza going in than I had in the past. At this point, I was more concerned that if I didn't get Eliza talking, it would mean that not only was my team a lost cause, but Eliza as well.

"Does she know about her father yet?" I asked.

Dr. March shook her head. "We tried to tell her a couple more times, but the second his name came up she shut us out."

I nodded. It was a card I hoped I didn't have to use, but I was prepared to. She needed to know, and I needed leverage.

Dr. March led me back to Eliza's door. The guard stepped aside when he saw me, and Dr. March let me in.

Eliza's head snapped in my direction when the door opened. This time, Dr. March stayed in the hallway, letting me be Eliza's sole point of contact. She sat up even straighter when I crossed the threshold. I took the chair—a new one—from its position at the foot of her bed and pulled it around to the side, angling it so I could see her. I also made sure she was positioned toward the window so everyone could see her face. She glanced behind me briefly, like she knew there was a room full of people watching, but she didn't ask any questions.

Eliza looked more worn-out close up, but she also seemed surprisingly alert and engaged. She was taking a series of slow breaths, like she was terrified of what I was about to do. This was something I more than understood.

"I'm sorry about last time," I said. She didn't move a muscle, not daring to trust me. "But I need you to be ready to talk." I kept my voice light and cautious. I had to approach this whole situation differently from last time. I didn't want to make her any more defensive or on edge than she already seemed to be.

She stared straight ahead, being careful not to make eye contact. "I can't talk to you." There was ice in her voice. I knew coming in she wasn't going to make this easy.

I bit my tongue, trying to keep from getting frustrated with her. "You need to tell me what they did to you. Because whatever it is, they're going to do it to other agents too." She squeezed her eyes closed tight, like she was trying to shut out the world. "They'll do it to Misty."

Her eyes snapped open. "How do you know that name?"

I scanned her face. Did she really not know? "You kept saying it." She scrunched up her nose, looking startled and confused. I continued. "I talked to her a couple days ago. She's helping us."

Eliza blinked a few times, like she was having a hard time processing everything I was throwing at her. "She is?"

I nodded. "She said—she said to tell you not to let them take your light."

Eliza inhaled sharply at that and slid away from me, pressing her back into the foot rail. She rocked gently back and forth, muttering like she was struggling with something internally. Then she forced herself still and met my eyes. "I can't tell you." Her voice was different this time. Like it hurt her not to be more helpful.

I took a breath, giving us a beat. I wanted this to go slow and quiet so she would separate it from both last time and from KATO. "At least help me understand. I know Misty meant something to you." She sat tense and stubbornly quiet. We didn't have time to draw this out. I hated what I was about to do, but I didn't have a choice. "How can you keep their secrets after what they've done to you and your father?"

Her hands moved to her ears just like Simmonds and March said they would, but I was ready. I was out of my chair in a second, catching hold of her wrists before she could shut me out.

"Leave. Him. Out of this!" she yelled at me, but I didn't back down. I shifted onto the bed, sitting in front of her with one knee tucked under me so we were eye to eye. "He's already in it." She started shaking her head again. "Eliza—" My voice cracked and I bit my lip, taking a minute. Then I found her eyes. "Eliza, they killed him."

She went rigid in front of me, searching my face, looking for any sign that I wasn't being honest. I was shattering her. "No. No, they can't have." She pulled her arms out of my grasp and shook her head hard and fast. It was the kind of thing a small child would do to escape an adult. But I wouldn't give her any space. Instead I shifted closer, coming just short of touching her. "They told me if I listened they'd let him go."

A pit dropped into my stomach, and I fought to keep myself from shaking. "Eliza, you've been with them for over a year. Do you really think they would *let* someone go?"

She held my gaze for another moment, then everything seemed to snap into place at once. She curled into a ball, burying her face in her hands. She was on the verge of hyperventilating. I leaned forward and dropped my head so it was right above hers. "Hey." I put my hand on her back. "Take a deep breath." She did what I said. In fact, she took several. And eventually she had gotten it together enough that I was sure she wouldn't pass out. When she started to sit up, I slid back a few inches, giving her some space.

"When?" Her voice was hoarse and I knew she was still in shock.

"About two months ago," I watched her closely, gauging her reaction.

She thought for a second, then shook her head. "That's not possible. They threatened him just before you took me."

I met her eyes evenly. I had an idea what she was feeling, because I had felt it with my mom. The only feeling I had no context for was how abrupt this was. I had been prepared—or at least, as prepared as I could be. "They were lying." I took care to speak as gently as possible, though I couldn't be sure it mattered. "I was in KATO's headquarters.

I located him in the morning and he was alive. One of our agents went to retrieve him a few hours later and they had killed him."

She looked away from me and I could practically see her mind trying to understand all of this. Then she leaned forward again, pressing her palms into her eyelids. "I knew. They didn't tell me but I think I knew."

I dipped my head low so I was closer to her. "If he was the reason you were holding out, we really need you to talk to us." She looked up at me. "What did they do to you?"

She was breathing deeply again. Like she was doing her best to keep from falling apart. Then she shook her head. "He wasn't the only reason. I still can't tell you anything."

I let out a long frustrated exhale, then pushed myself off the bed and started pacing. "How can you still be loyal to them?" I asked, snapping at her. I immediately felt bad about it, but we didn't have the luxury of time.

"I didn't say I don't *want* to talk," she said, firing back. Her voice was stronger and more forceful than it had ever been before. I liked it. She met my eyes with a fierce, determined look. "I said I *can't*."

I tilted my head to the side, studying her. "What exactly does that mean?"

She stared at the wall over my shoulder, her face contracted in deep concentration. "All right," she said. "I'll tell you what I can. But I don't know how far I'll get."

I looked back at the mirror, hoping they were all ready for this. I didn't know what to make of it, but she was finally opening up. I wasn't about to slow her down by asking questions.

"I can only say this once. So, I need you to listen." The more she talked, the more afraid she looked. Still, I nodded.

She took a deep breath, gathering her strength. "Gerex wasn't the only thing KATO injected me with," she said. I sat up a little straighter, feeling slightly more panicked.

"What do you mean?" I scanned her, trying to work out if she was either lying or hurt.

"They put something in me—a different injection." She hunched over, and I noticed her heart monitor start to spike. "If we start revealing secrets," the monitor went even faster, and Eliza leaned forward farther, holding her head in her hands in obvious pain. "The pressure builds—" The monitor started beeping at an alarming rate. I was sure it was due to her pain, but it seemed to be entirely too fast regardless. She started to talk again, but I grabbed her hand before she could.

"No, no, no," I said, sitting back down on the bed, closer to her. "Don't say anything. Don't give us anything else." She took a series of slow breaths, battling through the pain, and clearly pushing any memory of what she was about to say out of her mind. She was shaking so hard, and I knew it was out of fear.

I slid even closer to her and tugged her arm, trying to pull her to me, but she yanked away. Tears leaked down her face, but she didn't wipe them away. "It'll make it worse."

I nodded slowly and shifted away from her. I didn't understand, but she had to have her reasons. "We're going to figure something out," I said, glancing at the window, at everyone behind it, hopefully making it clear that this was not just a suggestion. This was a clear-cut mission.

"Where did they inject this one?" I asked.

Eliza didn't speak. She just pulled her hand up and rubbed at the base of her skull, right inside her hairline. I came around her a little bit more and pushed her hair out of the way so I could get a good look. Buried beneath the mess of waves was a small red bump. If she hadn't been there to point it out to me, I never would have found it, let alone thought twice about it. She sobbed silently and I struggled not to reach out for her. The whole thing made me sick to my stomach.

After a few minutes, Dr. March came in and gave her something to help her sleep. I disappeared quickly out the door, feeling suffocated.

I walked past the observation room, not even stopping to glance back when I heard the door open. I moved swiftly through the lobby and out into the hallway, walking briskly to the large window at the end. It wasn't the air I needed—it was the space.

I put my back against the wall next to the window and doubled over. This was different from a craving—though I could feel that too—this was more like a physical sickness. They had messed with her *brain*. It made perfect sense. KATO had been pushing drugs into its agents for years. I thought they couldn't get any worse, or any more terrible, but they had. If they had the ability to change how people thought and reacted—

I gulped down air but I couldn't seem to get enough. No matter how many breaths I took it felt like my lungs couldn't hold on to anything. I felt dizzy and sweaty, and I couldn't figure out which was more severe.

Big black boots appeared in front of me. I knew it was my father, and I attempted to turn away from him.

"Jocelyn." He tugged at my arms, trying to get me to straighten, but I couldn't. "Sweetie, I need you to listen to me." I pulled away again, but he put a hand on each shoulder, holding me tight. "Come on, you're going to hurt yourself."

He forced me straight and I swayed. I gripped his upper arms to stabilize myself.

"Good," he said. I looked into his eyes and I realized they were the same color as mine. "Now, I need you to breathe when I do, okay?" His breaths were slower—too slow—and I found it impossible to match. "Let's go, you can do it." I tried again, and this time I got closer. He held on to me, coaching me for another few rounds until my breathing leveled.

"You did good, kid." He held on to the back of my neck, refusing to let me look away. "You did real good."

"They got—in her head." I could barely get the words out.

"I know." He gave my shoulders a squeeze. "And we're all going to talk about that as soon as you're ready."

I nodded. "Can we just stay here for another minute?"

"We can stay here for as long as you need."

I leaned back against the wall, and for the first time I was truly glad my dad was there.

Chapter Twenty

TRUTHS

My father and I moved back into the observation room when I had calmed down enough. Even though my head seemed to have cleared, I was still rattled to the point that my insides felt unstable. Simmonds stood near the door with Dr. March next to him, going over Eliza's file. Travis was on the other side of the room, tucked in the corner, his forehead rested on the glass so he could still see Eliza.

The silence of the room rang in my ears. I met Travis's eyes briefly and I could see he was just as shaken as I was. I pulled my head away from him, looking back through the window at Eliza, who was sound asleep.

"How did we miss this?" I asked.

No one rushed to answer, but eventually, it was Travis who spoke up. "We missed it because she wanted us to."

I swallowed. He had asked me a similar question in the past and that was the reason I had given him.

"What do we know about this new drug?" Simmonds asked Dr. March.

"That's the scary thing." She was still paging through Eliza's file, her face growing more and more concerned. "Now, keep in mind that this is still new. I haven't had the time to investigate anything fully. But it doesn't look like this is a drug. I ran a very extensive toxicology on her when she came in, and aside from the Gerex, there isn't any trace of a foreign substance," she said. "Something else I don't like is that, from the looks of things, it was injected directly into her brain."

"What?" I asked. I had to have heard her wrong.

Dr. March nodded. "The bump on the back of her head is from the drill they had to use to get through her skull. That's why we can still see it. It's a very direct approach, though I wonder if it's fully necessary."

"So they did it for fun?" my dad asked.

"Given that it's KATO we're talking about, it's possible. But it's more likely that this method would yield the most immediate result." She sighed. "I can't begin to guess the specifics, but based on what I've seen, the symptoms she has, and what she's saying she can and can't do, I think this is related to her oxytocin output."

My eyebrows knitted together. "What does that mean?"

"Oxytocin is a hormone and neurotransmitter that's released when a person bonds with another, which includes sharing secrets," Dr. March explained. "I think whatever is going on isn't necessarily preventing her from talking, but it's attacking the area of the brain that releases oxytocin any time she attempts to share a secret. The pain that comes with that is what's keeping her in check."

"Can you fix her?" Travis asked, his voice hoarse.

Dr. March tipped her head to the side noncommittally. "I can run some more tests now that we have all of this new information, but I don't know how conclusive they'll be."

I rubbed my forehead, trying to get my brain moving. "Could it be related to her immune system?" I asked. "Jin Su was interested in her and he visited an immunologist."

Dr. March flipped through some more papers in Eliza's file. "It's a possibility. I ran a check on her immune system after that report came in and didn't find anything, but I can check again."

"Is there a chance this might kill her?" Simmonds asked.

Dr. March shrugged. "I don't know nearly enough to answer that. But I'll say that based on what I've seen, the body's reaction to that amount of pain could do some damage if the pain is prolonged. And my guess is to her, it feels like she might die."

"That's all KATO cares about," I said. "They probably told her it would kill her even if it's not true."

"All right," my dad said, running a hand through his hair. "What can we do about all of this now?"

"Regardless of any information we may already have, the most helpful thing would be to get a look at the original serum," Dr. March said. "That was crucial to understanding the Gerex."

"Do you think you can reverse the process?" I asked.

Dr. March gave me a halfhearted shrug. "I honestly don't know. But there's at least a chance if I get my hands on the serum."

"I want this one," I said to Simmonds. "I have a team of KATO agents who will be highly motivated to track this serum down. And between the four of us, we should have the intel and resources to pull it off."

"We don't even know where to go," Travis said. He sounded frustrated by the entire situation. "If it's in their headquarters, we're talking about another trip into North Korea. And we don't know where they're rebuilding."

"It can't be there," I said. "Even if it was there at one point, something this important would have been moved after we invaded. That location wasn't secure anymore."

"You think they took it outside of North Korea?" my dad asked, following my train of thought.

"If they have safe houses all over the world, why wouldn't they have an alternate facility outside of the country?" I asked.

He nodded. "It makes sense."

"If I'm right, they would've had to have outsourced the construction," I said. "We can get Centipede to find out who they used."

Simmonds ran a hand along his chin, seeming to be seriously considering this. "Reach out to your agents. See what they know and how they can help. I'm hesitant to rely on them so soon for something this important, but they may be our best option."

"I'll get right on it," I said, heading for the door.

"The rest of us will reconvene in my office," Simmonds said to the others. "We need to figure out an alternative solution."

. . .

I went back to my room so I could make contact without an audience. I sat cross-legged on my bed, running my fingers along the ruffles on the comforter.

I called Centipede first. When she didn't pick up, I moved on to Venom.

She answered immediately like she said she would. I didn't give her too many of the details—if we were doing this, it seemed best to go over everything in person when we were all together. I told her what the job would be: to locate a new developmental serum and re-trieve it.

"They make more drugs?" she asked when I was finished.

"Well, we're not so sure it's really a drug, but yeah, that's the general idea," I said.

There was a pause on her end, and I imagined she was thinking it over. "Yes, I will do this."

"Okay, I'll send you a meeting place when I—" She hung up before I could finish. As far as I was concerned, it was a successful communication.

Then I called Misty. She also picked up very quickly. "You have something already?"

"In part thanks to you," I said. "We got Python talking. Everything you said helped a lot."

"I'm glad." It sounded like she truly was.

I filled her in on our task, giving her the same light details I had given Venom. "We'll talk about everything when we meet. I just need to know if you're up for this." I didn't want to give her any more intel over the phone in case someone was listening.

"I am."

"Good. I'll be in touch when I know more," I said before we disconnected.

Now all I needed was Centipede. It was a while before she called back this time and I found myself pacing the room. The more time passed, the more anxious I became. I was afraid she'd either gotten caught or turned on us. Either one seemed like a real possibility.

Finally she called back and I picked up quickly.

"What do you need?" she asked. There was a hard edge to her

voice that I didn't like. One I hadn't heard since I'd first convinced her to join. My senses were on high alert.

"Is everything okay?"

"I don't have time for that," she said. "Tell me why you called."

Her attitude made my guard go up, but I told her the same thing I had told everyone else. By the time I was finished, her tone had changed significantly.

"A serum?" she asked. She tried to hide it, but I heard the note of fear in her voice. "What does it do?"

"I'd rather give the details in person," I said, hoping I didn't have to explain myself any more than that.

She was quiet for a few seconds. Then she asked, "Is it bad?"

I bit my lip before I answered. "Yeah," I said. "It's really bad."

She exhaled heavily—too heavily. "You need to get Python and everyone else out of the IDA."

I froze. My heart started to race as her words sunk in. "What's going on?"

"KATO found a way in," she said. "I don't know what their plan is, but I've been told I'll be pulled back in the near future." She paused. "They said once the ground team arrives, I won't be needed anymore."

"How long have you known about this?" I asked. I tried to focus on my breathing, struggling to stay calm.

"Six hours." The more we talked the softer her voice became.

I ground my teeth together. "And if I didn't call you, would you have called me?"

She was quiet then for entirely too long.

"Are you fucking kidding me?" I was livid and terrified, and I didn't know what to act on.

"You brought Venom—" She cut herself off. "It doesn't matter. Now you know. Do you want to keep talking to me or do something about it?"

I exhaled heavily through my nose. "We think the serum is being kept in a facility outside of North Korea. You need to find out who KATO used to build it."

"What?" she asked. "How am I supposed to do that?"

"Figure it out! You owe us." I hung up on her and raced out of my room, moving across campus in a dead sprint. I nearly took out a handful of agents who stood between me and the operations building.

I didn't hesitate to burst into Simmonds's office. Simmonds, Travis, and my father were all there and looked up abruptly when I came barreling through the door.

"Whatever relocation plan you're operating on, you need to accelerate it," I said as I tried to catch my breath. "KATO's coming."

"You're certain?" Simmonds asked.

"Centipede just confirmed it. KATO *really* wants Eliza back." I said nothing about the fact that Centipede nearly let us get hit. Ultimately she told us what we needed to know, but I wasn't so sure Simmonds would see it that way.

"We're upping relocation to an emergency final phase," Simmonds said. "Emergency procedure dictates the immediate grounding of in-progress missions and operational suspension until relocation is complete. Your mission will be put on hold in the meantime."

"Wait a minute." For the second time in two days my entire mission seemed seconds away from blowing up on me. I wouldn't let it happen. "I can still make this work. I'm working with KATO agents who aren't used to *any* support. All we need are comms so we can talk to each other."

He gave me a weary look. "You're suggesting that I authorize an IDA-sanctioned mission while the IDA is effectively shut down."

"It's *KATO*, and they're messing with people's minds." I put my fists on the edge of his desk, my knuckles digging into the edge. "We have the advantage now, but we don't know how long that will last. We can't risk waiting until we're fully operational. Not on this."

Simmonds's mouth formed a thin line. I couldn't tell if he was considering this or if he was irritated that I was pushing.

My dad shifted on his feet. "Roy, no one hates to admit this more than me," he said, "but she has a point."

Simmonds grimaced, but nodded. "I have a location in Lyon, France, that you can use as a safe house to meet with your team. I'll have you and Agent Elton dispatched on a special assignment before initiating the protocol. Your mission is to retrieve the serum and any development information you can get your hands on." He looked to my dad. "Chris, I'm assigning you as the supervising agent."

My dad shrugged. "If you didn't, I was assigning myself." Simmonds leveled him with a glare that made my dad smirk, and I felt myself relax a fraction.

"If it's all right, sir," Travis said, "I'd rather stick around here and help with the relocation." I felt like a bucket of ice water had been dropped on me. I could not have heard him right. "We have a lot of sensitive intel that needs to be protected."

I stared straight in front of me, stunned. No matter what he had said yesterday, I didn't believe he would really bail on me when it came down to it.

"I agree," Simmonds said, eyeing him. "I had thought Hawthorne and Mathers would be well suited for the role."

"They would be," Travis said. "But I'd rather it be me."

Simmonds looked to me for a moment, as if he were trying to feel me out, but I kept my expression neutral, giving nothing away. "Very well," he said. "I can't say I wouldn't feel better having you around."

My jaw locked. Travis had just *chosen* to stay behind. I tried to ignore the way my stomach churned, but it got harder each second. I was desperate to move on before anyone knew how much disappointment coursed through me.

"I'd like Nikki with me," I said. "She may not be able to go in the field, but with this she won't need to. We could use her perspective." And I needed someone on my side.

Simmonds thought for a moment, then nodded. "I'll allow it," he said. "I'd rather the two of you not be outnumbered anyway."

"Can I also get Sam to monitor the situation from the school's location?" I asked. He was someone else who had never questioned me.

Simmonds's eyebrows came together. "His building isn't equipped to run an operation out of. Its intent is for students to have a secure place to learn. They don't have the same resources as we do here."

"I don't need the resources," I said. "But having a hacker for any background information we may need could be helpful. Sam reached out after the move and offered me help. He's also proven he can handle it."

Simmonds nodded. "Very well, then. Agent Steely, I'll let you prepare for your assignment. I'll have Agent Edwards sent right to you and I'll touch base with Sam Lewis."

"Thank you, sir," I said. "I can contact Sam on the plane if you'd like. You've got enough to worry about."

"Excellent," Simmonds said. "I'll check in with you periodically, but for all intents and purposes, you are on your own."

I hurried out of the office, refusing to so much as glance in Travis's direction.

Chapter Twenty-One

HOME BASE

I pushed Travis out of my mind and put my focus on the mission, which was more important anyway. Sam was, as expected, delighted to be called on. I briefed him on the situation and prepped him for a search on KATO's builders once Centipede arrived. He said he'd start on what he could and told us to check back in when we were set up in France. When I was finished with him, I sent a message to the others with the safe house location.

It was early in the evening when we landed in Lyon—already dark with just enough movement on the street to blend in. The house was a row home located closer to the edge of the city.

There was a keypad next to the door. In order to access the house, my dad had to enter three different codes at specific intervals. We entered into a living room. It was a big space, fully furnished with traditional European furniture. The stiff high backs and carved wooden trim felt a little too nice for our purposes. There was a staircase on the left side heading to the second floor, and an archway in the back right corner that presumably lead to a kitchen.

"I'll get the equipment set up," Nikki said, taking in the room. She had been giddy for most of the flight, happy to get off the base. Despite the fact that we had next to no direct IDA support, we'd been sent with monitors, computers, and cameras that would allow us to set up a low-functioning command center in the living room.

We were up and running within the hour, and the girls were due just before midnight. In the meantime, we took inventory of the rest of the house. The kitchen was stocked with enough food to last us a month, though I was hoping we would be less than a week. My dad also rigged the bedroom doors so they were stuck open. It didn't seem like a good idea to give the girls too much privacy.

I found myself pacing the living room as my anxiety started to get the better of me. The four of us had never been together before and I was uneasy about how all of this would go. "You two can't say anything," I said, looking to Nikki and my dad. "I'll introduce you and give them your roles, but I've been in charge and, for the most part, they're listening to me. I can't be outranked."

"You can run it," my dad said. "But if things get out of hand, I'm stepping in." I didn't argue. His face was set and it was clear this wasn't a point of negotiation.

The first knock at the door came around eleven thirty. I glanced at the two of them.

My dad tipped his head to the side. "I guess it's showtime."

I drew a long tight breath and opened the door.

Misty stood on the other side. She hugged herself as she hunched in the doorway, like she was doing her best to be invisible.

"You're the first one here," I said, stepping aside so she could enter.

She shivered slightly as she crossed the threshold. I noticed her face was still purple where Centipede had hit her. "You know," she said, "I came here still thinking this could be a trap."

I shrugged. "I've been praying none of you went back to KATO with any of this."

Misty smiled lightly, then a voice on the stairs pulled everyone's attention.

"I am here."

My neck snapped up. It was Venom. She stood halfway down the stairs.

"How did you get in?" I asked, trying not to sound alarmed.

"Attic fan." There was a touch of pride in her voice and I had to remind myself that she was on our side—or at least she was supposed to be. She moved down the steps, swinging her arms ever so slightly. She stopped at the bottom step when she spotted Misty. "Who are you?"

Misty stiffened when Venom focused on her, so I stepped in to introduce them to each other.

"Oh, this will be fun," Misty said, shooting a concerned look in my direction.

They both noticed Nikki and my father, who were now standing, but I was waiting until everyone arrived to make those introductions. In the meantime, Misty had taken a seat on the couch while Venom paced behind it, rhythmically tilting her head from side to side.

Centipede finally showed up just before midnight, tension radiating off of her. She blew past me without so much as a second glance. "KATO is furious they found the IDA's headquarters empty."

"Did you get the intel we need?" I asked, shutting the door behind her.

She looked mildly offended. "Why do you think it took me so long to get here?"

"Do they suspect that you're tied to any of this?"

She shook her head. "They haven't pulled me back, so I don't think so."

"Good," I said. "Then we need to talk."

She looked me square in the eye like she knew what was coming. "You found out in time."

"We did." I kept my voice light. I didn't want to fight with her, but she needed to understand. "But part of being an informant means that you give us intel when you have it. Not when we call and ask for it."

She crossed her arms. "You're lucky you got anything at all."

My eyebrows shot up. "What is that supposed to mean?"

She shrugged. "You don't have control of this. Just look at who you've put together." She gestured to the others. "We've got a retrieval expert who can't fight and *her.*" She glared at Venom.

"Hold on," Misty said, jumping up from the couch, her finger in the air. "First, I can fight well enough to still be alive. And second, it sounds like I'm the only one here who has volunteered useful information. So you don't have a lot of room to talk."

"And what do you think is wrong with me?" Venom asked, her eyes locking on Centipede like a predator's.

Centipede waved her off, dismissively. "You've got one talent and you're effective, but I'm not convinced you're that skilled."

Venom took another step closer, head cocked. "Do you wish to see how skilled I am?"

"Okay, that's enough." I shifted between them, putting my arms out to keep them each in their place. They were staring each other down. At the moment it was more or less harmless, but I knew how quickly this could get out of control. They were KATO-trained, which meant they were programmed to compete against each other. And Centipede was provoking everyone. Nikki and my dad had both straightened up, ready to intervene if necessary. I shook my head once and they stood down.

I grabbed Centipede's shoulders and steered her toward the kitchen, away from the others. She pulled away from me once we'd crossed the threshold and paced the length of the kitchen.

"You need to bring it down," I said, keeping my voice low so the others couldn't hear. "You're going to set everyone off."

"So what?" Her breathing was heavy and full of tension.

"Is this really about Venom?" I asked. I knew she wasn't thrilled with the addition, but she didn't seem nearly this upset about it when we separated in Turkey.

"Of course it is!" she snapped. "You know what her reputation is!"

"I do." I crossed my arms as she picked up the pace. "But she's just as invested as you are."

She shook her head hard. "This is going to burn us all."

I sat back on my heels and watched her for a moment. The emotions rolled off of her. The tension and anger and fear reached me from the other side of the room, and I thought I understood why. "Today was really close, wasn't it?" I said. She came to a complete stop. "You thought they might have figured you out?"

She held my eyes and she seemed to be struggling with herself. Then she nodded slowly.

I tilted my head to the side. "What happened?"

When she spoke her voice was tight. "My handler asked if there was anything I could tell them that would help. And I said no." She swallowed hard. "Then he studied me for a long time. He asked question after question—even more than usual. I was sure—" She cut herself off and seemed to be working to maintain control. "They always know when we're keeping something from them."

"They don't, though," I said. "It's just another lie they want you to believe."

She exhaled heavily. "How did you do this for *months*?"

I shrugged a shoulder. "I'm sure it was a lot easier not having to look them in the eye." I was plenty terrified misleading them through the computer as it was.

"I don't want them to have this serum," she said. "They have enough control over me. I don't want them to have any more."

"Then let's go take it from them," I said.

After a moment she nodded, and I waited for her to be ready to head back to the living room. I followed her, my stomach twisting in knots. She had just proven the one thing I had been afraid of. That when it came down to it, there was a very good chance that their fear of KATO would pull them right back in.

Chapter Twenty-Two

POWER PLAY

Centipede had calmed down considerably by the time we rejoined the others. Misty and Venom were seated on opposite ends of the couch and seemed to be watching each other closely.

"Everything okay here?" I asked, coming up next to Nikki, who was standing a few feet away from Misty.

"Things are—*interesting*," she said with a smile.

Misty shifted on the couch. "She keeps staring at me."

I looked to Venom, who was, in fact, staring intently at Misty. She flicked her eyes up to look at me. "Her hair is very straight."

Misty's face twisted as she gave Venom a once-over. I was sure she was taking in the chaotic mess that sat on top of Venom's head.

"Okay," Nikki said, her voice entirely too upbeat for the situation. "Who wants to know why we're here?" She gestured to me, giving me the floor.

I introduced Nikki and my dad, though we had decided we should use code names as a precaution. So as far as these girls were concerned, they were Echo and Archer. Then I moved on to the serum.

"I'm going to start at the beginning, just so we're all on the same page," I said. I gave them all the rundown on Eliza—how we knew about her, where we found her, and how important she was to KATO.

I flipped through the files we'd brought with us, looking for a picture. "It took us a little bit to get her talking, but when she did, she showed us this mark on the back of her head." I found the photo of Eliza's head; the red bump was so small the camera barely captured the image. I passed it around, starting with Venom.

Misty went next, studying it closely. "This is where they injected her?"

I nodded. "She could barely tell us what had been done to her. When she did, it looked like her head was about to explode."

The three of them looked at me, seeming a little confused.

"That's not too much of an exaggeration," Nikki said.

"I do not understand," Venom said as Centipede took a turn with the picture.

"From what she could share, we know that she was injected with some kind of serum, which caused an intolerable amount of pressure in her head when she tried to spill KATO's secrets," I said. "Our doctor has some theories, but it's nothing we can confirm." The three of them watched me, and I could see them all struggling with the idea.

"They would control our *thoughts*?" Venom asked, her disdain as thick as her accent.

Misty's face twisted, and she looked as if she might throw up. "They can't—"

"They can and they will," Centipede said. Her disgust was palpable and her voice strong. It was clear she had moved past the fear that had locked her in place earlier in the night. "We're their puppets. Their *toys*. They want to keep us on our strings."

"This is why we are here?" Venom asked. "You want us to kill the serum makers?"

I met her eyes briefly, and I couldn't help but be unnerved at the flash of delight that came with her suggestion. "Not exactly," I said. "We need to understand the serum. In order to do that, we need the original serum and, ideally, its development records."

Venom cocked her head to the side abruptly. "What good will that do?"

"We have someone who might be able to make an antidote, but she can't do it without the original," I said.

"And you think we can get it?" Centipede asked. Her tone told me she thought the task was impossible.

"Eventually," I said. "First, I need to ask what you three know about this—or about anything that could be related. Eliza was pulled from a safe house in Russia where she was being experimented on, but before that she was headed for a field assignment like yours. Did any of you see anything in your safe houses?"

Venom titled her head up at me, looking strangely lost. "I don't know anything. I've been on assignment."

"We both have," Misty said. She seemed annoyed that she didn't have more to add.

I glanced at the two of them. "How long have you two been at your posts?"

"Eight months," Venom said.

"A year," Misty said.

I knew they had been there longer than I had been at the IDA, but I wasn't expecting it to be by so much.

"How long were you at yours?" Venom asked, clearly reading that I was surprised.

I opened my mouth to answer, but Centipede beat me to it. "Nearly four months," she said. I turned to her, startled that she knew the answer, but she just shrugged. "The day you left was one of my best at KATO. I thought you were dead." Her tone wasn't harsh, just factual. Still, it proved to be too cruel for my father's liking.

"Watch it," he said with an angry edge. It startled me. He'd been quiet, which I appreciated. Though it was clear that no matter how much he intended to separate me as a spy from me as a daughter, there were some things that would be asking too much.

"It's okay," I said, blowing off Centipede and turning back to Venom. "Yeah, it's been four months."

"Is there a plan?" Misty asked.

"We believe KATO has an alternate research facility outside of North Korea," I said. "Centipede found out the name of the builders they would have used. If we get the blueprints, I have someone who can find the building based on them."

Misty's eyes flicked to Centipede. "How did you get the intel?"

"Viper's not the only one who's picked up on some of KATO's back doors," she said. "I hadn't dared to try anything until today."

I eyed Centipede, mildly impressed. She may be even more valuable than I had anticipated.

"We're going to bring in our tech expert," Nikki said, moving us along. She turned to the monitor on top of the fireplace and pushed it on. "Everyone say hi to Command."

She stepped aside as Sam waved. "Hey, KATO girl. Or, I guess it's KATO *girls* now." He smirked to himself while I rolled my eyes at him.

"We have a name for you." I nodded to Centipede.

"KATO's had contact with Burry and Elmer Architecture," she said. "Dating back several years ago."

"Give me one second." He pushed a few keys on his keyboard. His face disappeared from the screen and was replaced with the intel he'd found. "Okay, here are the basics." He put a picture of the firm on the screen along with the address in Geneva, Switzerland.

"That's not far from here," Centipede said.

"It's about an hour and forty minutes by car," Sam said.

"An hour and ten if I'm driving," my dad said.

"All right, then," Sam said, laughing. "I guess you found your driver." He continued sending the intel to the screen. "I'll start going through the systems I have access to. I should be able to get a copy of the office layout. Mr. Burry is the CEO. I'll figure out where his office is. That'll give you access to every structure they've ever designed. And if you have me patched into the comms while you're in the field, I can tell you how to hack his password. If I were at the IDA, I could probably save you the trip."

"It's okay, it's close enough," I said. "We'll touch base with you before we head out tomorrow."

"Copy that." He disconnected, and I turned back to face the room.

"I'll work on getting us a van," my dad said, pulling out his phone and stepping out of the room.

"We can't move on the offices until tomorrow night," Nikki said, stepping forward. "In the meantime, there's a room upstairs for the three of you. We only have three rooms, so you'll have to share—but I've heard you're used to that."

Slowly, the three of them moved for the stairs.

"Did you tell them about the doors?" my dad asked, coming out of the kitchen.

I shook my head. "They can figure it out on their own."

He laughed lightly. "You two get some sleep. I'll keep watch for the night."

"Are you sure?" I asked. We had agreed that one person should be awake at all times with these girls in the house. But they were my responsibility. I should be the one up first.

He waved me on. "Go ahead. This is something I can do for you."

I shifted uncomfortably, unconvinced.

"Really." He tilted his head toward the stairs insistently. "Go."

Still, I hesitated, trying to come up with a better argument.

He sighed. "Jocelyn, I didn't just come here to supervise. I came to help you. Let me."

I blinked, giving my brain time to adjust to the idea. "Okay," I said after a moment. "Thank you."

He settled into the couch with a small smile on his face as Nikki and I headed upstairs.

. . .

I was the first one up the next morning, giving my dad an opportunity to get some sleep before the others woke. Sam had sent the office layout along, so I spent most of the morning combing through it, coming up with a more concrete plan. I went over it a few dozen times, considering every possible problem until a mug of tea appeared next to me. I glanced up, and found Nikki standing over me.

"Thanks," I said as she took a seat.

"Stop overthinking this," she said, as if she could read my mind. I had walked her through my plan when she first got up half an hour earlier. "It's a good plan—as good as we're going to get. You have a way in that should keep anyone from being detected, and we know the rough location of the blueprints. Obviously, anything can happen, but you've considered as many possibilities as you could."

I exhaled, nodding. "Yeah," I said, but I still felt anxious. I felt too—alone—and too trusted with all of this. It didn't matter that Nikki was making sense.

She shifted so she was facing me more fully. "Can I ask you something?" I nodded, though I was almost afraid of what was coming next. "While I'm *thrilled* to get out of the IDA, why am I here and not Travis?"

I bit my lip and sunk back into the couch. "Because he didn't want to be."

Nikki arched her eyebrows. "I know you said he was mad, but I have a hard time believing that."

I had briefed her on how the team came together on the plane ride over, so she was up to speed. "Well, he opted out and Simmonds let him. He didn't want to give Venom a chance."

"Yeah," she said, grimacing. "He can be—difficult—sometimes."

"When Travis asked to stay behind, I knew I needed backup," I said. "You've *always* given me a shot. I needed someone who would back me, and give them the same opportunity."

She smiled. "Well, you *did* pick the right person for that."

She sat with me for a few more minutes. When she stood to leave, she paused for a moment before gathering my plans in her arms.

"Wait, what are you doing?" I tried to take them back, but she pulled them out of my reach.

"You've thought about this enough. Stop second-guessing yourself and try to relax."

I glared after her, but she never looked back.

I spent most of the morning in the living room, keeping an eye on the stairs, waiting for one of the girls to surface. They ventured out a couple times when they were hungry—the safe house had plenty of protein bars and other food that could be grabbed and eaten quickly. They barely talked, which wasn't too surprising. That was the kind of environment they were used to. We were planning to move at eleven o'clock that night, giving us the cover of dark. At five, we met in the living room again to discuss the mission.

All four of us were going in. It was really a two-person job, but I knew there was no way anyone would be happy staying behind. Plus with more of us we could get through the search faster.

I brought Sam in for one last update before I went over the final plan.

"Do you have a name we should be looking for?" I asked him.

"There's a Park Bo Yeon listed from about three years ago," he said. "The money trail comes from North Korea. It has to be that. I also found that Burry upgraded his safe right around that time. I have a feeling that wasn't a coincidence."

I turned to the others. "Do any of you have safecracking experience?" As a rule, that was one skill KATO wasn't big on teaching. We had been trained to get people to open the safe for us and then kill them.

I was surprised when Misty raised her hand. "I taught myself," she said. "I may be able to hold my own in a fight, but it wasn't something I wanted to count on. I learned to use other methods when I could help it. I'm not an expert, but I have some experience."

I nodded. "It's more than the rest of us have."

"I'll send the safe details to Echo so you know what you're dealing with," Sam said. He disconnected as Nikki grabbed her tablet and headed for the printer. I turned back to the others.

"Venom, you're the quickest and quietest," I said. "You're going to get us in. Then we move to the office *together*. When we get there, I'll take the computer to get digital copies of the blueprints or anything else that's relevant. Venom, Centipede, you guys are going to search for the hard copies in case anything's written on them that hasn't been backed up electronically. Misty, you've got the safe. Who knows what we'll find in there. KATO will have done their best to get rid of a paper trail, but you can only build a building so quietly." I looked to each of them, but their expressions were too neutral for me to get a read on. "I know this is a little different from what you're used to, but it's the same job you've always been doing. Only this time, we all have the same mission."

"We got it," Centipede said.

Misty nodded. "It's pretty straightforward."

My dad handed out comms to each of us.

"What are these for?" Venom asked. She pinched the device between her thumb and forefinger, holding it close to her face, scrutinizing.

"They're so we can keep in touch with each other, and with Command and Echo, while we're on the assignment," I said.

"You also can't use your KATO code names in the field," Nikki said. "If someone from KATO were to overhear, your cover would be blown."

"Then what do we call ourselves?" Venom asked.

"I have new code names for each of you." Nikki smiled. "Centipede, you'll be Condor. Venom, you're Vulture, and Misty, you're Magpie."

I smirked at her. "Really? All birds?"

"It seemed fitting," she said with a shrug. "Here's what you need to know about the safe." She passed the papers off to Misty.

"What's your code name?" Centipede asked me.

"Raven."

My dad cleared his throat. "We leave here tonight at nine fifty. Be ready to go."

They all nodded and dispersed quickly again, separating between the upstairs and the kitchen. I found myself feeling uneasy. They had never worked like this before. It was a simple assignment, yet it felt like there were so many things that could go wrong.

Nikki came up next to me, meeting my eyes one more time. "You can do this," she said. I nodded, but there was a gnawing feeling in my gut that told me this wasn't going to be as easy as she made it out to be.

Chapter Twenty-Three

IN SWITZERLAND

Everyone was ready on time, and the ride into Switzerland was a quiet one. My dad had been accurate in his time estimation. We rolled up to the side entrance of the building an hour and twelve minutes after we had left. "I'll be on the back road when you're finished. If you need me, I'm on comms," he said, popping the earbud in. "Keep your heads down and stay together." Then he looked me dead in the eyes, silently telling me to be careful. I nodded once and led them out of the car.

"Command," I said into my comm. "We're right outside." Sam had told me once my tablet was within range of the security system, he should be able to get access.

"Copy," he said. "I have a live feed of the cameras. Security sees a loop from the past ten minutes. You guys are hidden."

Venom dropped down in front of the lock to pick it.

"Anything on the first floor?" I asked.

"There are security guards at the front desk," Sam said. "Otherwise the floor is clear."

"We're in," Centipede said as Venom cracked the lock.

Centipede took a step forward and I grabbed the back of her shirt, pulling her behind me. I needed to be the one to lead them in. She shot me a mildly irritated look, but she fell in line in front of

Misty, with Venom bringing up the rear. We crept down a hallway on the left side of the building, headed for the emergency staircase in the back. It would drop us off a little farther away from the CEO's office than I would have liked, but it was also the farthest from the front desk security.

"You're coming up on the fourth floor," Sam said as we snaked up the steps. "The office is at the end of the hallway and you'll have a clear shot to it."

I led them down the hall, stepping aside when we got to the office so Venom could get us in. She had us inside in under ten seconds.

It was a sizable office, with a large glass desk on one side and a white slatted door that ran along the back wall. I pulled the door open to reveal a shallow closet with filing cabinets that went from one side to the other. "You guys know what to do." The three of them pulled out flashlights and got to work, while I took a seat at the desk. "Okay, Command, talk me through this."

Misty came up behind me. "I can do it," she said. She held her flashlight between her teeth and started typing. A few seconds later I had access.

I pushed my comm in. "Never mind. I'm in."

"Wow," Sam said. "I'm impressed."

Misty stepped away like it was nothing. "Yeah," I said, "me too."

"All right," Sam said, "you're looking for a contract under the name Park from three years ago." Out of the corner of my eye I noticed Misty had found a safe hidden in a wall panel and was already working to crack it.

I focused on my own task. "I found him." There wasn't an address of the location anywhere in the file, but I wasn't expecting there to be. KATO wouldn't take that kind of risk. I had the prints up on the screen. Behind me, Venom and Centipede were riffling through the filing cabinet, while Misty had gotten the safe open and started combing through the documents. She found a large envelope and paged through it.

"I have emails from Park dated two days ago. It looks like there's some kind of security issue with the KATO building he wants fixed," Misty said. "I also have pictures. It seems that KATO threatened the CEO's family." She flipped through the photos and froze.

"What is it?" I asked. She turned the picture around. There was a house in the background, which I imagined was the Burrys'. In the foreground there was a hand holding a gun. A hand with a very distinctive scar on the webbing.

"Park Bo Yeon is an alias for Jin Su," Misty said. That got Centipede and Venom's attention. They both whipped around to stare at the picture. I saw a flash of fear in their eyes.

I breathed through my nose, trying to figure out how to handle this, but Sam interrupted before I got the chance. "Raven, I've got some kind of alarm going off in that office."

I tensed and saw the others had done the same. The room was quiet, so it had to be a silent alarm. "Can you shut it down?"

"I already did, but you've got two security guards headed your way," he said. "You won't make it out unseen. Find a place to hide."

I closed out of the blueprints and powered off the monitor. Misty closed the safe, taking the envelope with her, while Venom and Centipede shut the filing cabinets. I did a quick assessment of the room. There was a ventilation shaft coming out of the wall we could use. I got to work loosening the grate. Out of the corner of my eye, I saw Venom jump up to grab the lip of the shelf that ran along the top of the closet.

"You have about thirty seconds," Sam said.

Venom hoisted herself up and rolled to the back of the shelf. It was deep. The only way she'd be spotted is if the guard stood on the desk. Centipede eyed the jump, looking less than thrilled at the prospect, but followed Venom's lead. I pulled the vent out of the wall.

"Get in there and get as far back as you can," I said to Misty. She didn't ask questions. While she climbed in, I shut Venom and Centipede in the closet then jumped in the vent myself.

"Are you out of sight?" my dad asked.

"We are," I said. Even if we were found, we'd have the element of surprise. Though I'd have to imagine no one in this building could handle four KATO-trained spies even if they were prepared.

We weren't hidden for more than five seconds when I heard the key in the lock.

"This is probably a false alarm, but let's do a search," a man said in French. I sent a silent thanks to Sam for disabling the alarm so quickly—it had to be part of why the man believed this to be false. Misty and I were still as the flashlight splashed into the edge of the vent. We were far enough back not to be seen, but that did little to relax either of us.

I heard the closet door open and held my breath.

"It's clear," the second guard said.

Their flashlights ran around the room one final time before they left the office. None of us moved a muscle until Sam gave us the word.

I popped out of the air duct and opened the closet door for Centipede and Venom, who landed as Misty rolled out of the ventilation shaft.

"We need to get what we came for and get out of here," I said, sitting back down at the computer to finish copying the intel.

"She cannot come with us," Venom said. I looked back at her and found her staring at Misty.

"She's right," Centipede said. "Misty tripped the alarm. And *we* were nearly found because of her."

Misty shook her head. "I told you I wasn't an expert. None of you could do any better."

"Hey!" I snapped at them. This was their KATO training showing. We were taught to eliminate any weaknesses and at the moment that meant Misty. "We need to complete the *mission* right now."

"I think I have a copy of the blueprints in here," Misty said, shooting me a grateful look.

"Okay," I said, looking to Centipede and Venom. "Then you two do one last check for any files under the name Park or dated April of three years ago." Neither looked convinced, but they got back to work anyway. Their need to complete the mission overrode everything else.

We finished our tasks in silence. Centipede came up with a contract just as the digitals finished copying.

"You guys need to get out of there," Sam said in our ears. "The guards are still sweeping the building. It's only a matter of time before you're caught."

"We stick *together*," I said, eyeing each of them. They agreed, though Centipede and Venom were more reluctant. "Command, the back is still clear, right?"

"Yes. Go!"

We crept swiftly down the back staircase, down the hall, and out the side door. We moved for the back of the building, hurrying around the corner until I saw the van idling ahead of us. I jumped in the front seat, leaving the back for the others.

Centipede started on me the second the door closed. "How can you let her stay after her weakness?"

"I think we need to talk about who's involved in this," Misty argued. "That's more important."

"Not more important than being caught," Venom said.

"We are a team!" I spun in my seat to face all of them. "We don't kick someone out simply because they made a mistake. This isn't KATO!"

Centipede wasn't interested. "This is my life—"

"Whoa," my dad said. "What the hell is going on here?"

"The alarm went off because Misty opened the safe," I said. "Now these two want to kick her out."

"But I also found out Jin Su is involved," Misty said. "I found a picture."

My dad glanced at me uneasily, but didn't say anything. It turned out he didn't have to.

"Wait," Centipede said, leaning forward. "You don't seem as surprised as we are to find out he's a part of this." She looked between the two of us. "Has he been connected before now?"

I pursed my lips and my dad looked straight ahead.

"You knew the director of KATO was involved in this and you didn't tell us!" Centipede said, her voice raised.

"I—it didn't come up." I had made sure it didn't come up.

Each of their faces were hard with anger, even Misty's.

"You know how hard I worked to stay unknown—to make it this long," she said. "He's who I've been hiding from!" She stared at me, and it was clear that while she may have appreciated my support inside, it would only get me so much as far as this issue was concerned.

"With everything we're risking, you don't think we need to know that the person in charge of us could show up out of nowhere?" Centipede asked.

"I wasn't sure if we could trust you!" I argued back. "I didn't want you to know how close we were to the director until I was sure." Of course, there was more to it than that, but I was afraid of the damage the truth could do.

"You ask us to trust you and you can't trust us?" Venom asked. She didn't yell. She never yelled. But her voice chilled my soul. It looked like this approach wouldn't earn me any favors. "And you also want to keep weak people?"

"I'm not weak!" Misty snapped. "You needed someone to crack the safe and I did!"

I started to talk as Centipede initiated another attack. Then Venom jumped in, her voice raised loud enough to be heard, and Misty refused to go down quietly.

"All right," my dad said, attempting to cut through all four of us. It had little impact. "That's enough!" He shouted this time and the car finally got quiet. "Now, I don't want to hear another word out of any of you until we can get back to the house and figure this out."

"But we need—" Centipede started, but my father silenced her with a hard glare in the rearview mirror. The five of us stewed the entire ride home.

Chapter Twenty-Four

DEEPER ISSUES

Misty had dropped the envelope of papers on my lap shortly after my dad silenced us. It was what she pulled out of the safe. I flipped through it. It was the hard copy of KATO's blueprints along with the original and more recent correspondence between the agency and the architect. It looked like KATO found a history of corruption in the CEO and used it to blackmail him into the job three years ago. It also seemed that Burry was led to believe that this building was for a Korean corporation, though Jin Su had still made sure that Burry knew he was someone to be feared. The threats had started almost immediately after the two had entered into the agreement. It was a combination of both pictures and messages. It also looked like he had done something to rattle Burry's family, but the emails didn't discuss the details. The more current emails addressed the security problem Misty had mentioned.

I was almost positive KATO would never find out we had the intel. There's no way Burry was supposed to have held on to this information, and mentioning the theft would mean letting Jin Su know that he had it in the first place. Aside from the blueprints, I didn't think it would be too relevant to our operation, but I'd turn it over to Sam anyway.

Nikki was waiting in the living room when we got back. "Well, that looked like an eventful assignment."

I shook my head. "That's one word for it." I heard the girls talking and moving upstairs behind me, but I didn't so much as glance at them.

"You did a good job getting everybody out," Nikki said. She gestured to the monitor. "Command wants to talk to you."

I stepped past her to face Sam. "What's up?"

"I'm sorry I missed that alarm," he said. "I just went over the schematics again, and there's nothing there. It must have been added with the safe upgrade."

I waved him off. "Don't worry about it. You're on your own, and you didn't have much time to prep. You got us in and out, which is all that matters."

He smiled. "I actually did a little more than that." His eyes had a mischievous glint. "I was able to hold on to the building's network. That means I can monitor Burry's emails and find out if he's sending a crew anywhere."

"You're a genius." I pulled out the flashdrive with the blueprints. "I'm going to have Echo send you the blueprints and copies of some other documents we pulled so you can get that search started. There's supposedly a security issue. We'll make finding that our priority if you can work on getting a location for us."

"I'm on it," Sam said. "I'll check back when I have something."

I turned away from him and saw the others had resettled in the living room. They were all watching me, with varying degrees of hurt and anger on their faces.

"You know what," Nikki said as she grabbed a laptop. "I'm going to send this from the kitchen."

I glanced at her as she left, wishing I could follow. But hiding wouldn't fix this problem.

"You kept the director from us," Misty said, as if I needed the reminder.

"I had a good reason to—"

"You put us at risk!" Centipede talked over me. "Twice in one mission."

"Our *first* mission," Venom said. "And still, you keep the weak one."

Misty rounded on Venom. "I. Am not. Weak."

They were all shouting again, but not one of them was listening to anyone else. I tried to weigh in, but every time I talked they all got louder. It took a sharp whistle from my dad to silence them.

"Okay," he said, once everyone had shut up. "Everyone needs to take a breath." He looked at each of us. "We need to *talk* about what went wrong back there. Not yell. *Talk*."

"Where have you been?" Centipede asked him. "First Viper won't cut dead weight, and then we find out she's been lying to us."

I rounded on her. I had finally reached my limit. "In case you forgot, it was just yesterday that you were withholding information that would have gotten me recaptured and destroyed the agency that's trying to help you. So you don't have much room to talk." It was a low blow, especially given what I knew about her situation, but right then I didn't care.

Centipede squared herself to me. "You are asking me to risk *everything*!"

"All right, one thing at a time," my dad said, talking over us before another fight could break out. "As far as the mission goes, it looks to me that Misty volunteered to do a job none of you could do, and that you two"—he pointed at Centipede and Venom—"were ready to cut her off the instant it wasn't done perfectly." He was wearing an expression similar to the one Travis had after our first mission as partners.

"Yes, that is what needed to be done," Venom said, bowing her head. "She is a problem."

Misty opened her mouth to defend herself again, but my dad didn't give her the chance. "Misty got into that safe and got us intel that we would not otherwise have had."

"She almost got us caught," Centipede said. "How can we go into a KATO building with her?"

"It could have happened to any of you." I had forgotten how much patience my dad could have when the situation called for it. "You're on a team now. You don't abandon your team—especially in the field. You help each other."

Centipede crossed her arms. "You can't expect me to risk my life for someone—especially someone who doesn't tell the whole story." She glared at me.

"What do you want from me?" I asked her. "I needed your help and I was afraid none of you would sign on if you knew the director was poking around!" I hadn't meant to be so honest, but she had finally pushed me.

The three of them stared at me evenly.

"How long have you known?" Misty asked. Her eyebrows arched, pointedly.

I bit my tongue, wishing I could take it all back. But it was too late. "Since we pulled Eliza out of the safe house."

Centipede's eyes narrowed as her anger intensified. "*Before* you brought any of us into this."

I swallowed but forced myself to nod. "I needed you on board," I said. "My focus was on getting to KATO and this seemed like the best way."

"If that is your goal, I could kill him," Venom said, with a shrug. "You just have to find him for me."

"That won't solve our bigger problem," I said. Centipede opened her mouth again but I talked before she could. I couldn't hear any more from her right now. "We need a break." My dad looked at me sharply, and I shook him off before he could disagree. "Just an hour to clear our heads." We were talking circles and going nowhere.

He still looked like he wanted to say something, but Nikki, who had obviously been eavesdropping, appeared in the kitchen door. "If anyone is interested," she said, "there's training equipment in the basement. I found it while you guys were out."

Venom considered her for a moment, then nodded. "Yes, I would enjoy hitting something."

"I don't think we're finished with this," Centipede said. I shot her a weary look, and my dad stepped up to back me.

After a tense glare, Centipede followed Venom into the kitchen and toward the basement door.

"Is there room to run?" Misty asked.

Nikki shrugged. "It's tight, but you could probably make it work."

She joined the others, leaving me and my father alone.

"I understand what you're trying to do," he said, "but I'm not sure you have an hour to waste."

"We need to be able to go after the serum together and we are never going to get there like this," I said. "I need to talk to them, but they're not listening to me. I need a new approach, and I need them not to be here while I think this through."

My dad nodded. "I guess giving them time to cool down couldn't hurt."

"At the very least, I'll be more prepared to handle them," I said with a grimace. I really wasn't sure it would change anything. "For now, I'll start going over the blueprints. At least that way the hour won't be a complete waste."

"All right. I'm going to monitor the situation downstairs. I don't want Nikki left alone with them," he said. "I'll check in with you before we regroup."

I nodded as he left, appreciating that I could finally hear my own thoughts.

. . .

I had the prints spread across the coffee table. I'd taken the hour to page through them and do my best to get a rough understanding of the building. The deeper I got into this, the more detrimental the disagreement with the girls felt. I needed to win them back. But I knew better than anyone how fragile trust amongst KATO agents was. There was a chance I'd done too much damage.

"You ready to try this again?" my dad asked from the kitchen threshold.

"I'm honestly not sure," I said.

He crossed the room and sat down next to me, taking in the blue-prints on the table. "You know we got so caught up with the *excitement* earlier, we never talked about what you came away with."

I smiled lightly. "Yeah, I guess the mission was a success. And we didn't just get the prints. We also learned that the building has an issue with security."

"If you can find the flaw, you can use the weakness to get inside."

I slid back, pulling away from the plans. "Though none of that will matter if I can't get them on the same page again."

My dad nudged my knee reassuringly. "You will."

I glanced at him uncertainly. "What makes you so sure?"

"Well," he said, shrugging. "They're all still here."

I tilted my head, letting his words sink in. "They are, aren't they?'

He smiled. "Yeah."

He was right. If they were still here, they had to want this to work on some level. That meant I still had a chance. I scanned the blue-prints again. "Still, we don't have a lot of time. We need to find the security problem and take advantage of it before it gets fixed."

My dad shifted, running his hand along his jaw uncomfortably. "I've been trying really hard to let you do your job here, but I'm not going to be okay with you rushing into a KATO facility—with only KATO agents as backup—because you think you're on a clock."

I bit my lip hard, because his concern was perfectly valid. But we *needed* this serum. There wasn't time for my fears. "We *are* on a clock," I said. "And I can handle it." I wasn't sure I *wanted* to handle it, but I could.

His mouth formed a thin line and I kept my attention on the

papers so I didn't have to look at him. "What'll happen to you if you get caught?" he asked. "Or if one of those girls downstairs turns you in?" I closed my eyes, desperate to keep my mind away from that place, but my dad pushed. "I believe they *want* to be here," he said. "But if something goes wrong, I don't trust them to help you. If it's between them or you, they're going to look out for themselves. Tonight was proof enough of that."

I thought about Eliza, and of the damage KATO could do. "It doesn't matter. I can handle myself. We need this serum."

"It *does* matter." Something flared in his eyes, but he quieted it quickly. "You still won't tell me what happened to you in there." I tensed immediately, afraid of what might come next. "I'm not asking about it again," he said, reading me. "You've made yourself clear. But the fact that you won't talk says plenty."

"I'm good enough to do this," I said, speaking through my teeth. I *needed* to do this. KATO was too close to too much power.

"I believe you are. But not rushed and not alone like you are now." He leaned closer, as if to be sure I heard what he was saying. "I know you're in this to help Eliza and stop KATO, and I want you to do those things. But not at your own expense." He met my eyes fiercely. "You may be fearless, but I'm not. And I will not lose you again."

I drew a sharp breath, trying to sift through the series of emotions that came with what he was saying. It was too much at once, and I couldn't find the right words—or *any* words.

"Whether you find the flaw or not, you need to make a sound plan. Doing this any differently is too dangerous and I will tie you down to keep you here if I have to." He stood and headed back for the kitchen. "For now, we'll focus on getting this team back together. But you need to think this through."

I watched him go, struggling to keep up with everything he had just said, but I did my best to push it aside once his footsteps faded. I had a more crucial conversation to prepare for.

Chapter Twenty-Five

RESTORED

While I didn't appreciate that my father had threatened to hold me back from an assignment, it meant a lot that he cared enough to try. It also didn't hurt that he was right. Racing into the facility without a solid plan was stupid. Repairing things with Centipede, Venom, and Misty was the first step to doing this right, and I was prepared to do whatever I had to—even if it meant being completely honest with them.

I stood when I heard them coming up the stairs. The three of them entered the room looking sweaty, but no less angry than they had an hour ago.

I stepped aside, gesturing to them to take the couch.

Centipede crossed her arms. "I'd rather stand."

She was still looking for a fight, but I wasn't going to give it to her.

"If you didn't want this to work, you'd already be gone," I said, arching my eyebrow. "So let's sit and figure this out."

Her lips pursed, but she didn't move. After a moment, Misty caved and took a seat, followed closely by Venom. Centipede glared at them, annoyed, but joined them with a huff.

Once they were settled, I sat down in the chair closest to Misty.

"I'm sorry I didn't tell you about Jin Su," I said. They stayed quiet, but I knew I had surprised them. "I was asking a lot from each of you, and you should have known exactly what you were signing up for."

Each of their expressions held some combination of shock and uncertainty. Centipede recovered first. "I don't know how you can expect us to follow you anywhere."

"Would it help if I said you were right?" I stunned her back into silence. At KATO we didn't admit defeat in any form. Not ever. It was seen as another sign of weakness. And I'd just done it for the second time in this conversation. "I didn't really trust you. I wanted to, but—" I shook my head. My reasons were too complicated and ultimately beside the point. "But I'm trusting you now. And I'm hoping you'll trust me too."

"Must we trust everyone?" Venom asked, glaring at Misty.

Misty's head whipped around, but I spoke before she could.

"Yes," I said. "Because the only way we're going to survive is if we protect each other. We're teammates, and teammates have each other's backs no matter what." I met each of their eyes. "Misty may have been the reason those guards came to that office, but something like that could have happened to any one of us. The only thing that gets you kicked out of this group is betrayal."

Again, there was another long silence. They were quiet for so long I was beginning to grow concerned. Then Centipede spoke.

"So," she said, talking slowly. "If I agree to this, how would it work?"

I tried not to smile. The fact that she was asking this at all meant I all but had her. "We look out for one another. If one of us is in trouble, we help—we don't blame or threaten to cut someone out." They were watching me so intently they didn't seem to be blinking. "We consider each other before we act. If something happens and plans need to be changed mid-mission, you don't make any decision until you consider how it would affect each of us. And we don't keep intel from each other."

"That goes for you too?" Misty asked, eyeing me skeptically.

I nodded. "It does." Obviously, that wouldn't apply to IDA secrets, but if I had intel that was relevant to them, I would share it.

"Okay, then," she said, relaxing into the couch.

"If I see someone trying to hurt one of you," Venom said, "I will stop them."

"Right." I smiled lightly. "You should."

I turned to Centipede, eyeing her pointedly.

She sighed, resigned. "Your terms are acceptable."

I held her gaze. "You won't regret this."

"We'll see about that after this mission," she said, shifting forward. "What have you found out about the building?"

I walked them through what little I had worked out on my own, highlighting my intent to find the weakness if we could and build a plan around that. My dad had interrupted us shortly after, suggesting that we work in shifts, with one team studying the prints while the second team rests. This way we'd have people working on this around the clock. He had also proposed himself, Centipede, and Venom for the first shift. I started to argue, but he pushed the issue, and I'd had enough fighting for one day. So I caved and led my group up the stairs while the others got to work.

. . .

It was nearly four in the morning when we went to sleep, so it was almost noon when we got up. My dad briefed me on what they'd found, which wasn't much. Whatever the security issue was, it was difficult to nail down. However, they were able to isolate a few areas of weakness, if we ended up needing a different plan of attack.

Nikki, Misty, and I got to work at once. We passed pages back and forth, taking turns to make sure nothing got missed. I had done my best to learn everything I could about reading blueprints, but nothing seemed to tip me off to the problem that Jin Su had found.

"I don't know," Nikki said after a few hours. We had looked at these blueprints a million different ways, and I was going cross-eyed from all of the lines and symbols. "This security looks perfect."

"It can't be," I said. "Jin Su's emails were too insistent for that to be true."

"It's not surprising that it's so complex," Misty said. "It took KATO this long to find."

I fought the urge to pull my hair out. "We don't even have days, let alone the years it seems to have taken them."

A rhythmic beep shot through the room, making me freeze. I isolated the sound quickly. It was coming from the front door. Someone was trying to access the house.

I jumped to my feet and moved swiftly to the weapons case on the other side of the room. I had a gun in my hand just as the door opened. I whirled around, gun out, ready to fire.

"Whoa!" It was Travis. He had his hands up, eyeing me cautiously.

I pointed my gun at the floor and glared at him. "What are you doing here? And why are you sneaking in like this?"

"Yeah, Scorpion," Nikki said. She had a hand on Misty's arm, keeping her from joining me at the weapons case. "What *are* you doing here?" Travis narrowed his eyes in exasperation. "Oh, look at the time! We should go—call Command and give him an update." Nikki flashed a smile at me and grabbed Misty, pulling her to her feet.

"What?" Misty asked, startled. "Who is that?"

Nikki gathered half the blueprints and pushed Misty toward the stairs. "Just come with me. We have work to do." Misty was so confused, she didn't seem to be able to do anything other than what she was told.

I turned to Travis once they were gone, trying to decide how to feel. I hadn't liked doing this without him, but I also hadn't forgotten that he was the one who asked not to come.

He shrugged uncertainly. "I heard you needed help."

"I do need help." There was no point in denying it. We were dealing with KATO. "But I don't want to fight you for it."

His eyes settled on me, his face open and honest. "I didn't come here to fight. Really."

I arched an eyebrow. "You know there are still three KATO agents upstairs, right? Venom included."

He put his hands on his hips. "Can you please not make this harder than it has to be?"

I watched him for a moment, weighing my options. On some level, I wanted to be stubborn and send him away, but a bigger part of me hated that idea. So I nodded. "Fine." I put the gun away and came back to the couch. He followed my lead.

I let the quiet settle before speaking again. "I'm really surprised you showed up. You were dead against it when I left."

He let out a sigh so deep it could only have been fueled by exhaustion. "Yeah, well, you didn't seem to want me anywhere near this."

My forehead tightened. "What are you talking about?"

He squinted at me, like he couldn't tell if was serious or not. "I wouldn't blame you. After how I acted, I understand."

"Travis, I really don't know what you're talking about," I said, racking my brain

He twisted so his shoulders were squared to me. "I said I wasn't coming and you didn't put up a fight," he said. "What else was I supposed to think?"

It never occurred to me he would see it like this. I leaned forward, resting my elbows on my knees and lacing my fingers together. "I *did* want you here. Badly." I couldn't look at him when I spoke. I felt too exposed. "But if you didn't want to be a part of this, I wasn't going to beg you." I paused, summoning the strength to continue. "I didn't like when you weren't around."

He squeezed my forearm, and I pulled my eyes up to meet his. "It seems to me like you've done pretty well on your own." He smiled lightly and I knew he was trying to be reassuring, but I shook my head.

"That's not the issue. I can do a lot on my own. It's all I've ever known." I swallowed. "But I liked not *having* to. I liked having a partner and knowing you had my back."

He closed his eyes for a second and I could see he was starting to understand. "I'm sorry I let this get so bad."

I relaxed a fraction. "It wasn't just you."

"Yeah, but—" He shook his head, cutting himself off. Then his jaw flexed as he collected his thoughts. "I'm not used to being the second-best agent at the IDA." He tilted his head, so he was looking at me again. "I can handle that you're better than me. Because you are. You always have been. The only reason I'm alive at all is because you decided not to kill me."

"That's true," I said.

He fought off a smirk to glare at me. "The part I don't do well with is when people—when *you*—don't listen to me."

"You weren't listening to me either," I said, crossing my arms. "And I'm not going to do something just because you tell me to."

"I'm not saying you should." His voice strained as he tried to contain his frustration. "But you *never* tried to see my side of things with Venom." He looked to the floor. "I didn't really know what to do when that happened."

My brow furrowed as I thought back over our last exchange. He was right. I didn't want to hear what he had to say. "You have a point," I said. "But you didn't hear me out either."

His eyes widened slightly. "Oh, I heard what you were saying. I just didn't like it."

"I'm not sure that's any better."

He thought for a moment. "Yeah, I guess it's not," he said. "I'm sorry." Then he sighed. "We're good together because we make each other better. I make sure you don't get us killed." He looked at me pointedly. "But you push me to try things I never thought I could do. I am, without a doubt, a better agent because of you."

I nodded, seeing his point. "And you've made me think about things more," I said. "And made me less—reckless."

He smiled. "So, can I ask you something?" I nodded. "You fought me to keep this operation a lot harder than I expected, especially given the risks to you specifically. Why?"

I looked at the table in front of me, which was still covered in papers. I wasn't sure I wanted to share. But he was here, and asking, and willing to listen. And I didn't want to shut him out anymore. "At first, I hated how helpless it felt to lose the upper hand on KATO," I said. "This team seemed like the fastest and most effective way to chip away at them. But once I met these girls—" I hunched forward and rubbed the center of my forehead, trying not to think of how hard Misty worked to hide, the bruises on Centipede's neck, or what must have happened to make Venom so delighted by death. Travis put a hand on my back, sensing I needed the encouragement. I rolled my head to the side so I could look him in the eye. "It's easy to think of everyone at KATO as terrible people, but not all of them are. What happened to me is still happening to those girls. They're living my nightmares every day, and I asked them to take this huge risk. I need to make sure they make it out."

He moved his thumb across my spine and I couldn't help but feel calmer. "You have a good heart," he said, meeting my eyes.

Half a laugh snuck out of me, but it was powered by relief. "I'm really glad you're here."

"I am too," he said, tipping his head closer. "I promise I'll hear you out the next time we disagree on something if you'll do the same."

"Yeah. Okay." I bit my lip. "But if for some reason I don't, I need you to be there until I do."

He gave me a small smile. "I can live with that."

"And Venom?" I asked. "You know she's still here."

"I'm still not sure how I feel about her being involved," he said.

"But I trust you." He held my eyes, as if he needed to be certain I understood.

"Thank you."

He nodded, then took in the table in front of us. "Now, what are you working on here?" He pulled a page of the blueprints closer.

"It's the building that has the serum." Nikki had taken a handful of the pages upstairs, but had apparently left us with the lower floors.

"You're sure?" he asked.

I shrugged. "As sure as we can be. Jin Su's been in touch with the builder." Travis looked at me sharply. "He said in an email that the security was compromised in the building and threatened the builders so they would fix it. The only reason I can come up with for him to personally oversee this would be if the serum is involved."

"So you're trying to find the problem and use it to get easy access to the serum?"

"That's the idea," I said. "He said it's a security issue, but the six of us have been combing over these pages all day and can't find any serious weaknesses. Maybe you'll find something we didn't."

"Before we do that," he said, "you need to fill me in on what I've missed."

I launched into a detailed account of everything that had happened in the past few days. It felt like a balance had been restored, and I found myself more determined than ever.

My dad had called me fearless, but my conversation with Travis had reminded me that I wasn't. I was afraid of a lot. I just had no intentions of letting that fear stop me. I may not be fearless, but I certainly wasn't helpless. And that was a lesson KATO still needed to learn.

Chapter Twenty-Six

LOCKING IN

I had just finished bringing Travis up to speed when my tablet lit up on the table. It was Sam.

"KATO girl!" Then he caught sight of Travis. "And Agent Elton. I didn't realize you were around." Travis gave Sam a salute.

"Did you find a location?" I asked.

"Not yet," he said. "I'm working on a theory for that. But Nikki said you guys were having a hard time nailing down the security issue, and I think I have your answer."

"What did you find?" Travis asked.

"I was going through some of our CEO's emails and I found one from right after the building was finished." Sam pulled the email up on the screen. "Because CEO Burry was under the impression that he was building a corporate building, he had it wired with a high-tech, built-in, top-of-the-line security system. It wasn't until after he turned the building over to KATO that he realized his mistake."

I nodded, understanding. "KATO doesn't want an outside security system. They have their own security."

"Exactly," Sam said. "Now, Burry realized this and had the third party monitoring cut off before KATO moved in. But the thing with this advanced system is, in order to truly shut it down, you have to both deactivate the monitoring and deactivate the building on sight. Something, according to these emails, Burry was too afraid to do."

Travis leaned forward into the frame. "So what does that mean for us?"

Sam took the emails off the screen so we could see him again. "It means that this facility is still connected to the separate system. Even if it's not currently being monitored, the building is still live. If one of you can get inside the security company's offices, we can use this system to get into KATO's building, then hack into their security from there."

"So this is our way in," I said.

Sam nodded. "You guys sit tight for now. I'll check back in when I have a location." He disconnected and I dropped the tablet on top of the papers.

I leaned into the back of the couch. "There's nothing else we can do until we hear back from him."

Travis ran a hand along his jaw. "Is there someplace we can train while we wait?"

"Nikki says there's a training room in the basement," I said, smiling.

"Perfect." He gestured for me to lead the way.

. . .

I called Nikki down before we headed to the basement and filled her in on what Sam had said. She agreed to stay by her tablet in case he checked back in while we were training. Meanwhile, Misty had started looking over the few details Sam had come up with regarding the security situation. A lot of the technical details were over my head, but she seemed to know her way around a computer on our last mission. It wouldn't surprise me if hacking was another skill she picked up to avoid human interaction on KATO assignments.

Travis and I worked out for a little over an hour. We hadn't intended to go that long, but it had been a while since we had trained together and it seemed to be something we both missed. When we had finished, Travis settled in the living room to go over the blueprints. Since the rest of us had spent hours studying them, he still had some catching up to do.

Meanwhile, I moved into the kitchen. I wasn't all that hungry, but I knew I should eat. Nikki followed me.

"It's awfully strange Travis turned up out of the blue like that, huh?" she said, smirking.

I smiled sheepishly from behind an open cabinet. "Thank you."

She shrugged like it was nothing. "Your dad was worried about you going into this place without real IDA backup. And he wasn't the only one."

I settled on a protein bar, and leaned against the counter to eat it. "The backup definitely doesn't hurt. Especially now that a secondary location is coming into play."

She glanced at the clock on the wall. It was almost seven at night. "The others will probably be up soon."

"We should head back in," I said, tipping my head toward the living room. "I want to be ready to brief them."

My dad was the first one up, with Centipede and Venom not far behind him.

"Who are you?" Venom asked, eyes locking on Travis from the stairs.

"He's Scorpion. My partner," I said, introducing him. "He showed up to help a couple hours ago." My dad didn't seem all that surprised to find Travis sitting in the living room. He must have been in on this too.

"You were in Austria?" Centipede asked.

Travis nodded once. "I was."

Venom cocked her head to the side, then circled him slowly, scrutinizing. I watched Travis uncertainly, knowing how he felt about Venom. He looked uncomfortable, but didn't react otherwise. She turned back to me when she had finished her inspection. "His face is oddly shaped, but he looks useful."

Travis's expression told me that he was both clearly insulted and convinced Venom was as nuts as he had suspected. "My face is fine." He was slightly more defensive than necessary considering the source, and I had to fight to keep from smiling.

I brought us back to the issue at hand, walking my dad and the others through the details of what Sam had uncovered.

We had just finished going through the latest developments when Nikki appeared. "Command reached out. He has a location."

She turned the monitor on and Sam's face appeared on the screen on the mantel. "Wait until you hear how good I am," he said, smirking at the camera. "I scanned the world looking for a building that matched the blueprint, but came up empty. Then the architect sent an email ordering a small crew to Saudi Arabia. So I scanned the country again. Still nothing." He said all of this fairly quickly. "Then I took another look at the blueprints and noticed how strange the shape of the building is. It should be easy to find. Do you know why it isn't?" I had noticed some floors were a little longer than others, but I didn't think too much of it.

"Why?" Travis asked.

"Because they built it *in* a mountain." He pulled up the images. "I managed to get a thermal imaging scan and electrical outputs to confirm it."

"Okay," I said, taking this in. "So, we're going in a mountain."

"From what I can tell, the doors to the building line up with tunnels that were already in place," Sam said. "So, this is how it's situated." He showed us an outline of the mountain with the building inside it.

"Did you find out anything more about the independent security company?" I asked.

"They're called Phantac Security." He pulled up the company's logo. "They're an international company with offices around the world, including Saudi Arabia. They also have a base in France."

"Can we get access through the France location?"

Sam was quiet for a second as he double-checked something. "It looks like it. The monitoring for this particular building would have been in Saudia Arabia, but it appears it's all in one network, so we can get into this building from any Phantac office in the world. The one hitch is that one of you is going to have to run this on-site. Phantac's own security is *tight*. I could hack from here if I had time, but not if you're looking to move in the next twenty-four hours."

"Misty," I said, "can you get into their system?"

"I should be able to figure it out," she said with a one-shouldered shrug. "I've been looking over the intel, and it seems straightforward once you're on the inside. But this is a lot like the safe. I know my way around, but I'm not an expert."

"That's okay," Sam said. "I'll still be on comms to walk you through it. The French offices are in Paris. I'll send you the exact address."

"And I'll go with you," my dad said. My eyes jumped to him. "You'll need someone to keep the heat off of you if you're found. Besides, this isn't a job any of you should be doing alone."

Misty seemed uneasy, but nodded.

I looked to Sam. "We'll be in touch when we're ready to move."

He hung up and I turned back to the group.

"Now we need to plan our attack on the building," I said. "Retrieving the serum and any data related to it is our objective. And we want to do this as quietly as possible."

It took us two hours to sift through all the intel and come up with a cohesive plan.

"All right, each of us will be paired up," I said as we reached the final stages. "Echo, you're monitoring the situation from here. If we need to coordinate anything, we'll go through you."

Nikki held her cast out in front of her. "My broken arm and I will hold down the fort."

I smiled lightly. "Misty, you and Archer are in Paris; Venom, you're with Scorpion, going after the development files in the building supervisor's office." I glanced at Travis, hoping he would be okay with this. I knew how he felt about Venom. But when he didn't object,

I moved on. "Centipede, you're with me. We're getting the serum."

She nodded, agreeing easily.

"This will work if we each do our jobs," I said, looking to Centipede, Venom, and Misty in turn. They were silent and attentive. "We also need to keep our faces hidden," I said. "It can't get back to KATO that you're with us."

"That is no problem," Venom said. "I will kill anyone who sees us."

"We actually want to avoid doing that unless we absolutely have to," I said, trying not to be too harsh. "Once Misty is in the system, she'll get control of the cameras, so there won't be any record of you. We also have masks, hooded jackets, gloves, and everything we need to keep our identities hidden." My dad passed them around.

"What if something happens and they get a good look at us?" Centipede asked.

I swallowed. "Then we'll do what we have to." I still hadn't killed anyone that I was aware of since I started at the IDA. But I would not let Centipede or Venom's identities be exposed.

My answer hung in the air for a moment until Travis brought us back. "What's the on-site security like?"

I met his eyes, grateful for the redirection. "There will probably be guards stationed periodically throughout the facility," I said. "They're not spies. They're high-ranking soldiers with special clearance. I would bet their orders are to injure, not kill, if possible. KATO would undoubtedly want to interrogate any intruders."

"If you're retrieving something medical, there's a good possibility it'll need to be kept at a specific temperature," my dad said.

I reached inside my jacket and pulled out a small rectangular container. "Dr. March gave me this before we left. She said it will keep a sample at a consistent temperature for twenty-four hours. That should give us enough time to get back here and transfer it to the right environment."

"All right, then," my dad said. "I don't think there's anything else to discuss. You four need to get in the air." He looked to Misty. "I'll work on getting us a ride to Paris. Check in with each other as much as possible."

I exhaled a heavy, tight breath, and dug my hand into my side. I had kept my cool during the preparation because I needed them to feel confident. But we were going into another KATO facility, and that reality wasn't lost on me.

My dad came up next to me and grabbed ahold of my shoulders. "Be careful, okay?" His tone was serious, though not nearly as intense as it had been when we first started working together.

"I will." I flashed a smile at him. "I promise."

"I'll be listening, if you need anything," he said. He gave me a reassuring squeeze, and for a moment I felt calm. More calm than I ever could have hoped before a mission involving KATO. I stepped away from him, moving toward the door with the others.

. . .

Travis and I sat in the back of the plane, while Centipede and Venom each took a bench of their own closer to the front. We were headed for a mountain range in northern Saudi Arabia.

I was more in control than I ever had been when it came to dealing with KATO. This was an invasion we were initiating. We had a covert way in and a planned exit strategy. I was using three of their assets to pull everything together. Still, the closer we got to the mission, the more apprehensive I became. We were still dealing with KATO, and while they had yet to catch me, I couldn't shake the thought that it was only a matter of time. And I was also all too aware that I wasn't the only one at risk anymore.

I bounced my leg up and down, trying to release some anxiety. Travis put a hand on my knee, forcing it still.

He leaned into me. "You have done *everything* you can to be ready for this."

"I know," I said, exhaling slowly. "But it still doesn't feel like enough."

"You're not going in alone this time. I'll make sure you come back out."

I swallowed. "That's not all I'm worried about." My voice dropped even lower. "I know these girls are as invested as I could hope for, but there's still the very real possibility that they could turn on me. They've all proven they want to be here, but when they're threatened by KATO they get skittish. I know I have to keep them from feeling that way. I'm responsible for them, but I can only be so prepared."

"That sounds like it's a job for the both of us," he said, his eyebrows arched.

"Right. Sorry." I cringed. I'd gotten too used to this being my problem. I didn't mean to cut him out. "This just really needs to go well."

"It will." There was no trace of doubt in him.

"You are always way too sure when it comes to KATO," I said, sitting back in my seat.

He shook his head. "It's got nothing to do with them. I'm sure of *you*."

"I thought I was too reckless," I said, smirking.

"That's sort of what I'm counting on," he said, laughing. I shoved him and after a moment he got serious. "We both know you've come a long way. Although—" He cut himself off, eyeing me hesitantly.

I watched him questioningly, but he wasn't forthcoming. "Travis, just tell me," I said.

He debated for another beat before diving in. "I've told you a lot that you shouldn't be reckless, but that doesn't mean you should completely stifle yourself either."

My forehead tightened. "What are you talking about?"

"You told me once that you didn't want to get past your time at KATO because you wanted to use it against them. But you're not using it anymore, you're burying it. You have been ever since your dad showed up," he said. "You can't use that time as motivation if you're too busy pushing it aside."

I shifted uncomfortably. "Just because I haven't taken him through the deadly details doesn't mean I'm holding back in the field."

He eyed me, as if he knew something I didn't. "I think you're not being honest with him yet and that means you're hiding a piece of yourself when he's around. Which is an issue, because you are at your best when you're confronting problems, not hiding from them."

I didn't completely see his point, but I nodded anyway. "I'll keep that in mind."

He held my gaze for another beat, then shifted back, satisfied.

"You'll keep an eye on Venom, right?" I asked a few minutes later. "I know you have issues with her being here—"

"I meant it when I said that I trust you," he said, interrupting me. "I'll have her back."

I smiled lightly. "Thank you."

He tipped his head in acknowledgement. "Get some rest while you can."

I was too wired to sleep, but I closed my eyes anyway, doing my best to keep my nerves at bay.

Chapter Twenty-Seven

INSIDE

I ended up falling asleep halfway through the flight. I woke easily when the plane landed, though I found my eyes felt heavier than I would have liked. Fortunately, the adrenaline started to flood my system, kicking me into mission mode. Travis stood and looked back to me. "You good?"

I nodded. "Let me know if you need help with her," I said, gesturing to Venom.

"I've got her," he said. "But trust me, if she's a problem, you'll be the first to know."

We headed for the front of the plane. I came to a stop briefly next to Centipede. She gave me a scrutinizing look, which then turned to surprise. "Were you *asleep*?" I didn't know if she was jealous or appalled.

"Are you ready?" I asked. I rubbed any remnants of sleep out of my eyes.

She smirked. "I think the question is, are you?"

I rolled my eyes and stepped in front of her to disembark, pushing my comm into my ear, tugging the mask over my face, and flipping my hood up. The others followed my lead.

"Does everybody copy?" Sam asked when he saw all of our comms were online. We checked in, confirming the connection.

"Magpie and Archer are inside Phantac. They should have access to the building within the next ten minutes. Once that happens, Magpie will have the cameras and be able to guide you."

"Copy that, Command. We'll wait for her word to move in." I turned to the others. "We have fifteen minutes to reach our perimeter location starting now." Travis and I set our watches so each team had a clock running. Then we separated, taking different routes to avoid being detected.

We'd landed on flat ground a couple miles away from the mountain in question. According to Sam, the electrical output in the area was coming exclusively from the mountain, which suggested perimeter security was lacking. It made sense. KATO didn't have a ton of money. It paid for them to invest in internal security and trust that the mountain would keep them hidden.

The plan was to enter from the back of the mountain. We'd all be using the same door in and separating from there. We were moving in on foot, weaving between the smaller peaks as we closed in, using them as our cover for any unexpected guards. Centipede and I didn't speak as we crept through the desert area surrounding the back of the facility. Her head scanned rapidly from one side to the other, like a predator. We were both light on our feet, moving quickly, but not running. We had to save our energy for when we made it inside.

We got to our destination seconds before Travis and Venom. I pushed my comm in. "We're in position."

"Stand by," Sam said. We waited a few tense breaths before we heard his voice again. "Magpie, you're on."

"The cameras are looped and you're clear to move in."

The four of us acted at once. Venom had the door open in fifteen seconds and we stepped into a hallway that was quiet and empty, re-affirming that Misty had taken control.

"See you on the other side," Travis said. He and Venom headed to find the nearest staircase while Centipede and I moved just inside the door, ducking around a corner to keep ourselves out of sight. The plan was simple. Venom and Travis went to the top floor where they were sure to find the facility supervisor's office, which would have access to developmental files. Meanwhile Centipede and I went hunting for the serum.

"The blueprints say this floor has all of the labs," I said. If this serum was still in the developmental stages, this was the most likely place to find it.

"We need the biggest one first," Centipede said.

"I have eyes on it," Misty cut in. "It's around the corner. The door has a long scratch above the window."

Centipede made eye contact with me briefly and we took off down the hall, scanning each door we passed to be sure we didn't miss anything. We'd reached the end of the hall before we heard Misty's voice again. "Raven, Condor, you've got someone headed in your direction."

We came to a sudden stop, pressing our backs against the wall.

"A guard?" I asked in a quiet hiss.

"Negative. A lab coat," she said. I glanced at Centipede, who nod-ded, then stepped aside.

"Tell me when," I said. It was already determined that if we had a choice, I would be the one seen by other KATO workers. Even as covered as we were, I didn't want to risk Centipede's identity. I waited for Misty's cue, then whipped around the corner, using my elbow to strike the side of the researcher's head. He hit the ground before he even knew I was there.

"Anyone else in our path?" I asked.

Misty went quiet and I imagined she was checking all the camera angles. "The rest of your floor looks clear."

Centipede stepped out and joined me in the hallway. We made our way through the facility until we finally came to a stop in front of the door with a scratch running directly above the small rectangular window.

"A guard just stepped out of the stairs on the opposite side of your floor," Misty said. "He's around the corner, but moving fast." There weren't any alarms sounding, so we couldn't have been detected. But still, we needed to get out of the hall. I tried the door but it was locked. There was a keypad on the lock.

"Magpie," I said. "I need that lab opened."

"Give me a second."

Centipede locked eyes with me, and I saw a touch of panic.

Then keypad beeped softly and Centipede and I pushed our way inside. I shut the door firmly behind us. We silently pressed ourselves against the wall on either side of the door, waiting for word from Misty.

The room darkened and my heart sped up. The guard had to be standing in front of the window between us, blocking the light from the hall. I looked to Centipede, whose eyes were squeezed shut. I caught a tremor in her hand before she tucked it behind her back. He lingered for a little too long. Almost as if he knew there was something here he should be looking for.

"He passed you," Misty said as the light came back into the room.

"He'll clear the floor in the next ten seconds." I met Centipede's eyes briefly, neither of us moving an inch. Not until we were sure we were clear. Once we were, we didn't waste another second.

I looked around the room. It was a large space, big enough for five tables of microscopes and machines. There was a table in the corner that appeared to be for patients. Wires hung from the ceiling and IVs ran along the back. It led me to believe that a fair amount of experimentation happened here.

Centipede moved quickly for a door on my left. She had her hand on the knob, and I grabbed her wrist.

She shot me a confused look. "What?"

"We both need to be ready," I said. She grimaced in frustration. Her KATO mentality was showing and she knew it. We weren't trained to pause for any reason.

I pulled my gun out and gave her a nod. She yanked the door open, leaving me to sweep the room. It was small and sterile white. There was a refrigerator on the countertop. Inside was a series of syringes.

I took a tray of them out and placed them on the counter before lifting one up to study the Korean writing on the label.

Project: 08562

Eliza's file—the one we'd pulled from the director at her safe house—had said the same thing.

"This is it," I said to Centipede. "This is what we came for."

The excitement flashed in her eyes. We had two seconds to appreciate our success before a sound from the other room made us both freeze. The door to the main lab had opened, putting both of us on heightened alert. But there wasn't anything we could do. My heart pounded and I worked to stay collected. We had no way out and nowhere to hide. Why hadn't Misty warned us?

There wasn't enough time to ask any questions. It took all of three seconds for the guard to reach us, yelling in Korean, ordering us to put our hands up and get on our knees. He had his gun on us, giving us no choice but to obey.

I felt my hands start to shake slightly as the blood pulsed in my veins. The only reason I had managed to keep my head clear was because there weren't any agents in this room, but I knew how quickly that could change. Still, I couldn't let my fear show. Because I was certain that next to me, Centipede was even more terrified. I had to get us out of this.

The guard yanked the syringe out of my hands, then disarmed both of us before ripping off our masks. If he recognized either of us, he didn't say anything. I doubted he had a reason to know who Centipede was, but I was almost positive my face had to be on his radar.

He circled us before coming to a stop at our backs. I didn't have to feel the gun to know it was floating between us.

I was surprised when a woman in a lab coat crossed the threshold.

"You should not be here!" the guard snapped at her.

"I want to see who is stealing from my lab," she said. She wasn't an agent—her eyes didn't have the harsh dead look that came with that job. She also didn't seem nearly afraid enough to be a prisoner like my mom or Dr. Foster had been. She had to be a Korean native. I didn't see another explanation.

She studied me and Centipede closely, her face etched with fury.

She didn't seem to know me either, though that would make sense if she wasn't an agent. The guard passed the syringe off to the woman, and her lips formed a thin line.

Her eyes snapped to us and she leaned over so her face was inches from the both of us. "Did you think you would get away with this?" Centipede and I both stared straight ahead silently. "Taking my hard work? My chance at pride and honor?"

I turned my head as if I couldn't bear the shame, but really I was trying to get a better look at the guard positioned between us. He was centered with one foot behind each of us. I could work with that.

"I would not let you be taken away without seeing my face." Again, neither of us responded. "You have failed. My work will continue." Her lips twisted in a smile. "And you will be faced with harsh punishments."

That was all it took to set Centipede off. The reminder of the punishments KATO would deal out pushed away the small amount of control she'd been able to hold on to. She punched the woman in the face then jumped to her feet. I dove for Centipede, wrapping my arms around her legs and bringing her to the ground just as the guard fired off three shots.

I rolled away, hooking my legs around the guard's knees and tugging sharply until he fell. It was enough to jar him, giving me the opportunity to disarm him. I leapt up and whacked the side of his head with the butt of the gun, effectively knocking him out.

Then I rounded back on the woman, who was not looking nearly as confident as she was a minute ago. She backed away from me, spinning the syringe in her hand. I moved in slowly, debating the quickest and quietest way to take her down.

Then I heard gunshots from behind me. I turned sharply, afraid the guard had already woken up. Instead I found Centipede standing over him, gun in hand, and three bullets in the guard's chest. Her silencer quieted the shots, but it didn't eliminate the sound completely. We needed to get out of here. If backup came looking and found this guy dead, none of us would escape.

I opened my mouth to tell Centipede, but I never got the words out. I'd taken my eye off the scientist for too long and she took her chance. She charged at my back, and I felt something jab into my neck. I went cold. It was the needle. I knew it was. I just prayed she hadn't pushed down on the plunger. I elbowed her in the stomach, stunning her briefly.

Centipede reacted, coming in from behind and twisting the woman's neck until it snapped. She dropped cold. I pulled the syringe out of my neck. It was empty. The serum was in me.

My heart hammered and I fought to clear my head. This wasn't like the Gerex. There didn't seem to be an immediate response. Did that mean it didn't work? She had stabbed me out of self-defense. She wasn't a fighter. The needle with the serum was just a convenient weapon. She hadn't drilled a hole in my skull or aimed for a vein. Maybe that mattered. Maybe it wouldn't affect me. I didn't feel any different.

Centipede watched me wide-eyed. I shook my head—attempting to shake myself out of the shock—then moved toward the serum tray on the table—as if this was a problem that would disappear with enough activity.

"I'm sorry," she said. "I didn't mean—"

"I know." I grabbed a full syringe, closed it in the case Dr. March had given me, and tucked it in my jacket pocket. "We need to go."

Centipede was hunched over the dead guard, rooting through his pockets until she had come up with our masks. She tossed mine to me and we covered up again.

I picked up my gun from the floor before following Centipede into the hall and pushing my comm in. "Is anyone there?"

"Yes!" Misty sounded relieved. "They're onto us. They jammed our comm system but Command was able to override it."

"We were just ambushed," I said. The injection had me rattled and my patience was short.

"Are you both okay?"

"Yeah," I said, my voice cracking over the lie. "We have the serum. We just need to get out."

"Did they get control of anything else?" Centipede asked. "The cameras?"

"No," Misty said. "They seem to know the building has been compromised, but they haven't been able to take the system back from us." That's why they resorted to jamming our signal. They hoped to slow us down enough to find us.

"Can you get us a clean exit?" Whatever was in Eliza was now in me. I had no way of knowing how long it would be before I saw side effects, but I was sure I didn't want to be in a KATO building when it happened.

"Go back down the hall and out the way you came in," she directed. "No one's on your floor at the moment, but you have about seven guards sweeping the building."

"Copy," I said to her. "Scorpion, Vulture, where are you guys at?"

The line stayed quiet. I tried again, and still didn't get a response.

My heart dropped. Now that we were out of immediate danger, I realized that it had been a while since I had heard from either of them.

I had a terrible feeling churning in my stomach. "Magpie, where are the others?"

"Give me a second." The line went quiet. "They're in the supervisor's office," she said. "It looks like there are about five guards outside that door."

"Are they okay otherwise?" I asked. Centipede and I could handle five guards—especially if we got the jump on them.

"I don't know," she said. My heart pounded as my fear found a way to heighten. "There aren't any cameras in that office. All I know is that they made it inside."

They weren't okay. I knew they weren't. If they were, one of them would have responded. I ground my teeth together, my adrenaline elevating and giving me new life.

"You have guards three floors away and closing fast," Misty said.

Centipede looked to me, her eyes wide with panic. "We need to go." I understood the instinct. It was self-preservation. I didn't blame her.

"We can't leave them," I said. "They're part of our team, and I'm not leaving my partner behind." I wouldn't let my thoughts stay on Travis. I didn't want to think about what KATO would do to him—if they even let him live.

She held my eyes for a long moment, and I could see the internal debate waging in her. "I don't like this," she said, finally. "But lead the way."

I pushed my comm in. "Magpie, are the guards taking the stairs to us?"

"Yes."

"Do we have control of the elevator?" I asked. I was already running for it. Thanks to all the time I spent poring over the blueprints, I knew exactly where I was going. Centipede followed close.

"We do," Misty said. "I'm sending it your way."

"Make sure they can't see that it's operating," I said. "Have it drop us off a floor below the supervisor's office."

"Copy that."

Centipede and I stepped onto the elevator and there was another voice in our heads.

"Hey, Raven." It was Sam. "I'm patching you into Vulture and Scorpion's comms."

I held my breath, praying to hear Travis's voice.

But it wasn't Travis I heard. The voice that filled my ear turned everything inside me cold.

"You *will* tell me why you are in this office!" It was Jin Su.

He was here. And he was alone with Travis and Venom.

Chapter Twenty-Eight

BREAKING POINT

I stared at the metal doors in front of us, forcing my brain to process the information. Travis was trapped in a room with Jin Su, and there was a team of guards standing outside the office, presumably waiting for Jin Su's word to take them into custody. That was how the guards knew to jam our signal and look for more of us.

"We can't stay," Centipede said as we stepped off the elevator. Her voice was soft but insistent. "Not with him here." She shifted on her feet, her distress more apparent than ever.

I was afraid too, but it wasn't for myself; it was for Travis and Venom. I needed Centipede if I had any chance of saving them.

In my ear, Jin Su was talking again. "I expected better from you, Venom."

Venom started to speak. "I—" Her words shook with a fear I hadn't expected. Out of all of us, she had seemed the least afraid.

"Step away from her." That was Travis. His voice was a low protective growl. I heard a hard thud next and then Travis groaned. My heart beat faster, the terror coursing through me. I had to get to him.

"This is a trap I set," Venom said. "I brought him to you."

"No!" I snapped into my comm. I was losing her. Centipede started moving down the hall, and now it was a race. If Venom started talking she would turn Centipede and Misty in. But if

Centipede could somehow get there first and get her story out, she could take the credit for playing us. I was sure even Misty, thousands of miles away, was preparing to run and find a way to save herself. "Vulture, we're a team, remember? They can't tell you what to do. Don't give them that power!"

"Go on," Jin Su said to her. His voice was cold, and it was clear that while she would be in a severe amount of trouble either way, what she said next could very well save her life.

Venom kept talking—she had to—but she mumbled and stumbled over her words, buying time. I let out a breath. Down the hall, Centipede had stopped moving away from me. She rocked on her feet though, ready to make a break for it if she had to. I hadn't planned for this. I had no idea what I could possibly say to keep them with me, but I had to try. Then I remembered what Travis had told me on the plane.

"I know you're afraid of him. I am too," I said to Venom, speaking quickly. "And you shouldn't forget what he's done to you." I swallowed. The only person who ever knew I was afraid of anything was Travis, and even he always had to guess before I would admit to anything. But they needed to remember why we were doing this.

"*He* is responsible for the burns, and the beatings, and the cuts. He's the one who orders you to kill people you don't want to kill." Venom had stopped talking, and Jin Su was yelling, but I was too focused on my problem to make out what he was saying. "So you can be afraid, and go back to him like *they* trained you to, or you can use that fear to break them." I took a breath and pushed on, knowing I was running out of time. "We have more power right now than they ever wanted us to have. If you stay with me, we can give them something to be afraid of."

There was a long pause, then Venom spoke. "I—I have nothing to say." She was speaking to Jin Su. Her words were strong, despite her hesitancy. I looked down the hall at Centipede, who nodded.

"Vulture, Scorpion, we're coming for you." I turned to Centipede. "We need to split up. You take the closest set of stairs and I'll take the ones on the other side of the building. We'll come at the guards from either side. Once we're in the room, it's the four of us against Jin Su."

"Whatever you say." There was still fear in her eyes, but she was all in, and back in full mission mode.

We took off running.

"There are five guards outside the door, and now ten others searching for you," Misty said.

"Copy," I said. "Condor, I'll let you know when I'm outside the door. Wait for my signal."

I could hear the back-and-forth between Jin Su, Travis, and Venom. It would be only a matter of time before Jin Su lost his patience. He'd go after Travis first. He was expendable. He would probably suffer just enough to be an example to Venom before Jin Su killed him. I pushed every terrible outcome out of my mind and focused on what was in front of me.

I signaled Centipede when I was in position and we moved in as planned, creeping down the hall while the guards were focused on the door hiding Travis and Venom.

The guards had AK-47s pointed at the office, prepared for action. Centipede and I made eye contact, inching closer. Each of us had our gun drawn and trained on them. The last thing I wanted was to start shooting. I didn't want to give Jin Su any reason to get trigger-happy. Our best approach was for each of us to disarm two guards as quickly as possible, then we'd have the remaining agent outnumbered. I nodded at Centipede just once. It was enough to put her in motion.

We moved quickly and in sync. The fact that we were raised on the same training regimen couldn't have been more obvious. We were each able to knock out the two guards closest to us in quick, sharp movements. The fifth guard turned in Centipede's direction, gun out and ready to fire. I knocked his feet out from under him and Centipede kicked him hard in the face until he was unconscious.

I turned to the office door to make my move.

Then I heard a gunshot from the other side.

My whole world stopped. It had been only one shot—it had to have hit its target.

Time moved impossibly slow, and I felt hot and cold all at once. I forced my legs to work, pushing myself forward and nearly ripping the door off its hinges to get it open.

I took in the scene quickly.

Travis was on the ground—alive, but breathing hard next to a chair he appeared to have dove out of.

Venom was a few feet away from him, and next to her was Jin Su. Both Travis and Venom were mask-less. It wasn't hard to work out what had happened. Jin Su pulled a gun on Travis and Venom had tackled him as he fired. Now Jin Su was on his back next to her, his gun again pointed at Travis. He was poised to pull the trigger again, and there was no way Travis would be able to avoid it.

I didn't think. I reacted, burying bullets in Jin Su's chest until he went limp. It took four.

The shots from my gun seemed to echo through the room. I pivoted to Travis once I was positive Jin Su was down, taking in every detail. He was panting, and there was a sizable gash on his eyebrow that appeared to be bleeding steadily. Otherwise, he seemed okay. He locked eyes with me, looking as relieved and grateful as I felt. My hands felt like they were vibrating. I didn't know what to do. I wanted to get to him—to take a closer look. To be *sure*. But I couldn't seem to move.

"Half the guards in the building are headed your way," Misty said, snapping me back to the situation at hand.

Travis jumped up off the floor. "Get that door locked," he said to Centipede as he retrieved his gun from Jin Su's body. Centipede did as she was told.

Venom stood and took in the dead director. Then she turned to me with an expression of deep approval. "You did a very nice job."

I gaped at her for a moment, then turned to Travis. "Did you get the development file?"

"No," he said. "We only managed to knock out the facility supervisor." He gestured to the man next to the door, who I hadn't noticed. "Jin Su was already here when we got in. We weren't prepared."

"Guards are on your floor," Misty said. The office door rattled. They were right outside.

"We're out of time," I said. "I have the serum. It'll have to be enough." I didn't want any of us in this building for another second.

"Magpie," Travis said into his comm. "We need an out." He found his mask on the floor and tossed Venom's to her.

"There's an emergency exit in this office somewhere," I told her. I'd seen it on the blueprints.

"I found it," she said. "It's behind the first bookcase on the left, but I can't see how it opens."

"We'll figure it out," I said.

The four of us wordlessly spread out around the office, looking for any kind of lever or button that might open the bookcase.

A light moaning from the ground distracted all of us. The building supervisor was waking up. Venom moved the fastest. She was on him in a second, her foot hitting at the side of his neck. She leaned into him, twisting her hip just enough to make it crack. He went limp in an instant.

I swallowed, hating that she'd added another body to this mess. But I had no place to say anything.

"I found it!" Centipede said from behind the desk. She had the top drawer open and appeared to be pressing some kind of button underneath the top of the desk. The bookcase sprung to life, swinging out, with just enough room for a person to slip behind it. Venom darted through the door without a second glance, with Centipede right after her.

I took one more look at Jin Su dead on the ground. I had done that. And I would do it again if I had to.

"We need to move," Travis said, pushing me toward the door. He pulled the bookcase closed behind us. We were faced with a spiral staircase that snaked down the six-floor building. Venom bounded down the stairs as Centipede followed, still in complete business mode.

I pushed my comm in, doing my best to shove all of the insanity to the back of my mind. "Venom, don't go through whatever door is at the bottom until we're all together."

It felt like a basic note, but at this point, I wasn't taking anything for granted. She stopped at the base of the stairs and looked up at me, her head cocked. She seemed confused, but did what I had asked.

I pushed my comm in. "Magpie, do you know where this lets out?"

"It takes you to the first floor and drops you off right near an exit," she said. "Guards are there now, but they're moving. I'll tell you when it's clear."

"Copy," Travis said.

"We can just kill them," Venom said, as if it were the most obvious solution in the world. "They already know we're here."

Now even Centipede was looking at her like she had gone too far. She turned to me. "She's still unstable."

Venom rounded on her. "*You* are the unstable one."

I ignored Centipede and turned to Venom, gathering my patience to answer her question. "We can't afford to draw any more attention to ourselves."

She cocked her head to the side, considering me. "All right, then."

I let out a sigh of relief and looked to Travis. His wide-eyed expression matched how I felt, but he gave me a nod of approval.

"You're all clear," Misty said. "You're going out the door, then to the right. There will be another door in front of you, but then you're on your own. We don't have a camera on the outside."

Travis grimaced but pushed his comm in. "Copy that. We'll touch base when we're clear of the facility." Then he turned to me. "You get the door, I'll clear the area."

I moved past Centipede and Venom, quickly finding the door-knob. Travis raised his gun higher and stood next to the door. Centipede and Venom watched us.

Travis caught my eye and nodded. I pushed the door open and stepped back, giving him room to get out. He cleared the hallway quickly and motioned me toward the other door.

Again I waited for his signal. If we were going to run into another problem, it was going to be here. But we didn't have time to second-guess. Travis nodded again and I threw open the door.

It was quiet. He did a quick sweep in both directions. "Clear."

I motioned back to the others and they did as I asked, hurrying from one door to the next.

A few seconds later, we were out. There was a smaller peak a short distance away. That was where we needed to be. None of us spoke as we sprinted, guns still drawn, toward our goal. We stopped behind the crest to catch our breath.

I pushed my comm in, but took care to keep my voice low. "Magpie, we're covered."

"Copy," she said.

Then Sam cut in. "I managed to get satellite access. I'm seeing activity around the building. They're filtering their way outside now and heading in your direction. You have to keep moving."

I glanced at Travis and the girls. I could see hints of panic in both Centipede and Venom. The stakes were higher now than ever. The director was dead and they had been involved. There would be no talking themselves out of anything if they were caught now.

I pushed my comm in. "We're headed east toward the plane. Let us know if we're going to run into trouble."

"Don't worry," Sam said. "I've got a lock on your position and I'm tracking their movement. They won't sneak up on you."

"They're going to find us," Centipede said. Her voice was hard, cold, and factual.

"They *won't*," I said. I felt strong and determined, and my voice held the same power. It was enough to make them all look to me— startled. "I have fought too hard to accept that. We keep moving and we get to that plane before they get to us."

"We *killed* the director." Her voice cracked as the weight of it all hit her. "This was a mistake."

I pivoted around to face her. I could see she was shaking—she couldn't hide it, and I feared she was even closer to turning now than she was in that hallway. And this time it would be her choice, not Venom forcing her hand. After everything we had just escaped, we were so close to getting away.

I put my hands on her shoulders and looked her square in the eye. "There is nothing you can tell them that will make them go easy on you at this point," I said. "There's no such thing as 'worse' now. It will just be bad, and hard, and painful. You know who they are, and if you're okay with that, then fine. But that's your choice."

I turned and headed onward. Travis fell very quickly into step next to me. I felt him watching me. He carried his tablet with a map of the area pulled up. "Can I see that?"

He handed it over without a word. I led us through the desert, navigating around the peaks and through the valleys, toward the plane. I wasn't at all surprised when I looked behind me to find that not only was Venom still with us, but Centipede as well.

I nodded at her. "Good call."

Her jaw locked, but she didn't say anything.

"The serum's still okay, right?" Travis asked, taking the tablet back from me. I caught a glimpse of the blood leaking out of the eye-hole in his mask. The bleeding had lessened considerably, but it still looked bad.

I reached for my inside jacket pocket, letting the air rush over me as we moved. I ran my fingers over the case. "Yeah, it's safe."

He nodded as we ran.

Then Sam was in our ears. "You guys need to hurry up," he said. "They must have some kind of bead on you. They're fanned out and moving fast."

I glanced at Venom and for the first time, I noticed the fear in her eyes. Centipede was the same.

"Come on," Travis said. "None of you are getting caught tonight." He took off sprinting, and the rest of us followed his lead.

We bobbed and weaved and did everything we could to stay lost in the cover of dark. As we ran, I put Centipede and Venom in front of Travis and me, adding an extra layer of protection between them and KATO.

I heard voices coming up behind us and pushed my comm in. "That plane needs to be ready to take off when we get there."

"Copy that," Sam said. There was a tension in his voice that told me we were running out of time.

"How much farther?" I hissed at Travis. They had to be closing in on us.

"We're almost there," Travis said. "We should see the plane any second." And then I did. I dug deep and pushed on, letting the adrenaline carry me to the end.

Centipede arrived first, with Venom right behind her. Travis beat me by feet, but stepped aside, letting me get on first. I hurried up the stairs, only glancing back in time to see the KATO agents pouring out from around a peak behind us, charging forward. The engine was already going.

We were off and running in seconds. Venom and Centipede kept their heads down, but I pressed mine against the window. I needed to see that they couldn't get to me. That we were leaving them behind. They had their guns raised, preparing to fire as we left the ground. I heard a couple of the bullets hit the metal side, but we were already too far out of reach.

Chapter Twenty-Nine

REALITY

I didn't move a muscle until we were in the air. My heart still pounded furiously as every part of the mission caught up to me. I ripped my mask off my face and looked to Travis, sitting next to me, who had just done the same. "Are you— Is your eye—" I breathed hard through my nose, trying to sort through my thoughts. I reached for his eyebrow instead, wiping some of the smeared blood off with my sleeve. It had stopped bleeding completely now.

"I'm okay," he said.

Relief coursed through me. It didn't feel real until he had said it. I spoke quietly, so only he could hear me. "I have never been more afraid than when I heard that gun go off." I forced myself to look at him. "I thought you were dead."

He eyed me doubtfully. "You grew up in *KATO*," he said, as if I needed the reminder. "I have to believe you've been more afraid."

"Travis." I squeezed his wrist, trying to make him understand. "I haven't been. *Ever.*"

His entire expression softened and he seemed to realize what I was saying. "I'm okay," he said again. "Venom saved me from the first shot, and you saved all of us." He looked me square in my eyes, like he understood how much I needed to be reassured. "Because of *you*, I'm okay."

I exhaled heavily and leaned forward to rest my elbows on my knees, finally letting myself relax. I didn't say anything about the injection. I'd wait until we were back at the house and the girls were gone. I wanted to put one fire out before igniting another. I'd barely thought about the injection since I found out Jin Su had Travis and Venom anyway. It didn't matter as much in comparison.

Travis and I were sitting on a rear-facing bench toward the front of the plane, giving us a clear view of Venom and Centipede. They were both doing the same thing. They sat on the edge of their seats, tourniquets wrapped around their upper arms and needles going in to their veins. Gerex. My stomach clenched. It had been on this plane the whole time and I hadn't known. But I knew now.

My post-mission craving was kicking in. After nearly losing Travis, and now seeing Centipede and Venom doing what I wanted to do, I felt my control slipping. I needed to look away from them, but I couldn't. I was struggling to keep it together when Travis's hand closed over my shaking fist. It was enough to pull my focus. He took my hand in both of his and squeezed, as if he were trying to draw the craving out of me.

"Don't look at them," he said in my ear. I made myself face him. "Focus on me, okay? Not them."

I nodded and closed my eyes, doing my best to ignore them and regain my control. One of Travis's arms found its way around me. He pulled me into his shoulder, giving me the space to isolate myself from everything that made me weak.

Chapter Thirty

THE RETURN

We stayed like that for a long time, not speaking for what felt like hours—until I had gotten the craving back under control. Centipede and Venom seemed to have fallen asleep, which felt like its own miracle.

"Joss," Travis said, a note of concern in his voice. "Why is there blood on your neck?"

I pulled away from him, rubbing at the spot where the needle had punctured. I knew this wasn't something I could avoid, so I took a breath and told him what had happened. I tried to keep my voice neutral. If I could learn to be relaxed about the whole situation, maybe he would be too.

"Jocelyn—" he said when I had finished. There was an edge to his voice that indicated my calm was not translating.

"I don't feel any different," I said quickly. "She panicked and stabbed me. It's not like she had time to drill through my skull. Maybe it won't take." Though even I didn't completely believe what I was saying.

His face hardened. "She put that stuff *in* you." He leaned forward to look me in the eye, as if to make me understand just how serious this was. "You've seen what it does."

I bit my lip and felt my façade fall away. "I know," I said. My voice felt strained now, as the anxiety spiraled through me. Because he was right. No matter how calm I tried to be, there was no denying that this was really, *really* bad. Travis picked up on my tension.

He exhaled heavily, as if he was working to rein in his emotions. "We have the serum," he said eventually. "Dr. March will be able to figure out what to do."

I swallowed hard. "I hope you're right."

He nodded. His face was creased with worry, but his voice was sure. "I am." Then he tugged me back against him, holding me tighter. This time, it didn't feel like it was just for my sake.

. . .

Nikki and Misty were waiting for us in the living room when we finally made it back. I pushed my injection worries aside for now. Travis had agreed to keep that issue quiet until the girls were gone, and I'd told Centipede to keep her mouth shut too. I didn't know what my dad would do about it, but I suspected it would be better if this assignment was completely wrapped.

"You guys had us worried," Misty said, her big eyes so wide they practically took up her entire face.

"We had ourselves worried," I said.

Nikki caught a look at Travis's eye. "You need that cleaned," she said, gesturing to the first aid kit on the coffee table.

I looked around, searching for my dad, but I didn't see him anywhere. When I asked where he was, Nikki directed me to the kitchen.

"He's been in there since he and Misty got back," she said.

I eyed the doorway, trying not to feel intimidated. I had a lot of time to think on the plane—long enough to come to the conclusion that Travis had been right. I was a better agent when I wasn't hiding. The more I buried my time at KATO, the harder it was to use. And it had started when my father had shown up. I steeled myself and headed for the kitchen.

I found my dad leaning against the counter with his arms crossed, tense and rigid. His eyes jumped to me when I entered and relief spread across his face.

"I'm really glad you're back," he said.

I swallowed and nodded. "Yeah. Me too." He didn't say anything after that. I knew this was my window.

"The first time—" I hesitated. I wasn't as ready for this as I wanted to be but I pushed on anyway. "I was thirteen the first time I killed someone for KATO." My dad's jaw locked and he seemed to be struggling with both the reality of what I was saying and the disbelief that I had said anything at all on the subject. "It was a training exercise. We had to kill our opponent in order to stay in KATO."

Still he didn't say anything. I drew a shaky breath and kept talking. "I never wanted you to know what I did for them." I looked at the cabinets behind him. "I didn't want you to know how bad it really was."

Finally, he moved. He pushed himself off the counter and came closer to me. I didn't bolt even though I wanted to. He put his thumb on my chin and turned my head so I was facing him. I resisted for a moment, but I knew there was no point. It hurt to look him in the eye.

"It doesn't matter what you did," he said.

"It *does*." Now I stepped away from him. Because I needed him to understand. "It matters because when I had to pick between myself and innocent people, I picked *me*." I met his eyes again, preparing myself for what was sitting on my tongue. "And if I had to, I would do it again." And that was the thing I really didn't want him to know. That I would do it again.

He nodded, slowly letting my words sink in. "It's okay."

"No, it's not!" My voice broke. "Even tonight—"

"Jocelyn." He didn't yell, but his tone was firm enough to stop any argument. He waited until he was sure I was paying attention. "First, I am the one who left you in that position. So anything you did to survive is on me." There was a guilt in his face that made my chest ache. I didn't want to hear him apologize again, and I didn't want to argue fault.

His hands fell to my shoulders, making sure I was squared to him, then he continued. "You need to know that I am also so *proud* of you." My eyes widened in what I was sure was a mix of surprise and uncertainty. He gave my shoulders a squeeze. "You fought back. You found a way out of a situation that—" He cut himself off before the emotion got the better of him. "And in case you didn't notice, tonight you killed someone who was about to take out two people on your team. You've protected yourself, and you've protected your people. That is *never* something to apologize for."

He spoke with a certainty and intensity that gave me no choice but to believe him. I had been so afraid of my father showing up— of him finding out any details about the last ten years—that I never considered he might actually be *proud* of me. I was unprepared for all of it, and now I had more feelings than I knew how to sort through. I didn't even realize how much it all mattered until now. I didn't have any more words, but it was okay because he didn't seem to need them.

"I'm glad you told me," he said. "And you can tell me anything that happened there, whenever you want. Okay?"

I nodded, swallowing hard. His squeezed my shoulder one more time, then stepped away, moving toward the others in the living room.

I pinched the bridge of my nose once I was alone, breathing hard until the tightness in my chest loosened. I felt the tears gathering, and I squeezed my eyes shut before they could fall.

. . .

I rejoined the group once I got myself together. Nikki and my dad were packing up some equipment, while Travis sat on the couch with a fresh bandage above his eye. Centipede leaned against the wall by the steps next to Venom, who was studying the ends of her hair. Misty sat on one of the chairs, still looking tense from the mission.

"There you are," Centipede said, straightening.

I smiled. "I needed a minute."

"We are leaving," Venom said.

I nodded. "I had a feeling." We'd accomplished our goal. Now they all needed to get back to their posts.

Venom launched herself at me, hugging me tight—too tight really. Like no one had ever taught her how to be gentle with others. But there was something very endearing about it. I hugged her back once I'd recovered from the shock and couldn't help but laugh a little at one of KATO's deadliest assassins hugging their most wanted member. Eventually, she pulled back and looked me in the eye. "Thank you for picking me."

I smiled at her and nodded, not having the heart to point out that she had actually picked herself.

"Thank you for picking me too," Misty said, taking a step closer. She looked like she may have wanted to hug me as tight as Venom had, but she refrained. "And would you mind keeping me updated about Python?"

"Not at all," I said.

The two of them headed for the door, but Venom paused when she got to the threshold. "We'll do this again, yes?"

"Yeah," I said, smiling. "I'm sure we'll get the chance. Those phones you have work both ways. I'll reach out when we have something and you let me know if KATO tells you anything that might be helpful to us."

She gave me a single hard nod. "I can do that." Then she pivoted on her heel and took off without another word. Misty gave me one last smile before following her out.

I turned back to Centipede, who appeared to be in no rush to leave. She stepped up to me and seemed to be having a hard time looking me in the eye. "I'm—sorry." She stumbled over the words. "At the end there—I panicked. We killed the director, and they were after us—"

"I get it," I said. "But you can't keep doing that. I can't talk you into this every mission—especially *on* a mission."

"I know."

"You have to decide if you're in or out."

"I'm in," she said quickly. "Really."

I held her eyes. "Okay, then."

"It's strange," she said after a beat. "I'm terrified that they might find out what we did. Or that I'll show up back at headquarters and someone will have seen me. But the fact that they might not—that we might have gotten away with it, and that I could actually escape them. That feels really good."

"I know exactly what you mean." I smiled. "Remember that when you're inside."

"I will." She returned the smile and took a step for the door. "I need to tell KATO something," she said. "They're going to want to know where I was when I don't come back with you again."

I chewed on my cheek, thinking. "Give them this house. We'll leave enough behind so they'll know we were here, and I'll tell our director it's been burned. Just give us some time to clear out."

It wouldn't save her completely, but it was better than going back empty-handed. "Thank you," she said, letting out a small sigh of relief.

"You should check in with us on occasion, even if you don't have intel," I said. "Just so I know you're all right." She was the most vulnerable out of all of them.

She looked perplexed at first, and I knew it had been a very long time since anyone had said something like that to her. Eventually, she nodded. "I will let you know." Her gaze dropped to my neck, and when she spoke again there was a note of sincerity I wouldn't have thought her capable of a month ago. "Will you be okay?"

I rubbed the injection site, trying to hide my anxiety. "I guess we'll find out soon, won't we?"

Her eyes hardened, but she didn't push. "I'll be in touch," she said. And then, like the others, she was gone.

Nikki had taken the chair Misty vacated, and my dad sat in the other one. I flopped onto the couch next to Travis feeling like I could take my first true breath since I started this team. This experiment had been rocky and uncertain, but somehow it had all come together in the end.

Travis kicked my foot and gave me a very pointed look. When he had agreed to keep the injection to ourselves until the girls were gone, I didn't realize that it would be so literal. "You do it or I will," he said.

Nikki looked between the two of us. "What's going on?"

I took a moment to glance at her before focusing on my dad. "Something happened on the mission that you should know about," I said. I took the story slow, giving him time to adjust to the reality as I spoke. It did very little to help the situation.

"You were injected," my dad said, his voice quiet but intense. He leaned over the coffee table, and seemed to be fighting the urge to move closer.

I nodded, biting down hard on my lip. "I feel okay so far, though. I even shared some secrets on that mission after I was injected."

"That may not mean anything," he said. "Dr. March said that drilling into the skull was the most direct approach, not the *only* approach. Who knows how long it takes to kick in this way."

Both Travis and Nikki watched me closely. Nikki looked more shocked than anything else and Travis seemed to be even angrier and more worried than he had been the first time he'd heard.

"So," I said, inhaling slowly in a pathetic attempt to calm my nerves. "What do we do?"

My dad drummed his fingers on the table. "Get what you need

from this house," he said. "We're getting you and the serum to Dr. March at the new headquarters."

"Is it ready?" Nikki asked.

My dad glanced at her. "Yes," he said. "And that's the place with the tools and resources to fix this." He started moving around the room, collecting equipment. He worked quickly—too quickly.

"Do you even know where the new location is?" I asked.

"England," he said, heading for the stairs. "Let's go. I want that serum in Dr. March's hands by the end of the day."

Nikki set to work packing up the rest of the tech, while Travis started sorting through the papers we'd left scattered on the coffee table. I leaned forward, resting my head in my hands, giving myself one moment to allow everything to sink in.

KATO had found yet another way to damage me. Though even with that, I had three KATO agents, Eliza, and their special serum. They may have gotten some hits in, but I was starting to get mine. And I didn't plan on giving up any time soon.

Acknowledgments

First, to every reader of *Crossing the Line*, thank you for reading. And thank you for telling a friend, or ten—or the Internet. Thank you for loving Jocelyn so much. I hope you enjoyed reading this next chapter of her story as much as I did writing it.

Thanks to my awesome agent, Michelle Wolfson, for continuing to be so supportive, enthusiastic, and insightful. And thank you for reading this book in a weekend when I was pretty sure I needed to rewrite at least half of it for the third time. If left to my own devices, I would have done that rewrite, and this would have been a different (and worse-off) book. I can't thank you enough for your perspective—both then and on a regular basis.

To my fabulous editor, Jill Santopolo, for helping me tell the story I wanted to tell. I seriously don't know how you did it. I'd decided long before I turned this book in to you that the direction I wanted it to go in just wasn't plausible. You asked all the right questions and led me back to the book I wanted to write—which was also the book that needed to be written. Thank you for being so good at what you do. Also, thanks to Talia Benamy, whose notes were equally on point, and to Michael Green, Semadar Megged, Jennifer Chung, Kristin Smith, Maggie Edkins, Rob Farren, and everyone at Philomel and Penguin Young Readers for all of your hard work to make this book happen.

To my parents, sister, grandparents, aunts, uncles, cousins, and the rest of my extended family for being so excited and supportive of these books. I was in no way surprised by this enthusiasm, but it's been so amazing to see in action. I wouldn't want to call any other group my family.

To Jenn Lacko for imagining with me for the past twenty-eight years—especially over this past year and half, when my brain desperately needed a refreshing change of pace. To Caitlin Naylor for being such a fierce booking agent and for sending me a picture every time you come across my book in the wild. To Shannon Jenkins for telling absolutely everyone you crossed paths with about this series. And to Emily Irwin for offering to plaster NYC with *Crossing the Line* stickers (which I'm assuming you did, btw). I have the best street team an author could ask for.

Thanks to my coworkers at DCCC for being SO insanely encouraging. When I took this job, I seriously underestimated what it would mean to work with other writers. I'm so grateful for all of you. Extra thanks to Vicky Rostovich for taking my shifts when I needed just a *little* more time for this book—it really made all the difference.

To Michael Woody and Taylor Peca for being among my first fans and for being so dedicated. I'm truly grateful for both of you.

To everyone in the Sweet 16s and Sixteen to Read, your emails, tweets, and texts have made this whole publishing adventure a lot more fun.

To my amazing critique partners: Andrea Ridgley, thank you for seeing the potential in this early draft, for asking to read it again and again, and for helping me with the problems that came up. I truly would have been lost without your feedback. Dana Celona, thank you for having such a unique take on plot issues. Your ideas and perspective have always pointed me in a direction I hadn't thought of and did so much to shape this book. Jessie Furia, thank you for being appropriately horrified by the things that happen to my characters. It's how I know I'm going in the right direction. And for loving my crazy process, even though you want no part of it. (Though I think you secretly want me to teach you my ways. ;) And thank you all for reading this so many times. I never would have gotten this book in any kind of readable shape without you guys.

To my fresh eyes, thank you for waiting so patiently until I pulled this book together enough for you to read. Maggie McGrath, thank you for reading so quickly and calling me the second you were finished. And for everything you've done for me and these books. It's too much to list here, but know I am so grateful. Denise Mroz for being among my last new readers, even though it kills you to wait. For always being one of my biggest supporters, and the Ricky to my Julian. Also, for taking your assistant job so seriously. There is no one better at it than you. And to my cousin Kellsey Rogers for being the first person in my target audience to read my books. Your feedback means more than you know.

To my sister, Katie Rogers, for helping with all of the science and explaining everything over and over again when it was clear that I still didn't understand. (And for the record, I still *don't* understand. Sorry. You're probably going to have to try again.) Also, for reading and being so upset with *that* plotline (and equally happy to hear we were changing it).

And to my cousin Hunter Brutsche for the continued use of your brain. For answering my texts and phone calls, and always making time to help me figure out how to make the world work in my favor. This book, and this series, would not be able to exist without all of your help. I don't think there are enough words in the English language to fully convey just how thankful I am for everything you've done to make this series possible.